# ZOYA: RUPTURE

ALEXANDRA PUGACHEVSKY

SASHKINA

ISBN:979-8-9879977-5-8 (Paperback)
979-8-9879977-4-1 (eBook)

Author: Alexandra Pugachevsky
Cover Design: Damonza
Editor: Kirsten Rees | Book Editor & Author Coach

Instagram: @sashkina_author
Facebook: @sashkina.author
TikTok: @sashkina_author
Twitter: @sashkina
Website: sashkina.com
Email: sasha@sashkina.com

*To my parents*

*We made a run for it*
  *Bold, dumb, in broad daylight*

*Threw the guard over and*
  *Jumped head-first*

*We ran, breathing in unison*
  *Right in front of the guards*
  *Snow to our waists*

*The guards lined up, following orders*
  *The chainsaw screeched*
  *And they crossed us with the lead omens*

*The guards laid down, noses in snow*
  *While rabid dogs chased us*

*9 grams, how hot you are,*
  *How snug you are in your barrels*
  *They aimed and we were finished*

*We only had to make it to the horizon,*
  *But from their posts our fates were predetermined*
  *The snipers made us and mocked us*

*I wanted to see, to learn his name*

*Who'd dared to die with me?*
*Who'd risked his life with me?*

*We must have met somewhere*
*I came to and wheezed:*
*Buddy, what's your name?*
*What are you in for?*

*I was too late*
*A bullet crossed him out*
*Straight to the head, waist and shoulders*
*But I kept running, hoping I'd make it*

*Vladimir Vysotsky, Run for it, 1977*

# PROLOGUE

**Pittsburgh, May 1993**

*Is this what a bad trip feels like?*

Zoya jerked as saw a pink swirl, like a snake, flash before her eyes. She didn't remember falling asleep, wasn't sure she'd been asleep at all. Outside, the sun was shining, birds chirping, and Zoya decided there was no point looking at her watch. She knew it was late in the day. Bright circles floated before her eyes, and then moved to the ceiling. She felt dizzy and wanted to hide somewhere so that all these color adventures would be over as soon as possible. A purple snake shot straight at her head, a bright sliver of light gone as suddenly as it had appeared.

*Why, why did I do that?* Zoya tried, in vain, to push another snake away. *Why did I agree to drop acid? It was so stupid! We could have just danced!*

# CHAPTER 1

April 27th, 1993

"Hey, want to go to a rave on Saturday night?" Jessica smiled, as she produced a yellow piece of paper. The picture on it might have been a joker or a devil with a tail, standing behind the turntables. Date of the event, an outline of a sun, and the name of the rave, 'High Voltage', were printed at the top.

"What's a rave?" Zoya asked, unsure if she heard the word correctly. Despite living in the United States for over two years, she still had doubts about her English and was careful to double check new words.

"It's, umm, like this big party with loud music and dancing," Jessica clapped in excitement, "and really, really fun. The music will be great, and the night will be amazing! All these DJs! It's gonna be at the Irish Cultural Center, this semi-abandoned building in Frick Park, right by Allderdice." Allderdice was the name of their high school, located in their Pittsburgh neighborhood, Squirrel Hill.

Zoya was stunned – there were names of DJs, all of whom sounded like mythical creatures: Dub, Buddha, Dieseldude. A whole new world of music was unfolding before her, with DJs, records, and dancing.

"Wow, for real? Sounds cool! So we could walk there?" Zoya examined the flier and then stared at her friend in amazement.

"Nah, Matt will give us a ride! He's a promoter there!" Jessica smiled proudly.

Jessica had been dating a skater named Matt for several weeks. They'd met in Oakland, at a plaza which was a popular skater hangout. Jessica invited Zoya there, too, but Zoya didn't like that pastime. She found it very boring. The guys were skateboarding, while the girls watched, waiting for one of the skaters to approach and talk to them. All of the skaters dressed the same – in wide pants worn low, oversized Stussy T-shirts, and Vans sneakers.

But Jessica was one of the lucky few, Matt had come up to her and struck up a conversation. And right away, they started going out. Matt was very affectionate, looked at Jessica adoringly, gave her lollipops, and was always around. As a high school drop-out, he had a lot of free time on his hands.

It turned out that Matt had brought over a stack of bright yellow flyers and dumped them on Jessica's porch. He had been hired as a promoter and would get into the rave for free for his role in distributing the flyers. The rest of them had to pay $15 to get in.

"So what time do we have to be there?" Zoya asked.

"Oh, it starts at eight." Jessica shrugged.

"That's kinda late," Zoya frowned. "I don't think I can make it." Picturing her parents' faces, she tried to think of how to explain that she was going somewhere 'for a night out,' as her father kept repeating, and decided that the rave wasn't worth it.

"I know what we can do! It's for the whole night, but we can tell my parents that I'll sleep over at your place and your parents that you'll sleep over at mine. And Matt can take us home afterwards. It's really, really cool there. Matt's already been once. Everyone dances and has fun. And the music! It's like a concert, only better." Jessica's voice was high-pitched, as always, when she was scheming.

"Could we leave earlier? You know, like at one in the morning?" Zoya could hardly imagine staying out till dawn.

"Well, we'll see how it goes," Jessica answered vaguely. "Matt told me it's actually till five in the morning, and then people split after that."

"Umm, I'll see if André wants to go. It can be a double date!" Zoya smiled at her friend in excitement. "Won't that be awesome?"

"Alright, let me know, okay!" Jessica rolled her eyes, but Zoya decided to ignore her friend's reaction. Zoya suspected that Jessica didn't approve of André, but she never clarified why.

"See you," Zoya waved goodbye to her friend as she headed to André's.

André had moved to Pittsburgh from Paris in January 1993 and was finishing his first semester at an American university. He managed to get credit for some of his Ecole Nationale de l'Administration (ENA) coursework, and entered Carnegie Mellon University as a sophomore.

Ever since his move to Pittsburgh, Zoya spent most of her time thinking about André. He lived near the skater hangout spot, on South Bouquet Street in Oakland. If one walked across the skatepark and turned left, his house was at the very bottom of the street. Zoya liked the name of his street, and every time she went to visit André, she felt like she was about to see a beautiful, blooming garden.

André rented a room in a house with two other guys. He attended the prestigious Carnegie Mellon University, while his roommates, Rick and Mikey, studied at the Art Institute of Pittsburgh. In their spare time, the two of them rode skateboards around Pittsburgh and tagged the city with graffiti.

Rick was known by the tag 'Bandit', which he scrawled in black angular letters on a wide variety of surfaces, from bridges and building walls to postcards and notepads. Sometimes, Rick would draw a little guy in a cap who was spitting the tag out of his mouth. Mikey was into graffiti, too, but he drew entire sketches. Both had a large supply of spray paint in their rooms, which they used for tagging. Zoya knew that they regularly stole it from stores, and they even had several rehearsed variations of who distracted the clerk while the other stuffed cans into his wide skater pants.

André, unlike his roommates, was constantly studying. And when he wasn't studying, he was working. Almost immediately after moving to Pittsburgh from Paris, he found a part-time job tutoring French, and then, within a few weeks, started tutoring an introductory math course. He surrounded himself with a group of students who almost instantly demanded his full attention. Zoya felt like in return for paying for André's lessons, they demanded his soul. He had little time to spend with Zoya, and much less so for such idle pastimes as skateboarding or tagging.

This didn't come easily, Zoya could tell. His studies were in English, and he switched majors when she started at Carnegie Mellon, changing his from economics to mathematics. But he didn't give up. André had put together a strict schedule for himself, and followed it to a 't'. Before important exams, he did not leave the house at all and, Zoya suspected, possibly forgot to eat. Zoya had always considered herself to be a good student and was proud of herself for working hard at school. But when she saw how zealously André studied, she realized that she was no match for him. If he did not spend the entire day reading, he grew silent and a little unhappy.

Zoya made her way to André's place. She crossed the

plaza, carefully avoiding the skaters, and walked down South Bouquet Street to his house. She'd planned on dropping by to see him and was glad that now she could share the exciting invitation to a rave in person. Zoya knocked, but there was no answer. She knocked again, and then tried the door. It was unlocked so she walked inside.

"Hello?" Zoya probed, as she entered the dimly lit living room. It was sparsely furnished with an old couch and three crates that André's roommates used for a variety of purposes, from storage to seating.

"Je suis là![1]" She heard André's muffled voice coming from upstairs. Zoya climbed the stairs up to his bedroom and found André sitting at his desk, barricaded, as usual, by a pile of huge textbooks and notebooks.

"Salut, André, Jessica invited me to a party on Saturday, do you want to come? It's this fun dance, called a rave." Zoya spoke fast, trying to mimic the excitement of Jessica's description. "It's nearby, and we can dance all night."

"All night? Umm, no, I'll pass. I have a physics exam on Monday, I have to study." André narrowed his eyes.

*André needs to finish the semester and to get good grades, how silly of me to invite him to a rave!* Zoya thought right away, but said nothing.

"You see, Zoé," André addressed Zoya the French way, "I have to prove to my mother that I am capable. I have to excel here, in Pittsburgh. I have no choice. I have to save her, because she's still with that creep. With that bastard de Vigny." André stared into the distance. "Mother must understand that she was wrong to marry him."

"But, André, she's been with him for ten years. What exactly do you expect to happen? And you left home." Zoya tried to reason with him.

"I did, but still. She'll understand one day. I'll come home,

---

1. I am here (fr)

I mean, not home anymore, but when I go back to France in a couple of weeks, I'll go and see her. And when she realizes that I am fine, how well I am doing, she'll know she'd made a mistake and she shouldn't have trusted de Vigny."

"Wait, what? You mean you're going to France this summer?" Zoya swallowed hard. She had counted on a break from school to finally spend more time with her boyfriend, when he would be free from his endless exams, tests and tutoring. Zoya assumed that André, once free from his school year, which ended in mid-May, would devote his time fully to her.

She dreamed how they would stroll through her neighborhood, Squirrel Hill, how they would visit the Arabica Cafe, where they went on their first date in the city, and how they would walk together in Schenley Park. *Or maybe André would take me to Sandcastle? And then we could go to the pool all summer long and enjoy life and each other!*

"Of course, I am going to France. I am spending the summer there. I have to see my mother. And my uncle." André frowned. Zoya knew that André's paternal uncle, Count Orsini, had rescued him from the clutches of the dreaded psychiatrist and stepfather, Jean-Marie de Vigny, and helped him settle in Pittsburgh.

"But why didn't you tell me before?" Zoya sat on the edge of André's bed, trying to occupy as little space as possible.

"I guess, I don't know, I figured you knew?" André shrugged. "I'm flying to Paris first, and then I'll take the train to Lyon to see my uncle. So, I'll mostly be there."

"I see." Zoya tried to maintain her composure. She felt her eyes well up with tears. "So when do you leave?"

"Right after the finals."

"But that's in two weeks!" Zoya exclaimed. The tips of her fingers felt cold.

"I'll be back at the end of August. I am trying to sublet my room for the summer." André responded in a businesslike tone, as if he didn't notice her disappointment and shattered hopes. Zoya did her best to stay calm while listening to his explanations about why he had to return to France for the summer, and then quickly found an excuse to leave. Once at home, she burst into tears. She cried for a long time, and so bitterly that the following morning her face was swollen and her eyes were still red.

*I am never going to call him again!* Zoya decided with resentment, as she sat in her bedroom. *I am not going to answer his calls! He's probably lying. He probably doesn't care that he won't see me for the whole summer. I'm sure he'll find a girl in Lyon. Probably more than one. Or maybe he already has a girlfriend there, and that's why he is going back.* Zoya tormented herself, becoming acrimonious and nervous. And just when her thoughts of André's infidelity were at their peak, she got a call from Jessica.

"Hey, so did you make up your mind? Are you going? Is André coming, too?"

"Oh, umm, yes! I mean, no." Zoya was suddenly sure that she should go to the rave.

"What do you mean, Zoya?"

"I am going, but without André!" Zoya responded, twisting the cord of the phone so that it cut into her hand. She bit her lip in an effort to stop the tears. The desire to see André was too strong, and the thought of their imminent parting gnawed at her. Zoya wanted to punish André for his carelessness and for the fact that his desire to go to France for the summer was stronger than his love for her.

"Alright, cool, so remember, the rave is till like five in the morning," Jessica said.

"Yeah, that's crazy. What do people do there all night?"

"Dance, of course! And it's only fifteen bucks! And Matt will introduce us to his friends. He knows the DJs!"

"He does?"

"Yeah! He knows them real well. That's why they hired him as a promoter."

There was pride in Jessica's voice, and Zoya couldn't help but compare Matt to André. Matt was proving himself to be a good boyfriend, inviting Jessica to parties and even promising to introduce her to interesting people. *And André?* Zoya thought bitterly. *All he does is sit at home reading. And then he'll leave for the whole summer, and that's it!*

To get ready for 'High Voltage' they did what they always did – Jessica dragged Zoya to a thrift store. These trips had become their favorite pastime. Jessica loved shopping for clothes there, and Zoya got used to it, too, and accompanied her friend almost every weekend. Sometimes Jessica's mother, Jane came along, but there was a downside to her presence – Jane talked so much. She went on and on about everything in the world, about her students, about the events at the school where she worked as a Civics teacher, or memories of her childhood. Jane reminded Zoya of her own mother, who always had to be the center of attention and dominated every conversation.

# CHAPTER 2

May 1st, 1993

For the rave, according to Jessica, they needed very bright clothes.

"Everyone there is dressed in sequins, you need something different, not the usual. You have to stand out." Jessica nodded as if to emphasize the importance of her words.

"What are we going to find with sequins?"

"Umm, maybe a nice shirt, like a disco vintage one from the seventies, or some cool pants. Last time, I saw cute bright blue ones with silver stripes, those would do. Maybe we'll get lucky." Jessica sighed.

The trip to the store went very well. Jessica found a neon orange tank top, and Zoya got a blouse with sequins. They decided on wearing corduroy pants. Jessica thought they would be comfortable to dance in and would make them look stylish.

Matt was late picking them up, and they only got to the Irish Center at 10 p.m. The center turned out to be a long, one-story structure right in the middle of Frick Park. Surrounded by such thick woods, that even though the building was not far from Zoya's high school, it was hidden from view, so she never suspected it existed.

Just as they got out of the car, a group of girls in pants so wide that their feet were completely covered, in short T-shirts that exposed their belly buttons, and covered head-to-toe with bracelets and sequins, flew by. Zoya compared her outfit to theirs and immediately felt out of place.

One of the girls sucked on a lollipop, rolling her eyes in enjoyment. "That's one awesome trip!" she said dreamily. Her hair was arranged in two neat pigtails. The second girl took her by the hand and dragged her in the direction of the building. "Music! I hear music! Soup, let's run!"

And then, Zoya heard it. It wasn't music, but rhythmic thumps that merged into a pulsating and vibrating noise that made the ground shake. All her feelings of unease dissipated, and Zoya immediately wanted to move to that sound, to dance, to jump, to follow the beat, to do anything but stand still. Jessica had a similar reaction. She grabbed Zoya's hand and they rushed inside.

"Wait, Jessica, Zoya, you have to pay first!" Matt shouted after them. He pointed at an unassuming-looking guy who was standing at the entrance. The guy was dressed in an oversized white t-shirt and baggy jeans with a chain that hooked onto his belt and slipped into his pocket. He had a baseball hat on his head, turned sideways, with the Stussy emblem.

"Yo, Brad, wassup," Matt said.

Instead of answering, the guy reached out and smacked Matt's hand.

"Come on in," Brad said after a pause. "Are they with you?" He nodded toward the girls, giving them an assessing look.

"Yeah," Matt said.

"That'll be fifteen apiece," Brad declared after a short pause, glancing askance at the girls. "You know it's costing us a ton! We got Dieseldude to spin tonight."

"Yeah, that's rad," Matt said, not at all embarrassed by the admission fee the girls were charged.

"Yeah, they are paying him two hundred bucks for the night, he's getting full of himself." Brad shrugged in disapproval.

Matt nodded to Jessica, and she pulled out the money she'd prepared. The guy handed them two yellow bracelets, and they fastened them on their wrists. Zoya put hers on next to her amber bracelet that Yegor Vlasov had given her before she left for America. Ever since she moved to Pittsburgh from Moscow two and a half years ago, Zoya wore this bracelet on her left wrist.

"Come on, let's go!" Jessica pulled her along.

The girls went in, leaving Matt at the front door. It was dark inside, with strobe lights glinting brightly from somewhere in the back of the room. The venue was almost empty, but in the middle of it two or three figures were moving to the music. There was a strange smell. In the back, Zoya saw a DJ pressing one headphone tightly to his shoulder. He stood behind a table, next to which there were several crates bursting with records. A scrawny man was rummaging through them. A group of girls was sitting in the corner, laughing. Zoya fidgeted with her bracelet, wishing André was there.

"Dieseldude won't be here till midnight; let's keep moving." Matt emerged from the shadows and pulled them along.

They went through to another room, also pitch black. The music in the second room was incredibly loud. Zoya felt it going through her ribcage as if her whole body was pulsing to the beat. There, too, in the back of the room was a table, and behind it was an almost identical DJ, moving his hand on the turntables. And just like in the first room, next to the table were several crates bursting with records. But there were more people. Zoya could see several groups dancing.

"There! Do you feel it?" Matt spun into a dance. He spread his legs wide, waved his arms, and moved quickly to the beat of the music. Zoya froze in place, mesmerized by the sight. Jessica broke into a dance next to her boyfriend. And Zoya joined them. At first, she resisted moving as fast as the others, but then she relaxed. It was dark, and Zoya liked that no one could see her. The music was mesmerizing, swirling, pulling her along. The rhythm was crisp and tapping, and Zoya felt a part of that sound that went through her whole body. She gave herself completely to the dance.

The song roared: 'Let there be house,' words that Zoya found fascinating. *What kind of a house are they talking about? What does this have to do with a house?* Zoya wondered, as she moved to the beat. The DJ abruptly changed the record, and someone booed. Matt laughed at something, and then he and Jessica started kissing. Zoya stood apart, alone. She was too embarrassed to be dancing without them. Just as she decided to go somewhere and hide, a guy materialized next to her.

"Hey," he shouted in her ear so that Zoya jerked in surprise. "My name is Evan."

"Evan?" Zoya thought she heard wrong, the name sounded just like the Russian name Ivan.

"Yes! Evan! And you?"

"Zoya!" she shouted back. She had to lean into the guy, and this sudden intimacy felt unfamiliar and thrilling. She felt a wave of excitement.

"Where are you from?" shouted Evan.

Zoya did not know how to answer this question. She did not like to respond that she was from Russia, because that immediately led to questions about spies and jokes about the Cold War.

But Evan, without waiting for an answer, continued. "I live in Greensburg."

"Where is that?" Zoya leaned in closer, nearly touching Evan's ear with her lips.

Talking was very difficult: the music was blasting so loudly that it drowned out their conversation, but Zoya liked it that way. She thought it hid her accent.

"It's not far from Pittsburgh, forty minutes."

"Oh I live near here, in Squirrel Hill," said Zoya, glad that she could avoid mentioning Russia.

"Cool! Wanna go chill outside? My friends are out there," Evan suggested.

A strobe light flashed over Evan, and Zoya noticed that he was quite tall, strongly built, with nice facial features. Zoya thought that André would probably not approve of her new acquaintance with the handsome Evan. *But André probably wouldn't even care,* Zoya decided. *Because in a couple of weeks he is going to his uncle in Lyon, leaving me all alone for the whole summer.* And Zoya nodded in agreement. *So why not have a chat with this cute guy? Especially since Jessica has disappeared somewhere.* Zoya followed Evan outside.

They ended up on the slope at the rear of the building. Zoya could still hear the pulsating music, but it wasn't as loud as before. Groups of ravers were sitting there, chirping merrily. Zoya recognized one of them, the girl with the lollipop, whom she had spotted in the parking lot. The lollipop girl suddenly jumped up, smiled sweetly, as she ran up to Evan and kissed him on the cheek. She then took off. Zoya thought the girl was very pretty: with a short haircut, huge eyes, and an unusual, sunny smile.

"That was Nikki, she's also from Greensburg. We go dancing together," explained Evan.

"I see," Zoya responded, looking wistfully after the beautiful Nikki.

"How old are you?" asked Evan as they sat down next to each other.

"Sixteen."

"What?" Evan gasped. "So you're still in high school?"

"Yeah, I'm in tenth grade. Well, almost eleventh," Zoya

corrected herself. After all, the end of the school year was only a few weeks away. "And you? Where do you go to school?" Evan looked slightly older, and Zoya assumed he was studying at one of the local universities.

"I don't. I work. At the newspaper."

"A newspaper? Which one?" Zoya's eyes lit up as she imagined that Evan was a famous war correspondent, a journalist who traveled to the hotspots of the world and interviewed celebrities.

"The *PennySaver*, it comes out on Saturdays. You've seen it, right?"

Zoya knew the *PennySaver* very well. It was a newspaper that advertised the buying and selling of everything from crockery to inflatable boats. More experienced immigrants recommended it to Zoya's parents when they were looking to buy a car, and Zoya blamed the *PennySaver* for the fact that her parents bought a horrible, shabby, broken-down Chevrolet Caprice Classic in beige with a wood grain panel across its body.

"Yeah, I do." Zoya sighed, immediately remembering the last time their car had stalled in the middle of a hill and they had to wait for AAA to come and rescue them. "What do you do there?" She realized that journalism was out of the question.

"I do desktop publishing. I trained myself. They pay me by the hour, for the time being, but I am going to one day become full time staff, with a salary, benefits, all that. That's my goal." Evan looked straight at her, and his look was so determined that Zoya understood: *he will definitely get what he wants.* "What kind of music do you like?" he asked Zoya after a short pause.

"Umm, just stuff," Zoya decided not to share her musical preferences. *I can't tell this guy that I like the Russian band 'Kino' and Vladimir Vysotsky, can I?*

"Oh. Do you like techno? Trance, maybe? I love trance! Or drum 'n' bass?"

"What's that?" This was the first time Zoya had heard these techno labels.

"It's just different kinds of techno. At midnight, Diesel-dude is going to play, his set is always drum 'n' bass. But dancing to his music is kinda hard." Evan laughed. "And umm, do you like Bjork?"

"Who's that?"

"She's this singer from Iceland. I think you look like her. She's got this really cool voice."

"Iceland?" Zoya had a vague idea of what people from Iceland looked like, but her eyes glistened with pleasure.

"Yeah. Listen, wanna give me your number? I go dancing with my friends a lot, so maybe we can go together?" Evan asked.

"Sure," Zoya said but felt a knot form in her stomach. Events of the evening were unfolding rapidly. She thought again that André probably would not approve of her meeting this guy, but the resentment against André was stronger. So she wrote down her number on the back of a yellow flier and handed it to Evan.

"You want mine?" Evan carefully put the paper with Zoya's number in his pocket.

"Oh yeah!" Zoya waited while he scribbled it quickly on another yellow flier then accepted the paper with Evan's number.

"All right, see you 'round," he said and left, leaving Zoya on the hillside.

She looked at her watch – it was a quarter to midnight. Deciding that she needed to find Jessica, Zoya walked toward the building. She saw Nikki, dancing right near the entrance. *She is a Goddess!* Zoya thought, admiring Nikki's flat stomach, exposed by her tiny t-shirt. The girl moved to the beat of the music and twirled her hips very fast. A group of fans gathered around her, clapping and urging her on. Nikki was spinning faster and faster; it looked like she was about to float off and fly away. She complemented the dance with her hands, and Zoya could not tear herself away from the marvelous spectacle. *I'd like to learn to dance like that someday, too,* Zoya thought.

Jessica appeared next to her. "Hey. Where have you been? I've been looking all over for you," she yelled.

"I was sitting outside."

"By yourself?"

"No, there was this guy, Evan. Maybe you saw him. He has long hair, kinda like this," Zoya pointed to her shoulders, "and he's tall."

"Nah, I don't pay attention to guys with long hair. Too girly. They gotta have hair shorter than mine, at least!" Jessica laughed. She had a short haircut, which suited her very well. Zoya shrugged in response. She didn't think that Evan looked girly. Quite the opposite, she found him quite handsome if she were honest with herself.

"You wanna go listen to Dieseldude? He's famous." Zoya touched her friend's arm.

"Yeah, Matt told me about him too. He goes on in fifteen minutes."

"Let's go."

The girls moved toward the main hall, where the DJ was about to perform. They noticed a short, thin man move past them. He was carrying a huge crate full of records. The man had delicate features, plucked eyebrows, and was dressed in a neatly pressed shirt and pants. The crowd of ravers parted in front of him and Zoya heard whispers: "Dieseldude, Dieseldude's here! There he is!"

The miniature man glared in the direction of his admirers, did not respond to their greetings, and continued to purposefully drag the crate to the table. He reminded Zoya of an ant moving up an ant hill.

Jessica nudged Zoya and whispered, "It's him! That's Dieseldude! Wow!"

"That's awesome!" Zoya was impressed that they had just seen such a celebrity, even though she had first heard about Dieseldude only a few hours prior.

"Hey," Jessica whispered, "Umm, do you want to drop acid?"

"What??" Zoya's mouth gaped open as she stared at Jessica.

"You know, drop acid? Like try it out? This guy, Matt knows him, he sells hits for like only twenty bucks. We can split it. 'Cause I've never tried it, and I'm afraid to do it alone."

"Acid? Oh my God!" Zoya knew acid caused hallucinations. Rick, André's roommate, told her that in high school he took acid every weekend, and was tripping for eight or sometimes ten hours at a time. "That's when I decided to become an artist," Rick recalled his experiences with a happy smile.

His words rang in Zoya's ears: "But for a trip, for a proper trip, you have to make sure all the conditions are perfect. You have to be careful. Otherwise you can get so caught up that you have nightmares afterwards, and it can be real bad. Monsters appear. Well, that's if it goes wrong or if someone scares you. I usually only hang out in my room, in a familiar and tested environment."

After this story from Rick, Zoya decided she didn't ever want to try acid. She didn't like the idea of having visions for hours, at the risk of ending up with nightmares.

"We'll be fine. Matt's got our backs, he promised," Jessica reassured her.

"Matt? You guys talked about it?"

"Well, yeah. He said if anything goes wrong, he'll definitely help us. He's an expert at this. Please," Jessica gave a pleading look, and Zoya suddenly agreed. *We'll only take half a dose each, and in such a cool place; nothing bad can happen.*

"Okay," Zoya whispered in her friend's ear.

"Yay! It's gonna be so much fun! There he is." Jessica pointed to a guy who immediately dashed over to them. Jessica went to hand him the money, but the guy shook his head and gestured to follow him outside.

Once there, on the same slope, where Zoya had sat with Evan, the guy said two words: "High five". He then held out his hand to Jessica, slapped her hand so that she could transfer the money into his, while slipping something into hers. He then grinned and immediately disappeared. Jessica clutched something in her hand, squeezing her fingers in a tight ball.

"Jessica, show me. I wanna see!" Zoya nudged, but her friend refused to open her fist.

"Let's go to the bathroom," she replied and headed back in. The girls went into the bathroom and locked themselves in the last stall for privacy. It was only there that Jessica agreed to open her palm. There was a tiny pale pink piece of paper in the middle of it.

"What is that? Is that acid?" Zoya asked, staring at the cute and colorful wafer. It seemed so innocent.

"Yeah, I guess so. I'm gonna split it in half." Jessica carefully picked up the paper with her fingernails and tore it in two. She handed one piece to Zoya.

"What do I do?"

"Nothing; you just need to put it on your tongue, and that's it, then you'll have a trip. Matt explained it to me."

"Are you sure that's it?" Zoya was afraid the tiny paper would slip away from her.

"Yes, of course, it's like, super easy." Jessica quickly placed the piece of paper on her tongue. "See," she said with a lisp, sticking her tongue out. Zoya obediently repeated after her friend. The piece of paper looked so harmless that Zoya felt silly. After a few seconds, she spit it out of her mouth.

"Why did you do that!?" Jessica yelped.

"It's not working! I don't feel anything." Zoya shrugged. "But whatever."

"It takes a while. You gotta wait. But now you won't have a trip! You ruined everything."

"Who cares?" Zoya breathed a sigh of relief: she had done her best, split acid with her friend, and everything would be all right. She didn't want the acid to work anyway.

"Wanna go dance?" Zoya suggested. "Now that Diesel-dude's on."

"Yeah, let's do it. We are gonna have so much fun!" Jessica squirmed and raced out of the bathroom.

The girls went into the main hall. The ant-like man Zoya had noticed earlier was standing behind the turntables, moving the fingers of his right hand on the record and bobbing his head to the beat at the same time. From time to time, Dieseldude jerked and moved something on a strange-looking apparatus that was next to the turntables. The girls got closer to the DJ, and Zoya noticed that Dieseldude had a pierced lip, and had a tiny, circular earring in his left eyebrow.

An enthusiastic crowd formed around him and watched his every move. Zoya started to watch, but then she noticed Evan standing next to Nikki. He smiled back and waved, inviting Zoya over. She went over to her new acquaintance and said hello.

Zoya tried dancing, but she soon found out that moving to Dieseldude's music was not easy. The rhythm was breaking up, and the sounds layered on top of each other in an unpredictable progression. Just when Zoya thought she had figured it out and moved to the beat, the music stopped and started again, and she had to speed up again to keep up with the rhythm. Zoya didn't like that. Evan, on the other hand, moved slowly, smoothly, and appeared to be enjoying himself.

"Well, what do you think? Isn't he awesome?" Evan yelled into her ear.

"Umm, I dunno," Zoya tried to answer as diplomatically as possible, without offending Evan, since he obviously likes Dieseldude.

"It's called breakbeat, jungle, that kind of music. You'll get used to it. It was weird for me to dance to it at first, too." Evan gave Zoya a sympathetic look. "It's okay." He nodded encouragingly and continued his strange body movements.

Zoya stopped dancing and saw Jessica leaning against the wall.

"Are you okay?" Zoya touched her friend's hand.

"Yeah!!" Jessica gave her a crooked smile. "I think it's working. I can see some circles," she pointed somewhere at a distance. "Are there circles there?" Zoya looked to where Jessica was pointing and saw a bright pink spiral.

"There is no circle there, there is a spiral," she answered. "Oh!!!"

"Yeah, that's what I am talking about! Oh, Zoya, I'm scared! What's going to happen?"

"Let's sit outside," Zoya suggested, now desperate to get out of the crowded room.

"Okay." Jessica squealed. "Where's Matt? Have you seen him?"

"No, I haven't." Zoya felt panic rising at the pit of her stomach. *What if we both have a bad trip? Who would help us?*

The girls went outside and sat on the grass, on the slope where Zoya and Evan had been earlier. Nearby was a group of people speaking animatedly. Zoya heard a strange word: PLUR, PLUR, a guy was vigorously nodding and repeating: "Yeah! PLUR forever!"

Suddenly, the girl who was sitting the closest to Zoya and Jessica looked in Zoya's direction and asked:

"PLUR! Whatcha think?"

"What is that?" Zoya asked.

"It's our motto! All ravers! PLUR! Peace, Love, Unity,

Respect! Get it?" The girl handed her a lollipop. "Here, this is for you! PLUR!!!"

The rest of the group cheered. Zoya felt them welcoming her, despite the fact that they were total strangers. She looked at Jessica. Someone had also handed her a lollipop, and Jessica twirled it in her hand, looking at it with great interest.

"Are you all right?" Zoya leaned in to see the expression on her friend's face.

"Yes!!! He spoke to me!" Jessica smiled at the candy.

"Who?"

"The lollipop!!! He said something to me, but I couldn't hear." Jessica turned the lollipop around and gently stroked the shiny surface with her finger. "Say it! Please, little guy, say it again! There's something you want to tell me! I know it. Come on, honey, come on, don't be shy."

A bright pink spiral flashed before Zoya's eyes. *Maybe we should look for Matt? He promised to help if things went wrong,* flashed through her head. She looked at Jessica, who was still enthralled by the lollipop, which definitely meant that something wasn't right. *I shouldn't leave her alone,* Zoya hesitated, but then decided that getting help was more important. Zoya got up and headed quickly in the direction of the main hall.

The place had gotten very crowded, and it was nearly impossible to make out faces in the darkness. Instead of Dieseldude, another DJ was spinning. The walls were vibrating to the rhythm. Zoya headed straight to the spot where she'd seen Evan and Nikki dancing, but he wasn't there.

She made her way back to the exit, maneuvering through the crowd. Zoya looked around. Groups of strangers were wandering. Two people were kissing. Someone was smoking. She strained to make out a familiar face, but didn't recognize anyone. A man jogged past her. There was shouting, "Look, a naked man!", then laughter. Zoya felt fear gripping her insides: *What if Matt left us here? What then?*

A bright pink spiral floated in front of her eyes again and encircled her. Zoya was sure that if she didn't get rid of it at once, the spiral would strangle her, like a snake. She waved her hand in front of her eyes and the snake disappeared, and at the same moment Zoya saw Evan standing next to her.

"What are you doing?" he asked, giving her a concerned look. "What's up with your hands?"

"Evan! It's you!" Zoya yelped. She felt like leaping and giving him a hug. "Please, I'm sorry, but I have to go home. I live close to here. And so does my friend, we need to leave. Could you take us home, please?" Zoya swept her hand over her eyes again to remove another snake.

"Sure. Umm, you didn't take anything, did you?" Evan asked with interest.

"I kinda did. It was such a little scrap of paper, I didn't think it would work. Jessica and I split it," said Zoya. She badly wanted to share the experience of the evening with someone.

"Where did you get it?"

"We bought it here, from some guy. Jessica's boyfriend knows him."

"You shouldn't have done that." Evan shook his head and sighed.

The persistent pink snake floated in front of Zoya's face again, but she managed to push it away. But this time, the snake outmaneuvered her – it swam further away, and then transformed into purple patterns. Zoya peered into them and realized that they were hieroglyphics.

*I am like Schliemann,* Zoya thought of the famous archeologist, *I gotta crack the code!* And then she thought back to the spirals she saw at St. Anne's after being drugged with Klonopin and lithium by the evil psychiatrist de Vigny.

Before she could develop that thought any further, one of the signs turned into a dancing man, and then another, and all these purple men suddenly stood in a row and began twirling their arms and legs and dancing to the beat. Another thought flashed through her mind. *No, no, what did Sherlock Holmes do? How did he solve The Adventure of the Dancing Men?*

"Hey, Zoya! What are you doing?" Evan reached for her hand, and that stopped the flashes. "You know, you really shouldn't have done that. I never take drugs. I'm straight-edge. And you, too, remember. Please don't do that again. Let's go, I'll take you home. I was about to leave anyway."

"How do I stop it?" Zoya asked in a small voice.

"Don't worry, it'll pass. Stay home, draw, don't go anywhere, you'll stop tripping by tomorrow night."

"By tomorrow night?? What?" Zoya saw the pink snake again. The snake hissed and stuck out a bright crimson split tongue. One part of the tongue swam to the right, and the other began to grow, rapidly increasing in size, and was about to touch Zoya's face. She tried to dodge it, but a part of the tongue extended and wrapped itself around her neck.

"Aaaa!" Zoya yelled, twisting, so as to avoid the snake tongue. "We need to get Jessica, too."

"Oh, sure," Evan shrugged indefinitely. "Let's look for her, then. Maybe she's dancing."

"No, she was over there on the lawn. I left her there, and I went to look for Matt. That's her boyfriend. He drove us here."

"Okay. Let's go to the lawn, then."

Zoya followed Evan and was glad that her new acquaintance was so thoughtful. They went down to the slope, where Zoya immediately saw Jessica. Her friend was cooing something softly to the lollipop.

"Is that her?" Evan asked.

Zoya nodded and sighed.

"Jessica, come on, let's go." Zoya gently touched her friend's shoulder.

"Where to? What for? We just got here! It's so nice here!" Jessica gave her a hazy look. *Am I like this now, too?* Zoya worried. The snake hissed again, and Zoya involuntarily reached for Evan's hand. When she held his hand, she wasn't as scared. Evan was tall and strong and could repel any snake.

"Jessica! Is your name Jessica?" Evan stood in front of her. "I'll take you and Zoya home. You just tell me where to go, I know the area."

"Are you the long-haired one? Like a girl! I remember!" Jessica giggled.

"Yes, that's me." Evan grinned. "Come on, let's go."

Jessica obediently got up and followed Evan and Zoya to the parking lot.

"Here, this is my car." Evan pointed carelessly at a black Saab. "I only drive European cars."

"Why?" Zoya asked. She'd never heard anyone say that.

"I like it that way. And always a manual." Evan opened the door for Zoya and she sat in the front. Jessica got in the back. "Do you know where to go?"

Zoya nodded.

"First we'll take Jessica, then you," Evan said, starting the car.

They drove off and within ten minutes unloaded Jessica outside her house. Just then, Zoya remembered that they had lied to their parents about spending the night at each other's homes. *How will they explain their sudden appearance at home in the wee hours of the morning?* But it was too late. Jessica had already disappeared inside.

"How do we get to your place?" Evan looked at Zoya carefully, and she noticed that he was wearing glasses. "How did I not pay attention before?" Zoya wondered. The glasses had black frames and emphasized the blue of his eyes.

"I live right down the street. You take Beechwood and then turn right on Aylesboro," Zoya said. The names of these streets had become familiar after two years of living in Pittsburgh, though at first Zoya found them sounding grandiose.

"So you and Jessica go to the same high school?"

"Yeah, Allderdice."

"How long have you been friends?"

"Umm, about a year," Zoya said.

"Oh, I thought maybe a long time. You take such good care of her."

"Thanks, but no, I was born in Russia. I moved to Pittsburgh right before high school."

"Cool. I was just thinking maybe I heard an accent. Oh, wow. I have Polish roots. My last name is Kalina. Does it sound Polish to you?"

"Oh yeah, it does."

Zoya saw the pink snake again, and was terrified that she would soon have to face it on her own. The car stopped in front of her house.

"Okay, I'm going. I have to work in the morning. Bye. It was nice to meet you."

"Nice to meet you, too." Zoya pulled at the door, but Evan touched her elbow gently.

"Yeah, listen, don't drop acid anymore. I'll call you after work. You try to get some sleep."

Zoya nodded in response.

When she entered the apartment, the clock showed half past four in the morning. Her parents were asleep. Zoya rustled cautiously into her room, but then she got a strong urge to look at herself in the mirror. She tiptoed into the bathroom. Staring from her reflection were the eyes of a snake with pink rays coming out of them, and she averted her eyes in fear, but a second later, when she looked at herself in the mirror again, the vision was gone. With trembling hands, Zoya turned the water on, and, as it poured from the faucet, she heard music, as if the water was beating a rhythm against the sink. She bobbed her head to the rhythm, and then splashed washed on her face. Water made her feel better, the visions receded.

*Phew, finally! Over, at last,* thought Zoya, *now I can go to sleep*. She snuck into her room and crawled into bed. But sleeping was out of the question. Colorful spirals flew around the room. Zoya watched them move closer, then farther away. The spirals grew larger, then shrunk, and when she closed her eyes, they completely consumed her being.

After a few minutes, Zoya remembered what Evan said about drawing. She turned on the light, pulled out the markers she hadn't touched in over six months, since the day she had written her letter to André, and sat at her desk. Once she started drawing, she remembered the snail she had drawn in Moscow after her conversation with Inna Lvovna.

*Temporal branches* flashed through her mind. *Snail. Escargot.* Zoya thought of Paris and how she had finally visited it a few weeks ago.

*Did I actually get to go to Paris? How could it have been me, the same me who had just danced at a rave; and how could I have been to France and visited amazing palaces and admired castles and looked at paintings, and now I had just been to a real rave! And everyone was dancing! And PLUR! How weird!?* Zoya was reeling in amazement over the previous night's events in her head. *And they are so cool! Nikki is such a good dancer! Maybe Evan will introduce us.*

Zoya really wanted to dance as well as Nikki and to be as pretty as her. *PLUR! PLUR! Peace, love, unity, respect! Peace, love, unity, respect! How wonderful.* Zoya wanted to be back at the rave, to be surrounded by the people who were so friendly and welcoming. She closed her eyes. The pink snake receded, and she fell asleep.

# CHAPTER 3

"Zoya! Zoya! Phone for you!" She heard her father's voice.

"I'm coming!" she whispered. Her voice was hoarse.

"Hurry up. It's half past one. Why are you still asleep?" Her father shrieked into the receiver with his horrible Russian accent: "Sleep, she iz sleep," but Zoya had already jumped out of the room and tried to snatch the phone.

"Papa, I'm awake!"

"Phone for you. The Bear!"

Zoya sighed at her father's nickname for André, as she snatched the receiver.

"Hello," said Zoya, gripping the handset with sweaty palms. She tried her best to make her greeting sound calm and confident, but her voice trembled.

"Zoya! Hello." She blushed, hearing his familiar voice. A bright purple swirl floated before her eyes and disappeared. "Are you all right?" André could always sense her mood. Sometimes it seemed to Zoya that he was sitting right inside of her head, watching her. *Oh no, what do I do? Do I have to tell him about dropping acid last night?* She panicked.

"Yes," Zoya croaked.

"How did it go yesterday? I thought about you. I miss you very much." This phrase André always said in French: "Tu me manques beaucoup[1]", to which Zoya always replied: "Et toi aussi.[2]" This exchange of remarks has become a well-rehearsed ritual.

"Oh it was nothing much; we danced a lot," answered Zoya, sticking to the facts. She knew that if she began to lie, André would sense it at once.

"And how was the music? Did you like it?"

"Yes! Very much. And there was this DJ there, he's tiny, but very famous. He had a pierced lip, and he played this music. I didn't understand it, but it was called 'drum 'n' bass'. It's very hard to dance to it, but you can listen to it. But Evan told me I'd get used to it." Zoya bit her tongue, but it was too late.

"Who's Evan? Not Matt?" André enquired. Zoya thought she heard steely notes in his tone.

"Evan is his friend," Zoya lied. "He gave us a ride home."

"What about Matt? Why not him?" Zoya felt like she was drowning. Only a miracle would save her now.

"It's just that Matt's a promoter, he didn't have time to take us back, although he offered. But he was busy, and then Evan said it was on his way, so we went with him. We got back around two in the morning."

"So that's not too late. Why were you still asleep when I called?" Zoya was struck again by André's all-seeing eye.

"I just couldn't sleep afterwards, but the rave was cool, I had fun."

"I see. Maybe I'll go there with you next time," André promised. "I get off at around five tonight, wanna meet at the Beehive?"

------

1. I miss you a lot (fr)
2. you too (fr)

The Beehive was their favorite place in Oakland. It was a kind of a club, cafe, concert hall, and movie theater all in one. It was located in an inconspicuous building right on Forbes Avenue, near the University of Pittsburgh, and attracted a crowd of misfits. One could easily find groups of punks, skaters, ravers, and various fringe groups from all over Pittsburgh there.

Maroon curtains covered the bay windows, making the interior of the Beehive feel like perpetual twilight. The cafe was run by a wiry guy named Isaac, who had his ears pierced in at least ten places, his arms covered with tattoos, and his pants festooned with thick chains. Isaac liked André, and would usually discuss Heidegger with him. Around Isaac, Zoya felt invisible – he never noticed her.

When she went to the cafe with André, Isaac looked straight through her, took an order only from André, and never acknowledged her existence other than as an appendage to André. But she didn't mind. On the contrary, she was grateful to be ignored and surreptitiously examined Isaac, impressed by his eccentricity.

Any other day, Zoya would have gladly agreed to go to the Beehive. She loved meeting André there. She could sit and stare at him for hours, simply admiring him – so handsome and incredible he seemed to her. But the day after her first rave, she was not yet back to normal, and André would notice something was off right away. She was still seeing the strange spirals before her eyes. And also a terrible fatigue and a feeling of withdrawal in her body... Zoya remembered that Evan had warned her that the trip could last until the evening.

The problem was that she had never refused André anything and had a hard time coming up with a plausible excuse to refuse the meeting. *Could I say no? André had exams and tutoring, and who knew: if we do not meet today, when else would he find time for me?* So Zoya, despite herself, said yes. They agreed to meet at five.

After hanging up, Zoya returned to her room. The clothes she had worn to the rave, and had thrown on the floor, reeked of cigarettes. Zoya sniffed and realized that her hair smelled like smoke, too. She felt sick to her stomach. Pink circles swirled in front of her eyes and she felt a strong urge to lie down, but instead Zoya forced herself to take a shower. She had to get ready to see André.

Water brought relief. As Zoya soaped her hair with Pantene, the smell of shampoo so familiar since moving to America, now drowned out the cigarettes and her mood improved. Even the irritating pink circles retreated. After taking a shower, Zoya threw the putrid rave clothes into the bathtub to soak them. She thought about André's first and only meeting with her parents.

After learning that André's last name was Orsini, Zoya's father immediately rechristened him 'the Bear' and savored the opportunity to use the nickname. Zoya's father didn't like André but she did not know why. Nothing could change her father's attitude: neither the fact that André insisted on speaking Russian to him, nor the fact that he was invariably polite and courteous.

From the start, Zoya's father decided that André was not worthy of a relationship with his daughter. Upon learning that Zoya was dating the Frenchman, her father casually remarked: "The French are a despicable nation. Sneaky. Dostoevsky captured it in 'The Gambler'. This is a well-known fact. It's perfectly reflected in his works."

The argument that André was of Corsican descent didn't work on her father. After his first conversation with André, he concluded that André was not to be trusted and that he had few prospects in life based on his inferior knowledge of math and science.

"And what do they teach them there?" Her father raised

his hands up in indignation after having a conversation with André about his program at Carnegie Mellon. "We covered stuff like that in high school. It's the basics. Derivatives. I'm just blown away. And this Carnegie Mellon is a prestigious university? What a joke!"

Zoya never knew how to respond to her father's reaction. *What was a joke – was it André or his university? Or both?* Arguing with her father was useless. Once he made up his mind about something, he rarely changed it.

It wasn't Zoya's idea to introduce André to her parents, and she only did it upon André's insistence. He had come over to the Kassatkins' for tea, and brought a bouquet of flowers, which he handed to Zoya's mother. Introducing himself in Russian, he carefully pronounced every word he had practiced and memorized.

André could not roll the 'r' the Russian way, and had a strong French accent, and Zoya noticed that her father winced, as André finished his introduction. The Frenchman shook hands with Zoya's father, and they all sat down at the table. Ahead of André's visit, Zoya scrubbed the kitchen for hours to make it look decent and appealing. She cleaned the sink and the stove, which was usually covered in soot. Zoya had even changed the tablecloth, replacing it with a new, white one. But the kitchen still seemed dirty and squalid, and Zoya was embarrassed by her surroundings. She'd tried to dissuade André from coming over to meet her parents, but to no avail.

"We don't have anything to hide, do we? We're in a serious relationship. And besides, I think your parents would want to know where you spend your time."

Mentioning the fact that their relationship was 'serious' made Zoya nervous. *It can't be that serious, because we haven't even had sex yet!* She reasoned. But André had explicitly told her that they would not have sex until Zoya was 'older'. *If he really loved me, he wouldn't wait so long,* she fumed, mulling over their conversations on the topic.

"And then, Zoya, you are barely sixteen, you know very well that our relationship is against the law in America! I can be arrested and deported from the country!" André would explain if they talked about this issue.

"André! It's not like I'm going to run and complain about you."

"I don't want to break the law. I am not some kind of a pervert. I could go to prison!"

"So when we met and I was twelve and you were fifteen, everything was okay, but now it's not?" Zoya countered. "And just because you turned eighteen it's different?"

"I'm nineteen now. And, according to American law, yes." André would kiss her on the nose, and Zoya's eyes would feel tears starting. She wished that André would be so over-taken with passion, that he would rip off her clothes at once, rather than treat her as if she were a little girl.

"But we're in love, aren't we?" Zoya would parry.

"Yes, we are," André would answer and give her a long stare, burning her with his gray eyes. That look made Zoya so hot with desire that she wanted only one thing: that André would take her right there and then, make her his and never let her go. But instead, he would say that there was no hurry, and that when everything would happen 'for real', she would be grateful. And so, Zoya would fall silent.

André's meeting with her parents was doomed from the start. Her father tried to establish André's interests beyond his studies, asked the young man if he liked Russian litera-ture, and then tried to tell him about the 'Belkin Tales' and the iconic role of this work in Russian literature, then assured Zoya's suitor that even if he ever managed to read Pushkin in Russian, he would not understand anything, because to understand Pushkin one must have a Russian soul. And all foreigners lacked it. And at the end, her father told André about the incompatibility of Russians with other nations, using Leskov's 'Iron Will' as an example.

"This German fellow, the character in his story, was a very decent man. Very well-mannered, intelligent, but he couldn't adapt to life in Russia," said Peter Kassatkin, pouring Andrei another steaming hot mug of tea. Zoya's mother didn't stop her husband. The whole time, Zoya's father spoke in Russian, not caring whether André could understand him. And André politely nodded and kept silent. After that meeting, Zoya never brought André to her house again, and he did not insist on it either.

Zoya checked herself in the mirror and then remembered that André was leaving for the whole summer, thereby crushing all her plans. She'd imagined their relationship blossoming over the summer, and she would start a job at the library, working there as an assistant, or a 'page'.

She got the library job thanks Melissa, who also went to Allderdice. Melissa was a year older than Zoya. She wore bright makeup, smoked, bleached and permed her hair, and slept with a senior. Melissa had taken a liking to Zoya after they met in gym class. Both of them fell behind, when they had to do several laps around the school. Melissa told Zoya that she hated running and 'her lungs were no good' because of smoking, and Zoya immediately shared her failed attempt to join the running club and even mentioned how she fell right in front of their handsome classmate, Danny, and they both laughed. Zoya and Melissa started spending time together, chatting and laughing in gym, and one day Melissa suggested that Zoya should get a job at the library. Responsibilities of a library assistant, according to Melissa, were to shelve books, help patrons check them out, and organize magazines and tapes, when requested.

"I'm so bored there, they're all nerds. The rest of the library assistants are assholes. And the worst is this idiot, Tiffany, who quotes the Bible all the time. And she's such a goody two shoes. I can't stand it. You should work there, we'll have so much fun together!"

"Oh! Yeah! I'd love that!" Zoya's heart leaped at the thought of being able to spend all that time around books. A job at the library didn't seem like work at all.

"Just come over there one day when I am there, I'll introduce you," Melissa promised.

Despite her bad-girl exterior, Melissa was a hard worker, and the librarians loved her. Melissa recommended Zoya to the head librarian, Miss Specter, and now all Zoya had to do was to wait until summer break began, get her official work permit, and start working.

But besides the job at the library, Zoya didn't have any other plans. *How will I spend the rest of the summer*? The thought gnawed at Zoya. *I will be all alone! André would be gone, and Jessica is going on vacation with her parents.* And then Zoya remembered Evan.

Zoya gasped, leaped to pull out her pants from the tub, checked her pockets and produced the yellow High Voltage flier with Evan's number that miraculously survived. Zoya could still make out the number. Zoya clutched the paper as she proceeded to her bedroom, carefully placed it on her desk and copied Evan's number in her notebook, deciding that she would definitely have to see him again.

# CHAPTER 4

**M**ay 2nd, 1993

At four o'clock, Zoya was fully dressed and ready to go. To get to the Beehive, she had to take the bus down Forbes Avenue, and on Sundays they rarely ran. Zoya was putting her shoes on, when she heard her father's voice booming in her ear.

"Zoya, where are you going?"

"I'm going out for a walk," Zoya lied, not wanting to mention André unnecessarily, so as not to cause a tirade about the unreliability of the French.

"With whom? With Sofie? Weren't you together last night?" Zoya understood that her father was referring to Jessica – he often confused the names of her friends, and sometimes Zoya wondered if he did it on purpose.

"Yes, last night we had a sleepover. It's an American thing," Zoya said, hoping that her father would be impressed by her integration into American society. When Zoya first told her parents about Jessica, they were even glad that she'd made a real American friend. "But I am just going for a walk now."

"I don't understand why you had to be gone all night. What time will you be back?"

"Nine o'clock."

"You have school tomorrow. You should get some rest."

"Papa, don't worry, it's okay."

The fact that her father expressed concern about school was unusual. He never got into such details, and Zoya was sure that her father didn't know what time school started in the morning, or the names of her teachers.

"Zoya, I don't like you disappearing at night. It's not good. You should be home. With us. You're a girl."

"Papa, come on."

"I'm really worried about you. Just keep that in mind. You're going out, and I'm going to be on pins and needles. And your mother, too. We were up all night waiting for you."

"You were up all night?" Zoya opened her eyes wide. When she got home in the middle of the night, the apartment was quiet, and she was sure her parents had been asleep.

"We were up all night waiting for you. Mind you, if you go out again tonight, it could really wreak havoc on our health. Now go … if your conscience allows you. We'll see you at eight o'clock tonight. No later."

Zoya's heart sank. *My parents are old, they're almost fifty. Or more like forty-five, but they're still old. Papa has high blood pressure; I can't stress them out. What should I do? Papa needs to rest, he gets so tired at work.*

Recently, Zoya's father got a job at PPG. It was a real American job as a junior engineer at a big chemical firm in Pittsburgh, a prestigious position among immigrants and getting it was a small miracle. Peter Kassatkin finally was employed after searching for two years in vain, when they despaired that he would ever find a job.

Lydia, Alexei Kulikov's mother, played a key role in helping Zoya's father get a job. When she and Alexei visited the Kassatkins for the New Year's celebration in 1993, she promised to show his resume to her boss, Moishe, and kept her promise. Zoya's father was called for an interview and started working in March of that year. And now, a few weeks later, Zoya's parents still could not believe their luck and gushed over Lydia's generosity and their fantastic good fortune daily.

Only Zoya knew that it wasn't Lydia or luck that helped her father get the job. The real reason was her New Year's wish. On New Year's eve, Zoya had made two wishes: for her father to get a real job and for her to be with André. Now both of these wishes had come true.

Zoya left the apartment with a heavy heart. The thought that her parents had been waiting up for her all night nagged at her. *Could they have heard everything? When I couldn't sleep, when I was drawing? But weren't they sleeping? It was so quiet. Did Papa lie to me? To make me feel guilty? But he wouldn't do that.*

Zoya mulled over the conversation with her father, as she arrived at the bus stop and squeezed herself into the shadiest corner of the stop. She sighed, trying to seem as inconspicuous as possible – there was always a chance that a fellow Russian immigrant would see her and then immediately report to her parents that they had run into Zoya at a bus stop. And then questions would follow. At last, the bus arrived and Zoya was distracted from her sad thoughts.

Once onboard, Zoya had calmed down. She sat, looking out the window, dreaming how she would soon see André. Suddenly, a bright pink arrow flashed before her eyes. It wasn't curved, like the snakes she had seen earlier, but straight and pointed, ready to strike. Zoya flinched - she had managed to forget the events of the previous night, but now fear gripped her throat.

*What if these visions will haunt me the rest of my life? What if they never go away? Why? Why did I do it? I shouldn't have listened to Jessica!* Zoya fretted. *I didn't want to drop acid in the first place. But at least I made a friend. I should call Evan.* Zoya remembered the long-haired guy again, and decided to call him once she got back home.

When Zoya walked into the Beehive, André was already sitting by the window, in their favorite spot. It was hard to see in the dimly lit cafe, and Zoya hesitated at the door, while her eyes adjusted to the twilight. She felt his eyes on her before she saw him, and moved in his direction.

"I ordered you a mocha, your favorite." André moved the cup toward her and smiled, and Zoya melted at the sight of his slightly slanting dark-gray eyes. His handsome features never ceased to amaze her. Zoya liked everything about him: his masculine chin, the straight nose, the shape of his eyes, and his slightly curly brown hair.

"Thank you." Zoya smiled and pushed her chair closer to his. Ever since André had told her that mocha was named after a Yemeni city, where coffee was invented, Zoya felt a strong affinity to the drink.

"So, what did you think? You liked it?" asked André. He looked at Zoya attentively.

"Mocha? Yeah, it's so good!" She lifted her cup and took a sip.

"No, the rave." André pierced Zoya with testing eyes, and she shivered under his gaze. She was certain he could see right through her. *It's just a matter of time before he finds out about the acid and that I exchanged numbers with Evan.*

"Umm, well, I dunno." She hid the fact that she really enjoyed High Voltage. So much so that she thought about going to another rave again, as soon as possible. Zoya loved everything about the rave: the music, and the people, and how friendly they all were, how they all welcomed her, their sincere smiles, and the beautiful dancers who moved so well to the music, and the fact that she saw a famous DJ named Dieseldude.

"You know, I kind of wish I had gone there with you. I am

ready for the exam, so I could have come last night." André sighed.

"Oh! Sure! We can go together again another time; it turns out that they happen almost every week," said Zoya and immediately stopped herself. For a second, she had forgotten that André was about to leave for France for the whole summer. Her face dropped. The thought of separating from André for three long months was unbearable.

"Zoé, don't worry. We'll see each other soon, it's only three months, that's all. I give you my word." André took her hand, and Zoya felt an electric shock from his touch. She loved the warmth of his fingers in her palm.

"Three and a half," Zoya corrected André and frowned.

"Okay, three and a half. But it's not that long. I hadn't seen you in over two years before, and it was no big deal. Right?" André gave Zoya a pleading look, as if begging her to agree with his calculations.

"Yes, but it was different then. We were younger then, and anyway…"

"But back then, we didn't know we'd ever be in the same city! Same country even! Now all we have to do is wait out the summer."

"Why are you going away at all? Why do you have to leave in the first place?" Zoya couldn't help asking the question that had been nagging at her. She immediately regretted her words, because a look of dissatisfaction crossed André's face. His was the look of a man who did not like to be questioned.

Zoya knew that her words would make him unhappy, but she could not reconcile herself with the idea that André had chosen a trip to Lyon over a whole summer with her.

"Because it's important to me: I left home on bad terms, I have to find out some things and try to mend my relationship with Maman. My uncle agrees with me. Otherwise, all is lost."

"What is lost?"

"My relationship with her. If I don't work things out with her now, it'll be too late."

"That makes sense," Zoya nodded in agreement and then looked up at André: "What about de Vigny? Will you see him?" André had told Zoya several times about his stepfather, a scary doctor who tried to poison him with pills, and then locked him up in an asylum to get access to his inheritance. André miraculously escaped from the clutches of the evil man with the help of his uncle.

"I don't know. I hope not. But my mother may not agree to a meeting without de Vigny. She trusts him. And I must be able to persuade her that he is doing something wrong. It won't be easy. Do you understand?"

"Of course I do. But that's terrible!" Zoya threw her hands up in frustration.

For a moment, she had forgotten about her desire to spend the whole summer with André. Now, Zoya was heartily rooting for him and hoping for his victory over the terrible doctor.

"I don't understand it myself. While my father was alive, everything was different. She was normal, I don't know, a regular mother. And then it was like she had been switched. As soon as de Vigny came along, she immediately fell under his spell."

"Maybe he's drugging her, too, like he did with you? Maybe he's giving her some pills?" Zoya jumped at the thought.

"Oh! That hadn't occurred to me. You're really something! You are so smart!" André looked at Zoya with admiration, and her cheeks turned beet red at the thought that she said something that he would find useful. "It must be true. When my dad died, she was depressed and she met de Vigny, and he treated her. I only found out later, it was all hidden from me; but maybe he still gives her some pills?"

"That sounds about right." Zoya felt like Sherlock Holmes applying deductive reasoning. "But if that's the case, you'll have to talk to your uncle. If she is being drugged, she won't be able to be open with you."

"Yes, that's right. I'll have to talk to my uncle about all this. Why didn't I think of this before?" André shook his head. "I was wrong to resent her, if this scoundrel had been poisoning her all these years."

"Well, that has not yet been proven," said Zoya. She didn't want André to forgive his mother so quickly.

"I think you're right. You're so good! That's why they say, two heads are better than one!" André kissed Zoya on the cheek. "Do you want to go for a walk?"

Zoya had already finished her mocha and was looking at the traces of hot chocolate at the bottom of the cup. She remembered that they would have to part soon, and tears welled up in her eyes.

"Zoé, what are you thinking about?" André caressed her hand. "Are you worried about me leaving again?"

"Yes." Zoya nodded and realized that tears had already started streaming on their own. She sighed heavily, trying to stop them, but it didn't help. Then started rubbing her eyes. She felt that her nose was red and that she had to leave the cafe immediately, or she would cry right there. Behind the bar was the perennial skinny Isaac, and she didn't want him to see her in tears.

"Let's go to Flagstaff?" André was always very sensitive to her moods and he knew that it was her favorite and would make her feel better.

Flagstaff was a hill near Oakland that overlooked the Pittsburgh skyline. On Sunday nights in the summer, families with little children spread out blankets and food, preparing for the free movie shown there, while at the top of the hill, in the farthest corner from the screen, teenagers reigned.

André stood up and gave Zoya his hand, and then took

her in his arms. "Zoé, don't cry, please. We'll see each other before I leave, and everything will be fine. It will. I promise you. I'll write you a letter every day, okay? Every day."

"Okay," Zoya muttered back. She liked the idea of writing to André every day, it would be wonderful, and they could keep in touch..

"I'll also try to call you, once a week. I hope you won't be too busy to answer the phone with your library job." André kissed her on the nose.

Zoya calmed down and they walked down the half-empty Forbes Avenue toward Schenley Park. There were few passersby, almost no cars, as all the bustle of Oakland quieted down on Sundays. Only an occasional student scurried past them. The plaza that was usually crowded with skaters was nearly empty.

"Ollie! Do an ollie!" Zoya overheard. There was a rumble of the skateboard against the pavement, followed by cheers of approval. The girls stood around and looked at the skaters with adoration. Zoya glanced disdainfully in their direction, gripping André's hand tighter. She had a real boyfriend and didn't need the attention of skaters.

They put the Cathedral of Learning, a tall tower that was the symbol of the University of Pittsburgh and loomed sternly over Oakland, behind them. Zoya had already visited the Cathedral of Learning twice, during the obligatory tour that newly arrived immigrants received. Inside, the building was Gothic in style, right down to the soaring ceilings and the mosaics.

Seeing the tower, Zoya's thoughts drifted to the strange architectural style, which imitated the European tradition, gone out of fashion over five hundred years ago. *I wonder why they decided to build something like this in Pittsburgh, of all places,* she wondered. Architecture in America had always been a mystery to her, from the expansive Victorian mansions, one of which housed their apartment, to the squat buildings with flattened ceilings that were built on the outskirts of the city.

They turned by the Hillman Library, passed the Phipps Museum and Botanical Garden, and came to a huge clearing on the hillside, the very Flagstaff. Zoya looked at the now-empty slope, remembered the free movies that were shown there, and made a mental note to add Flagstaff to her summer plans.

"Let's sit here, okay?" André suggested, pointing to a spot on the grass.

Zoya nodded, but turned her attention to Downtown and the Pittsburgh skyline. That site depressed her. Downtown Pittsburgh was of little interest, and she rarely went there. A few times Zoya had gone to the Kaufmann's basement that sold discounted clothes, but those bargains were nothing compared to 'Nate's'. But most of all, downtown reminded Zoya of Point State park, where three rivers converged: Ohio, Monongahela, and Allegheny, and the Regatta Festival.

The Regatta was a summer competition of boats accompanied by fireworks. In honor of the Regatta, every year there was a festival at the Point State Park in Downtown Pittsburgh, complete with musical acts, hordes of people, and souvenirs. Zoya had been to the Regatta festival twice already since arriving in Pittsburgh in February 1991, and both times she found it insufferable. Both times, Vera and Simon Shapiro, their new Pittsburgh acquaintances, whose daughter was also named Zoya, brought the Kassatkins there.

Vera and Simon's daughter attended Harvard, and Vera liked to emphasize the fact that her daughter's Harvard achievements were exceptional and beyond anyone else's reach. No matter how hard Zoya tried to ignore Vera Shapiro and not pay attention to her words, she failed.

On the way to the festival, Vera Shapiro was invariably in high spirits and offered practical advice on where to park, what time of day to go to the Regatta, and how to save money. Vera carried with her a neatly packed bag of sandwiches, feeding her husband and their son, the laggard Alex.

Fortunately for Zoya, her Harvard namesake had stayed in Boston for the summer, where, according to Vera, the young Shapiro took on a prestigious internship to attain even more success and conquer new heights. Vera would interrupt the stories of her daughter's achievement with a cooing, "Simon, Alex, have a bite, I brought you ham and cheese sandwiches. They are tasty. Yum, yum!" Simon and Alex turned up their noses at her in unison. Alex, a huge lout who adored Howard Stern, mumbled an indefinite response, and Vera's husband Simon, a coroner, explained that one shouldn't eat ham in the heat because ham was an instant pathogen.

The Kassatkins came to the festival unprepared – they did not pack any sandwiches, even the pathogenic ham and cheese ones, and had no money to buy food at the festival. As a result, Zoya wandered around, listening to the rumbling in her stomach and suffering from the fact that she badly wanted something to eat, and would readily settle for the ham regardless of how much harm it would cause her, but she was too embarrassed to ask Vera for food. The unsuspecting Vera Shapiro chippered on and on about her daughter's success, and Zoya's irritation mounted and reached a boiling point. Hearing that Zoya Shapiro was a benchmark for academic success, Zoya formed a determination to outdo her Harvard namesake.

Sitting next to André, Zoya yet again thought of the upcoming summer. The end of the school year was still a few weeks away, but she already felt free. And Zoya made a decision that, despite André's departure and their separation until the end of August, she was going to have the best summer of her life. She would go to Flagstaff to watch free movies, start working at the library as a page, and try to go to another rave. *Or maybe even a few more raves?* Zoya pondered her choices. *I'll just have to make sure Jessica stays away from that crap.* Zoya shuddered, as she thought of the acid she and Jessica dropped, and immediately a pink snake tried to coil itself around her neck.

"Zoé, Zoé! Can you hear me?" André tugged at her sleeve.

"Oh, yeah," she responded, "I do now." As she said this, Zoya smiled. She liked to admit that occasionally her thoughts went somewhere very far away.

"You were thinking about something weird again. Will you tell me?" André looked at Zoya and then, without waiting for an answer, kissed her. It was a passionate, intimate kiss, and Zoya lit up at his touch.

*Oh is it going to happen?* Her heart leaped at the thought, and immediately she felt a knot forming in her stomach. This was not at all how she had imagined their first time. *It's not going to happen outside, on a hill, is it?* Zoya froze and pulled back. André stroked her face, whispering, "I will miss you, mon amour[1]."

Tears flooded Zoya's eyes. She pressed her whole body against André, leaned against him and they sat like that until it got dark. André offered to walk Zoya home, but she refused. André walked her to the bus stop, and she welcomed the opportunity to be alone on the bus, to look out the window and think things over.

The bus arrived a little late, and Zoya didn't get off at her stop until half past eight. She was in a great mood. She would get home early, and her relationship with André was going very well. *André is so romantic and sweet!* Zoya smiled as she remembered their evening together. She could still feel his touch and a hot kiss goodbye. Suddenly, a piercing scream interrupted her daydreaming:

"Zoya!! Zoya!! You're back!"

Her mother rushed straight at her, disheveled, wearing

---

1.  my love (fr)

slippers. Her father was running after her. Zoya saw that her mother was wearing an old house dress she had brought from Moscow, and a worn trench coat thrown over it, though it was warm outside.

"Peter! She is back!" Zoya's mother burst into tears.

"Zoya! We were so worried. How can you do this to us? Where have you been? We thought something had happened to you!" her father yelled, bulging his eyes at Zoya.

"How could you!? You've lost all sense of shame!" Her mother wailed, pulling at her hair.

"Ella, don't worry, everything is fine." Zoya's dad reassured his wife, not paying any attention to the culprit – Zoya, who stood nearby, incredulous. "She's selfish, she does it on purpose, to play on your nerves."

"Ah! Peter! Could this be true? But why?" Zoya's mother stared at her with disgust.

Dumbstruck, Zoya was desperately trying to get her bearings and understand what had happened. She shifted her eyes from her mother to her father and back, to figure out why her return had caused such a reaction. Why had her parents rushed to the bus stop to look for her? They had never done that before. She was back before her scheduled time, and when she left, everything had been fine.

*If they don't stop screaming, they are going to wake up the whole street,* Zoya thought ruefully, as she assessed the situation. Rare passersby stopped to stare at the Kassatkins. At last, her father took her mother by the hand, and they followed in the direction of the house. Zoya remained standing still, but suddenly her father turned around and shouted:

"What's wrong with you? Are you kidding me? Aren't you coming home?"

"What did I do?" Zoya finally regained the power of speech.

"How dare you? You're half an hour late! Your mother

and I were about to lose our minds with worry! We were on pins and needles all night. You promised you'd be home by eight!"

"No I didn't! I said nine. I am early." Zoya started crying. The injustice of her father's words cut like a knife.

"When you have kids of your own, you'll see! You'll understand! No one will love you like we do! Nobody!" her father yelled.

Her mother burst into tears again. "We raised a selfish pig! She is a monster! Peter! She doesn't love us!"

"Ella, don't worry, she'll understand; one day she'll have kids of her own, and then she'll understand!" Zoya's father looked over his shoulder menacingly at his daughter, who was following her parents dejectedly, her shoulders drooping. At that moment, Zoya wished for one thing – to get away, as far as possible, from these hysterical people who for some reason were her mother and father.

As soon as they got home, her parents' attitude softened. They stopped screaming and stopped paying attention to Zoya. Taking advantage of the lull, Zoya snuck into her room. *I am going straight to bed,* Zoya decided. She did not dare to call Jessica or Evan, for the fear of going out into the living room where she could once again become the target of her parents' indignation. Zoya was about to change into pajamas, when her father barged into her bedroom without knocking, followed by her mother. Her parents rarely spoke to her together, and their coordinated appearance did not bode well for Zoya. Her father, arms crossed, stood near the door, and her mother sat on the chair by the desk. Zoya hated it when anyone sat in that particular chair, but she did not dare correct her mother.

"Zoya, we need to talk." Her mother started the conversation with a sigh.

"Zoya, we're worried about you. Your mother and I. You have to understand: we're strangers here in America. We are nobodies. What if something happens to you? You don't feel sorry for us at all, disappearing in the middle of the night."

"This is unbearable!" Zoya heard hysterical notes in her mother's voice.

"Strangers call you! Men!" her father agreed.

"What men?" Zoya leaped. The only man who could have called her was André, and she had spent the evening with him. And then it hit Zoya, and the thought both pleased and horrified her. *So it had to be Evan who had called me! Evan!* Zoya felt ashamed that she was so flattered by his attention. *I am only supposed to be with André. So why do I need Evan? Why am I so excited by his call?*

"Zoya! Aren't you listening to a word I am saying? Why are you smiling?" her father grumbled.

"Peter, she's mocking us. Look at her! She's enjoying herself! I can't stand this! It's just impossible." Her mother's voice cracked, as she turned away, showing the greatest degree of disappointment, and now sat with her back turned to Zoya.

"Zoya, you have to apologize to your mother!" her father ordered. "See how she is suffering, how worried she is about you! Don't you feel sorry for your mother? You will never have a second mother! She does everything for you, and this is how you respond? You don't appreciate us at all!"

"Apologize?" Zoya choked with indignation. "I didn't do anything wrong!"

"What do you mean you didn't do anything wrong? You disappeared all night, and then you go out again the following evening! We were worried, we couldn't find you! We looked all over the neighborhood!"

"But why? I told you I'd be back at nine. I even got there early."

"I suppose there was some confusion. But it doesn't matter. What's important is that you should be home. Resting, spending time with us, not going anywhere."

"But why not?"

"Apologize to your mother! Look how she is suffering." Zoya's father pointed to his wife, who immediately frowned and gave a look full of disdain. She hated her mother's grimaces, when she shut herself up and kept silent, showing her resentment.

"Ella, don't worry, my love." Zoya's father approached and stroked her mother's hand.

"I don't need an apology! Not like this!" Ella Kassatkina grumbled through her teeth. There was a crack in her voice.

Zoya knew that there would be no truce and return to normalcy without an apology. Her mother could spend hours, even days, suffering in silence. And her father would hover and would do anything to comfort her. Now that she found out about Evan's call, Zoya wanted to get in touch with him, and for that to happen, she needed to appease her parents. So she made a concession.

"Mama, I'm sorry, I won't do it anymore!" Zoya whispered, forcing an apology.

"What did you say? I can't hear you." Her mother turned in Zoya's direction. Her face was streaked with tears and her nose beet red.

"I won't do it again!" Zoya squeezed out, despite being on the verge of screaming, internally seething at the injustice.

"Okay, I guess this will do," her mother threw her hands up in frustration and rose from Zoya's chair.

"Well, hug, you made up," Zoya's father fussed, relieved to finally have achieved peace and quiet at home.

"I don't want to hug her!" Ella snorted. "I've gone through too much!"

"Ella, come on, don't be a child." Zoya's father urged her.

"All right, fine," her mother turned to face her. Zoya got up from the bed and walked over to her mother.

"Ah, my girls! Well, finally. Let's have some tea, shall we?" Zoya's father announced, clearly relieved.

"Papa, who called me?" Zoya dared to ask.

"Some guy named Evan. Where do you find them? What does he want?"

"I dunno."

"Why is his name Evan? Is he Polish?"

"How did you know?"

"What do you mean, what else could he be? I just guessed, his name sounded Polish. Polish is okay, even interesting. There are a lot of Poles living here, and Serbs and Croats, which is surprising." Zoya's father cleared his throat and started a lecture about ethnography and immigration to Pittsburgh over the last century, and how the steel industry had changed the demographics of the city, but Zoya interrupted him:

"Papa, what did he say?"

"Evan? I don't remember." Her father shrugged.

# CHAPTER 5

Zoya climbed into bed. She thought of calling Evan, but could not find any energy to do so. After the fight with her parents, she felt broken. Her memory of the events of Saturday night, the rave, the music, and even the charm of her evening with André evaporated. And all that remained was an oppressive feeling of guilt.

Her eyes filled with tears at the injustice of her parents' behavior. Objectively, Zoya didn't feel she had done anything wrong. She told them that she would be back home at nine, which was a completely reasonable hour. Not only that, she even came home earlier than promised! Zoya clenched her fist in anger. The scene her parents had caused, or rather, her mother had instigated – of that Zoya was sure, because without her mother, her father would have never been in such a state – made Zoya question her parents.

*They are just out to get me!* Zoya fumed as she laid in bed. *They just can't accept that things in America are different! All they want to do is talk about Russia, they don't even want to become actual Americans!* Zoya shook her head thinking back to her father's opinion of The Simpsons as a 'kids cartoon', and not subtle satire of the American way of life. *I guess the less they know about my life, the better.* Zoya concluded before falling asleep.

The following morning, right before classes started, Zoya bumped into Jessica. Her friend looked haggard.

"Hey," Jessica muttered, not at all her usual chipper self.

"Hi, how are you?" asked Zoya.

"Oh, just awful! I could barely sleep, and all day yesterday I felt like crap. And you?"

"I fell asleep in the morning and then I kept seeing things, but I'm okay now." Zoya remembered the pink squiggles and the snake that tried to strangle her and shuddered.

"You're lucky. I could barely get out of bed!" Jessica sighed, walking along next to Zoya. The hallway was filled with students, rushing to class.

"That's 'cause I spat out that hit almost right away. And I kinda was thinking, we shouldn't have taken it at all."

"Why not? It's still something new. It was fun to try." Jessica shrugged, giving Zoya a defiant look.

"I'm not doing that again." Zoya shook her head.

"Neither am I … I guess," Jessica mumbled.

"What about Matt? Did you talk to him?"

"He's coming over today after school. He seemed okay. Said he missed me."

"Did he say why he didn't give us a ride back? I mean, he promised you he'd look after us after we took the hit, but then he just disappeared!" Zoya threw her hands up in exasperation.

"He was happy, 'cause he's now officially a promoter."

"That's it?"

"Yeah." Jessica raised her eyebrows, showing that the conversation didn't please her. The bell rang, and it was time to go to class.

Zoya had French. After their trip to France over spring break that year, Zoya had grown even more fond of Monsieur

Mbia, her French teacher. He shared with Zoya his life story, and told her about living in Paris as a young man after leaving Cameroon in the 1960s. Zoya enjoyed her trip to France immensely. Even the presence of the annoying Grisha Kantorovich, who whispered nasty things to Zoya, did not ruin the trip.

The trip to Paris that Zoya took with her class was technically her third visit, but the first one that was real. The other two trips she'd undertaken in different temporal branches, in an alternate reality, or in a dream state, depending on whether she were to believe explanations that Inna Lvovna, her Moscow neighbor, had given her. Zoya found it ironic that the one time that she did make it to Paris, André was no longer living there in reality, since he had moved to Pittsburgh just a few months prior, in January 1993. And yet, her time with him in that temporal branch or dream or whatever it was, had felt so real.

Once in Paris with her school trip, Zoya badly wanted to visit le Marais, André's neighborhood, and see the place where the Templar fortress once stood. She dreamt of the narrow streets, and of walking on the same cobblestones, where seven hundred years ago Templar knights met their fate. The place that she had seen in her dream, the second time she'd visited Paris. But her school group's time in Paris was limited to only three days, while they spent the majority of the trip traveling through the Loire Valley. And as much as Zoya resented visiting the castles in the Loire Valley, she did not make an effort to see le Marais while in Paris.

As soon as Zoya returned to Pittsburgh from France, she called André.

"France was so great! And Paris! But we were on a sightseeing bus the whole time. We didn't manage to walk at all," Zoya complained to André.

"What a pity! I'd love to go back there with you and show you the city," André said. He loved dreaming of future trips they would take together. He had already promised Zoya that they would visit the Sahara Desert to see the place where Antoine de Saint-Exupéry's plane crashed, and would go to Moscow and stop by the 'Vernissage' again, and would also travel together to New York, where André dreamed of finding a job.

Although Zoya considered his dreams to be silly fantasies, she never showed André that she doubted him. *Where would we get the money to travel to Moscow together? Who actually goes to the Sahara? And the job in New York? André still had to graduate from university first. And then, where was New York, and where was André?*

At the end of class, Mr. Mbia asked Zoya and Grisha to stay behind. Zoya sighed. She tried to minimize her interactions with her unpleasant classmate. In his presence, Zoya felt on edge. As if, at any moment, he was about to burst out with an insult. But she dared not disobey Mr. Mbia.

"Guys, I would like to invite you to my house!" announced Monsieur Mbia, cleaning his huge glasses. He smiled happily. "I've decided to bring our French Club to my home to celebrate the trip to France. What do you think of that?"

"Oh, thank you, Monsieur Mbia!" Zoya clapped her hands, forgetting all about Kantorovich. "How wonderful! And when?"

"Ahem," Grisha cleared his throat, "Monsieur Mbia, I don't quite understand, will you invite the whole French Club over? Or only those who have been to France? Not everyone paid for the trip." Grisha enjoyed emphasizing that the trip to France had not been cheap and that it was only for a select few.

"The whole club, Grégoire," answered Monsieur Mbia, as his eyes sparkled. Zoya noticed a steely note in her teacher's voice, which was unusual. "I want all of my students to have a chance to hear about our trip, not just those who happened to be in France in April."

"Well, I'm not going then," Grisha grunted. "I thought we were going to talk about the trip together. Why do we need to meet with everyone else?"

"Okay, Grégoire, it's your choice. Zoé, I hope you'll come? In two weeks, on the fifteenth of May, it will be a Saturday."

"Of course, Monsieur Mbia, I will be there." Zoya nodded.

"Perfect. I live near the school, I'll share my address later."

"Is there anything you need us to bring?" Zoya asked. Grisha threw a displeased look at her.

"I have not thought everything through yet," said Mr. Mbia. "I will ask my wife. And I hope to introduce you to my sister."

"Your twin? Fatima?" Zoya burst out and then caught herself, but it was too late.

Monsieur Mbia looked up at her in surprise and took off his glasses. Grisha stepped closer and leaned in. Zoya could smell the sweat coming from his silk shirt decorated with burgundy parrots.

"Umm…" Zoya stammered. *Am I having weird visions of Paris again? Didn't that all go away? What if I am about to give myself away?* Worries flashed through her head. Zoya vividly recalled the dream she had had of Paris and Fatima, who had rescued her from Saint Anne's mental hospital. "You once mentioned her," she responded after a short pause, "I have a very good memory!" The teacher had, indeed, mentioned his sister one day, right after the end of the winter break, and Zoya clutched at the straw.

"Yes, she actually visited us in January, and I guess I'd mentioned her, but you even remembered her name. That's impressive, Zoé." Monsieur Mbia looked at Zoya curiously, and she fidgeted under his gaze.

*Not that nightmare again*, Zoya blushed, remembering her

New Year's dream about the two Templars, who were supposedly past incarnations of Zoya and André, and how she had ended up at Saint Anne's, the infamous mental hospital in Paris, where André's stepfather, the psychiatrist de Vigny, took her hostage, and how she had a miraculous escape from the hospital with the help of Fatima, Monsieur Mbia's twin sister. *But what a vivid dream that was, so realistic!* Zoya thought. She remembered how she and André made love at the very end of that dream, and blushed. *I am glad those crazy dreams ended and I can live a normal life!* Zoya thought.

"Yes, Monsieur Mbia, I remember names very well, it's kind of this quirk I have," Zoya mumbled. Grisha Kantorovich chuckled.

"So, remember, on the fifteenth of May, we'll meet at my place. And you, Grégoire, maybe you'll change your mind?" Monsieur Mbia finished cleaning his glasses and put them on.

"Hmm," Grisha mumbled an indistinct response, grabbed his leather briefcase and left the classroom without saying goodbye.

"Bye, Monsieur Mbia," Zoya smiled at the teacher, "Thank you for the invitation".

*The end of the school year will be so much fun!* Zoya thought, exiting the classroom. There was an extra bounce to her step, as she thought of the invitation to Mr. Mbia's place. *And maybe I'll get to meet Fatima! I could try to find out about those Templars.*

At that thought, Zoya froze in place. *The burning! The betrayal!* She remembered Robert's gut-wrenching screams before he was burned alive, and the fact that, according to Fatima, Johannes, the traitor, was André's past incarnation. Zoya could almost feel the fire as it approached Robert's feet. The man was, according to Fatima, Zoya's past incarnation, but Johannes-André had betrayed his friend, condemning him to death. The image of de Vigny's contorted face as

Master Templar flashed before her eyes, inciting Johannes to betray his friend.

*No, no, it's all nonsense. Not that de Vigny guy again,* thought Zoya. *That's just ridiculous. Why am I obsessed with some creep? First he's an evil psychiatrist, torturing my double, Zoé, and then he's the Master Templar. And the whole story of Robert, Johannes, the Templars, and a fire? Their connection to de Vigny as the Master Templar? Whatever! And Acre!*

At the thought of Acre, a city in the Holy Land that she had seen in her dream, she hesitated. *I guess I should check if this place actually exists. I've never heard of it, so when I find out that there is no Acre, I will know for sure that everything I saw then was just a dream. I'll just stop by the library and say hi to Melissa. I can't wait to start working there with her! It'll be fun!* Zoya thought. Her mood improved. *Then I will definitely call Evan back. And I gotta say bye to André. I hope he doesn't get too busy with his exams.* More than anything, Zoya liked to have a well-organized schedule, and now, having planned out the rest of the day, she was happy.

She could barely wait for the school day to end, so she could finally walk over to the library and look up Acre. *Why didn't I think of doing this before?* Zoya sighed in frustration. *I would have sorted everything by now. All I need is to make sure there was no Acre and then I can just forget about that whole weird dream forever.* Zoya remembered how carefully she had avoided asking questions about the Templars during their trip to Paris, fearing that she might descend into a dream state, ending up on a parallel time branch, and once again have visions of their burning.

Most of all, Zoya worried that their group would visit the area where the Templar fortress had once stood. A part of her imagined that, as soon as she was there again with the group, she would suddenly plunge into her nightmares of the two templar knights, Robert and Johannes, but, to her great relief, her group avoided that part of Paris altogether. Nor did anyone mention the monument to Jacques de Molay, the last Grand Master Templar, which André had shown her.

And by the second day of the excursion, Zoya had completely calmed down, deciding that the dreams about the Templars and her stay in St. Anne's were merely the fruit of her imagination. Now she longed to make sure that there was no Acre either, and thereby erase the Templars from her life forever. *At least I'll live like a normal person, without all that weird stuff,* Zoya decided.

Immediately after school, without wasting a moment, she headed to the library. Zoya briskly walked up Shady Avenue, turned left by the Beth Shalom Synagogue, which occupied a whole corner of Shady and Beacon, then turned right onto Murray Avenue and found herself at the library fifteen minutes after school ended. She searched for Melissa, but her friend was nowhere to be found. As Zoya looked around the library, she walked past the most secluded part of the space.

It was the very corner where Zoya had taken Alexei Kulikov at the end of last year, right before the New Year's celebration. She remembered their conversation and how easy it was to talk to Alexei. *He is the only friend who can really understand what I'm going through,* thought Zoya and sighed. Alexei had been selected for a summer internship at Carnegie Mellon, but Zoya's father flatly refused to let him stay at their apartment, and he had to cancel the trip.

No matter how hard Zoya and her mother tried to convince Peter Kassatkin that he was being unreasonable, no matter how many hefty arguments they made about 'old friends from Moscow', and not even the fact that it had been thanks to Lydia and her recommendation that he had found a job, Zoya's father was adamant. He muttered that 'I have to keep him out. Zoya doesn't need him'. Her mother had to apologize and promise Lydia that Alexei could come and stay with them the following summer, when they would move to a house of their own.

The idea of buying a house started the day after Zoya's father found a job as a chemical engineer. Or, more precisely, it materialized after a skirmish, initiated by Zoya's mother.

"Peter, I figured everything out. We only need a certification of your employment, a few paystubs, and we will be able to get a mortgage. We can see a few houses over the weekend. There are some very decent ones nearby, in Greenfield," Zoya's mother said.

"Okay, Ella. Just go ahead, I don't need to see them. I don't have time."

"How's that? There is this woman, Tatiana, from Odessa, she is a real estate agent now, got her license, she will show us everything. Very pleasant, very nice, great woman."

"I don't want to see anything."

"Peter, but why?"

"Because I'm tired."

"But it will be over the weekend, you'll have time to rest. We need to move out of this horrible apartment. Another winter like the last one and I will lose it."

"We used to have a nice apartment."

"Peter? What apartment? Where?" Zoya's mother took the bait.

"Back in Moscow. We had the most wonderful apartment, in the city center, with thick gorgeous walls and a great view. And guess what? We abandoned everything to move to this hell-hole, in the middle of nowhere, for no reason at all. And now we freeze in the winter, and in the summer it's like a hot swamp. It's impossible to live here. America is not for normal people at all. Only scoundrels survive here."

"Peter, how can you?! Zoya can hear us."

"So what? Let her hear the truth!"

"But we immigrated because of Zoya, so that she could have a better life!" That was her mother's most convincing argument, used in only the most difficult situations. It usually worked, and, upon hearing about Zoya's promising future in

America, Zoya's father usually calmed down, but recently the situation had changed.

"What about Zoya? I'm not so sure she's better off here. Look at her friends, the hoodlums that she spends time with."

"Shhh, Peter, she will hear us."

"Ella, please don't shut me up; you came up with all this, it was your idea to move here. And now we are nobodies and we still don't know what will happen to Zoya here or how she will turn out."

And then the skirmish turned into a full-fledged fight, with accusations of dictatorship by Zoya's father and finally, her mother's sobbing. Zoya hated when her parents fought, especially since she knew for sure that her mother would win anyway and, as always, would have her way through tantrums and tears. Zoya's father could not stand his wife's emotional manipulations and in the end always gave up.

Zoya checked her watch—it was only 2:45pm. *Melissa usually starts work at three*, she remembered, as she let out a sigh and headed to the card catalog. Well versed in the Dewey decimal system, within minutes Zoya stood in front of the right shelf. She was peering into the spines of books, trying to find the most promising volume, when suddenly a thick, brown tome with gilding on the cover fell right on top of her head. Zoya gasped and jumped back. The book tumbled on the floor with a thump. On the cover Zoya read its title: *The History of the Knights Templar*.

With shaking hands, Zoya picked up the book and flipped through the pages. There were no library stamps and the spine of the book was free from any identifiers. Zoya looked around – no one had seen what had happened, and she began flipping through the pages. The paper was thick, embossed, of impressive quality. She checked the year of publication and gasped when she saw that it was published in 1914, which made the volume almost eighty years old. *Wow!* Zoya thought. *It's an antique!*

And then an illustration caught her eye: a man wearing a templar cloak with a red cross on his chest, with a tortured look on his face was tied with ropes to a cross. A fire burnt under his feet, and the flames almost touched him. Behind him was the Cathedral of Notre Dame. The man had an expression of intense suffering, mixed with defiance on his face.

*Like Zoya Kosmodemyanskaya,* flashed in Zoya's mind. She immediately remembered her dream and Robert's agony on the day of the execution. A wave of anger and indignation at the traitor Johannes rose in Zoya. *If it weren't for that bastard, if he didn't obey de Vigny, then none of this would have happened! Robert would have remained alive, and everything would have been different.*

Zoya immediately stopped herself: *I came to the library in order to find evidence that all my Templar memories were silly fantasies, not to avenge Robert.* She forced herself to look at the list of names in the Index of the book. Under letter 'A', at the very top of the page, the very first word was 'Acre'. An electric current jolted through her body.

*So it's real? Acre exists?* With trembling hands, Zoya turned to the pages that mentioned the city. She read that the Templars suffered a terrible defeat in Acre in 1291, and after that, the knights had been forced to return to Europe, having lost their only stronghold in the Holy Land. The book also contained a map of the fortress in Acre, and Zoya peered at the image. She slammed the book shut.

*Enough, this is enough! It was a dream, it was nothing!* She pushed the book away in revulsion. *The name of the city is just a coincidence. I could have heard about Acre somewhere, and then I dreamed about it.* But something forced her to reconsider. Zoya reached for the book again, flipped the volume in her hands, and then surreptitiously stuffed it in her backpack. *It's not a library book anyway; I'll keep it just in case,* Zoya reassured herself. *I'll return later, but I need to take a look at it at home.*

Zoya was on her way out, when someone called her name. Zoya's hands started sweating, and her heart was beating fast. *Did someone notice? Does anyone know I stole the book?! What's going to happen?* Zoya forced herself to stop and turned around. She saw Melissa, who was walking over to her. Her lips were painted bright red and she smelled of cigarettes mixed with perfume.

"Hi! How are you? When are you starting here?"

"Hi!" Zoya felt like giving Melissa a hug, so relieved she was that she didn't get busted for stealing a book from the library. "Right after the school year ends."

"I can't wait for you to start! It's boring as hell here," Melissa glared to the side and whispered: "There, see, it's that idiot Tiffany, she's the one who keeps quoting the Bible." Zoya saw a stooped, pale girl pushing a cart full of books in front of her.

"I can't even look at her, she is so pathetic, and I have to work with her! Can you imagine? I keep hoping that she'll leave, and you'll get her shifts. Or we could ask to work at the same time, you and me. Oh, Miss Specter's coming, I gotta run." Melissa hurried off.

Upon returning home, Zoya shoved the Templar book into the farthest corner of the blue shelf that divided their living room in two parts. *No one will find it here,* Zoya thought, *I'll look at it later.*

She sat on the couch and frowned. So much homework to do, but she also wanted to see André. *Only a few days till he leaves, and then what?* Zoya thought wearily, as she stared blankly at the turned off TV. At home, her positive attitude and confidence that André's departure would go smoothly and that she would take the separation well instantly disappeared. Zoya grew wistful. With less than a week left before her boyfriend's flight to France, she worried when they would see each other again, and hated herself for not making plans with André to say goodbye. But worst of all was the uncertainty over three-and-a-half long months of his absence.

*I've got to do something with myself, I've got to think of something, otherwise I won't be able to stand it.* The persistent thoughts pierced her mind. *I can't sit at home, I need to go somewhere, hang out with someone; Jessica?* And then, Zoya remembered Evan. *Yes! Of course! How could I forget? I need to call him!*

Zoya leaped off the couch and ran to her room, where she had hidden the yellow piece of paper with Evan's number. She then galloped back to the phone, which was in the living room. Zoya swiftly dialed the number and heard one long ring tone. Something clicked and she heard a hoarse woman's voice.

"Hello, oh, speak up," the other end of the line groaned.

Zoya hesitated. She didn't expect anyone other than Evan to answer.

"Ah, sorry, I think I got the wrong number," she muttered and immediately hung up. Zoya felt like she was about to burst into tears. Staring at the phone, Zoya pondered her options. *I can't believe I got the wrong number! I was really hoping to see Evan again, and his friend Nikki seems so nice.*

Her shoulders drooped as she retreated to her room and sat down to do her homework. Zoya placed the paper with Evan's number on her desk and from time to time looked at it. A strange premonition overwhelmed her, as if something terrible were about to happen. Zoya couldn't understand why she felt that way, but it frightened her. She pushed the thought away, but it gnawed at her, no matter how hard she focused on her textbook. At last, she heard voices coming from the living room – her parents had returned home.

Instead of greeting them, like she normally would, Zoya burst into tears. She flopped onto the bed and wept. Her whole life had been turned upside down. She would never be back in Moscow again, where she had been so happy, where her parents were actual parents not some strangers, and where André was a romantic hero, who took her on walks around the city and gave her a tiger cub figurine painted in the Gzhel style, and where Alexei Kulikov was a friend and a classmate and not the guy her father despised, and where there were no raves, Evan, and acid.

But the crying didn't last long. Zoya's misery was interrupted by a phone call and her father shouting:

"Zoya, where are you? That Polack is on the line for you again!"

After wiping her tears, she rushed into the living room. Zoya averted her eyes as she took the receiver from her father.

"Hello?" Zoya muttered. She tried to make her voice cheerful, but tears came to her eyes and she felt terribly sad again.

"Zoya, hello!" She heard Evan's bright voice and immediately imagined him, tall, friendly, caring, with long hair and nice features, and square glasses that made him look serious and reliable. "Did you call? My mom told me some girl called and hung up. I thought maybe it was you."

"Yes, it was me." Zoya blushed. "I thought I got the wrong number."

"It's my fault for not telling you that I live with my mother. She never leaves the house. She's on disability."

"Oh, I see." Zoya was surprised at how open Evan was about his living situation, but that made her trust him more.

"How have you been? How are you feeling? How's the withdrawal?"

"What withdrawal?" Zoya flinched as she turned to make sure her father wasn't within earshot.

"Well, you just dropped acid two days ago, so you're probably in a bad mood or something. You gotta be careful the first few days. I've babysat a lot of people through bad trips and stuff."

"Umm, I dunno, I guess I am not in a great mood." Zoya wiped another tear that rolled down her cheek.

"That's 'cause you dropped acid. Don't take any more, okay? You'll be better off without it. Trust me."

"Okay, I didn't like it that much anyway," Zoya admitted.

"Great. Hey, why don't we go dancing this weekend? There's this club, you wanna check it out?"

"This weekend?" Zoya's mouth gaped open as she scrambled to figure out her plans. Or, rather, her only plan, which was to see André before he left. She needed to find out when he would be free first, before agreeing to go dancing with her new acquaintance. But then a thought flashed through her mind: *If André wants to see me, he'll find the time.* And she agreed: "Yes! Sounds great!"

"So, on Saturdays at this club there's great music. It's called 'Pegasus'. Actually, it's a gay club, but you can dance like crazy there and I know the DJ. Anyway, you'll love it there."

"Okay, so Saturday night then?"

"Yeah, I can pick you up at five o'clock."

"Cool." Her hands got clammy as she thought of André: *what if he wants to see me on Saturday night? What if I am not available when he wants to say goodbye?* But then Zoya reassured herself of having made the right choice. *I'll figure something out! It will all work out on its own.*

"Bye! See you Saturday, then," Evan said.

"Bye, then!" As soon as she hung up the receiver, her father rushed over to ask her questions:

"What does he want? Evan? Is that his name?" Her father, usually confused about her friends' names, had been quick to remember the name of her new acquaintance.

"Yes. Evan."

"So? Where will you go? When?"

"Papa, I don't know yet, we just agreed to meet."

"I heard everything. Are you going out again tonight? Your mother and I can barely stand it, you're wearing us out."

"Papa, I don't know yet. I am not going anywhere tonight."

"Zoya, keep in mind, you're gonna kill us with your escapades."

"Papa, I gotta go, I still have homework to do." Zoya maneuvered out from her father's line of questioning and rushed into her room. She firmly closed the door behind her with a sigh of relief and stared at her textbooks.

# CHAPTER 6

After speaking with Evan, Zoya waited for a call from André. *He is about to leave Pittsburgh, he'll want to see me. I guess he'll call today,* she thought, as she reviewed her homework. She had been certain that he would call on Monday to set up a date for the following day. When that didn't happen, Zoya expected him to call on Tuesday. *He is probably busy, but today he will call for sure,* she thought, as she waited by the phone.

When the call didn't come on Tuesday night, Zoya was furious. All of Wednesday, she spent in agony. She had almost buried their relationship and fantasies of revenge occupied her mind. On the way to school, Zoya imagined how she would show André what a mistake he had made in rejecting her, and how she would spend the entire summer at raves with Evan and his friends.

She wasn't entirely sure if she liked Evan romantically and wanted to spend the whole summer in his company, and he didn't seem to like her all that much, but she wanted to punish André and make him suffer. *And what better way to do that than with a rival?* Evan was a great opponent, so tall and handsome.

In her revenge fantasy he turned into a romantic hero, and was gently, but firmly holding her hand, as they walked past André's house. Seeing them together, André immediately felt remorse and tried to win Zoya back, but it was too late. She was happy with Evan. André suffered alone, sobbing and crying out of a sense of his own insignificance and frustration at the fact that he had lost her forever.

By Thursday, Zoya's revenge plot had gotten more elaborate, and now included an open confrontation between André and Evan. She had not yet decided who would have the upper hand, when she heard the phone ring and went to answer it. It was André. Hearing her boyfriend's voice, Zoya leaped in surprise. She had just gone over the revenge scenario several times in her head, and had gotten to her favorite part, where Evan rolled up his sleeves and was about to punch André in the face.

"Zoya, hello!" André sounded happy and completely at peace with himself.

"Hi," Zoya grumbled, trying to hide her surprise. In her imagination, they had long ago broken up and she had been in a happy and stable relationship with Evan.

"Zoya, I turned everything in! And ahead of time! I had to hand in my essay tomorrow, but I finished it all today. And my students are all gone. Can we see each other? Are you free tomorrow?"

"Oh, André!" Zoya was so touched by his words. She turned red from shame for planning to take revenge on her boyfriend for four whole days, while he was busy studying. "I missed you so much!" Zoya blurted out and bit her tongue. *He is probably going to think I am stupid and romantic,* she sighed.

"Zoya, you have no idea how much I missed you. I thought about you all the time, but I knew that if I distracted myself from classes, I wouldn't pass my exams and I'd get bad grades. And then they would kick me out of the university and take away my visa."

"André, I don't even know what to say." Zoya's cheeks were burning. *I am a terrible person! Poor André was only trying to do his best, he had no choice, he couldn't call, and what did I do? I spent four days being angry!*

"Don't say anything; I know I should have called you, at least for a minute, but I've hardly slept since Sunday."

"No way!"

"Yeah, I've been studying, I took naps here and there, but I had to focus on my work."

"You must be very tired!" Zoya widened her eyes. She could not imagine what it would be like not to sleep for four days.

"Yeah, I'm very tired, and I'm just about to go to bed. I wanted to talk to you about meeting up tomorrow, and then I will probably pass out." André sniggered.

"I have school tomorrow, it ends at two. And then I'm free," answered Zoya, elated. She could already picture André picking her up outside of the school building, and how everyone would see her cute boyfriend kissing her near the exit, and how all the girls in her class would be envious and ask her who André was.

"Great! How about we meet early? Can you skip school?"

"Cut school? What for?"

"Then we could spend more time together," André suggested nonchalantly.

Zoya went cold inside. André had just told her how hard he had been studying, not sleeping for days on end in order to pass his exams, and there he was, suggesting that she skip school for him? *Doesn't he care that I am a good student and take school seriously?* Zoya's heart sank as she grasped the receiver.

"But I have school... I can't skip school. What if someone finds out and they call my parents?" Zoya responded, her voice shaking. In reality, she knew very well that she could easily skip school if she wanted to, and maybe even would have offered to do it herself, but she was offended by the ease with which André asked her to do it.

"I was hoping you would make an exception for me. Remember, I'm going away for the whole summer soon. I so want to see you," said André, completely unaware of Zoya's internal struggle. *Why couldn't I be older and study at the university already? And then we could even rent a house together, and André would not remind me of the fact that I am younger and he could go to jail if we were to have sex. And I could go to France with André for the summer, too.* Zoya fumed inside, trying to reconcile her disgruntlement with being flattered by André's desire to see her.

After a pause she sighed. "I dunno, maybe." Internally, she had already surrendered, as she usually did, once André applied even a little bit of pressure. She couldn't resist him. "I'll have to think about it. I'll check: if there are no exams tomorrow, then maybe I can," she answered, trying to sound as vague as possible.

"Oh! Great! Then I'll see you tomorrow? In the morning?"

Zoya made a precise calculation in her head: she always left home at 7:00 a.m. sharp. She could get to André's in twenty to twenty-five minutes, depending on the bus. But she decided not to tell him the exact time in case the bus was running late. And Zoya didn't like being late. "A little after eight, if I do end up skipping school."

"Oh, that's a little too early. How about a little later? 'Cause I want to get a good night's sleep, and I am so tired," André said, his tone stern.

"Look, let's just meet after school. I'm either going to school or not; it's not like I'm going to wander the streets and wait for you to wake up tomorrow morning." To Zoya's surprise, her voice acquired a steely undertone, and she wondered where she got that firmness.

"Okay, okay, let's meet in the morning. I'll try to get up

early and be ready. And we'll be together all day, all day! I promise! That's it then, I'm going to bed. See you tomorrow, my love. Bisous, bisous[1]!" André made a smooching sound, and Zoya responded in the same way. She found this manner of saying goodbye both funny and adorable.

Zoya hung up. The call left her feeling confused. It was as if she had just negotiated a complex transaction rather than agree to meet with her boyfriend. She felt unloved. The meeting with André made her nervous and she regretted agreeing to skip school so easily.

Zoya checked her assignments for Friday to make sure that she had nothing particularly important at school that day. If Zoya ever skipped school, it was to go shopping to Nate's with Jessica. From Squirrel Hill it was two bus rides away, near Century III Mall. 'Nate's' sold clothes and household goods at a deep discount, mostly due to manufacturing defects. It took hours of sorting and digging through piles of clothing to find a decent item of clothing at Nate's, thereby justifying the trip. And only when they found that gem, would Zoya and Jessica try on the clothes and select what was needed. Then, they would switch the price tags.

Substituting price tags had been Jessica's idea. During one of their trips to Nate's, Jessica mentioned that she didn't see the point of paying the posted price for the merchandise. "They got the clothes for free anyway, and we had to work our asses off to sift through all the crap," Jessica reasoned, sharing her idea with Zoya. "What difference does it make to them if we pay $2.99 or $5.99? But it makes a big difference to us. We need the money."

Switching price tags was a complex task, and required precision and focus. At Nate's, price tags were attached sloppily, with pins, and it was easy enough to switch them, but first one had to find a similar item at a lower price. The store

---

1.  kiss, kiss (fr)

had a system of codes by the type of clothing: all dresses had one code, and all pants another. Therefore, price tags had to be changed accordingly, replacing the price of one type of pants with a lower price taken off another pair of pants, and so on. The first time she and Jessica tried this, Zoya's hands were shaking. She was in a near panic. They hid in a corner of the fitting room and changed the price tag on the pants they liked from $5.99 to $1.99.

Zoya whispered, "Isn't that too low? Will they believe us?"

"Well, they do sell pants for two dollars here, just another brand." Jessica shrugged, pointing to the crumpled pair with the broken zipper.

"That's true." Zoya nodded. Her heart was beating so fast, she felt like it was going to burst out of her chest.

"Let's go," Jessica hissed, and they picked up the clothes and proceeded to the checkout counter.

They purposely put more items in the cart and hid the culprit pants in the middle of the pile. Zoya could not help but stare at her feet, while Jessica got all the items out of the shopping cart. The cashier, a middle aged redhead, indifferently scanned their purchase, threw a contemptuous look at them, and Zoya and Jessica left the store. They walked slowly to the exit, just like they had agreed before. "Just remember, we gotta act like we own the place," Jessica instructed Zoya when they first discussed their plan. As soon as they stepped outside, they hugged each other and shrieked in excitement. They had just discovered a goldmine! Zoya and Jessica managed to save $4 and now they could change price tags of other items and buy clothes at Nate's for thrift store prices.

But those trips to Nate's were rare. Zoya didn't like skipping school. She took honors classes and was enrolled in a prestigious program for gifted students. Zoya had to maintain a high GPA to get into a good college, and she had another motivation – her competition with her namesake and nemesis, Zoya Shapiro. *Even if I don't get into Harvard, I still gotta get into a good school,* Zoya reasoned.

*I should have just told him I can't skip school tomorrow,* Zoya sighed as she sat in her room and surveyed a pile of papers she needed to review for school. But it was too late to change her mind. André would be waiting for her.

On Friday morning, Zoya got up even earlier than usual. She carefully picked out her clothes and even put on the adorable lace thong. She bought them with Jessica at Nate's back in February, when Zoya still thought she and André were about to have sex. Zoya had read in *Cosmopolitan* magazine that thongs were sexy and romantic and the type of underwear that men really liked.

Wearing thongs was pure torture. The underwear cut into her skin in the most horrible way, and Zoya, having once tried wearing them to school, decided to never put them on again. But her thong was a beautiful soft pink color, and it remained in the underwear drawer. Now, Zoya was happy to have sexy underwear.

*What if André decides to take my virginity? What if today is the day and everything happens just like in my dream in Paris?* Zoya blushed at the thought.

After a quick breakfast, Zoya left the apartment, glad that she had managed to sneak out of the house before her parents woke up. She arrived at the bus stop a little earlier than expected, and right away the bus pulled up. It came ahead of schedule, and Zoya thought it a good sign. Ten minutes later, she was already in Oakland. She got off at South Bouquet Street, and headed toward André's house.

As she approached André's doorstep, Zoya checked her watch. It was still before eight, and Zoya's palms sweated as she thought that she was too early. *Maybe he's still asleep? What if no one opens the door?* Zoya tried to slow down her pace, then wondered if she should turn around and walk back to the Beehive, but the desire to see André was too strong. She knocked carefully and stepped away from the door, prepared to wait. But it opened immediately. One of the roommates, Mikey, had a girlfriend, Sibyl, and Zoya had nearly forgotten about her existence until the girl opened the door for her that morning.

Mikey had dark brown hair and piercing black eyes. He constantly talked about his Italian roots and alluded to his connection to the mafia. Zoya did not find him one bit attractive, and, though she'd never admit it, he reminded her of a cockroach. But Mikey was very popular with the opposite sex. In the short time that Zoya had known Mikey, she had met quite a few of his conquests. Among them were: Marie, the artist with a pierced eyebrow; the adorable waitress, Annette; the alcoholic, Julie; and now there was Sibyl, who turned out to be the most resilient. She appeared in the middle of March and almost immediately moved into Mikey's room. Zoya really liked Sibyl the one time she met her previously. Mikey's new girlfriend was French-Canadian and was very proud of her heritage. Sybil was petite, and had long blond hair that covered her waist. Like the first time Zoya met her, Sybil was dressed simply, in jeans and a white T-shirt, but managed to look very elegant.

"Hey!" said Zoya. "Long time, no see!"

"Hi, come on in." Sybil fixed her hair and smiled. "André asked me to open the door for you, just in case you come over early. I am always the first to get up." Sybil winked at Zoya.

Zoya was surprised that André had somehow predicted her early arrival, but then she remembered that he often guessed her actions even before she knew how exactly she would act. A wave of tenderness overtook her. *He is the best!* Zoya thought.

"I'm making breakfast," Sybil remarked. "Mikey says you can't mess up scrambled eggs." She shrugged. "You want something to eat?"

When Zoya first saw André's place, she couldn't stop

admiring the well-equipped kitchen. It had an arsenal of pots, pans, skillets, and other items that Zoya had never suspected even existed. She soon found out why – Mikey had a passion for cooking. He had been raised by his Italian grandmother, and had been helping her in the kitchen his entire life. Mikey was used to eating only high-quality, homemade Italian food. He even made spaghetti from scratch, claiming it was easy.

"Thank you, Sybil, I already had breakfast," Zoya answered. All she wanted was to see André. "I am gonna go upstairs," she announced, and, without waiting for an answer, headed upstairs, to André's room. His door was closed, and Zoya's heart sank at the thought that André was still asleep. She knocked gently and was relieved to hear his voice:

"Zoya, is that you?"

"Yeah."

She froze in anticipation. She missed André so much and only now fully felt the impact of their short separation. Her hands trembling, Zoya stepped inside. She expected to find a half-asleep André there, tired, lethargic and unprepared to see her. Instead, he was fully dressed, freshly shaven, and sitting on the bed with a mug of coffee in his hands. Seeing Zoya, he handed her a mug of tea, prepared just the way she liked it.

"How did you know that I would arrive early?" Zoya could not hide her surprise.

"I figured you'd normally be off to school at seven in the morning. And it would take you half an hour to get to me." André grinned, and Zoya could not hold back and threw herself into his arms.

"Wait, wait, I am about to scald myself," André said, putting the hot drink on the side table.

"I missed you so much," Zoya whispered, covering his face with kisses.

Zoya almost never expressed her true feelings. But when

she saw André this time, she could not control her emotions. She was both happy and sad, and the great power of their love overwhelmed her. André kissed her back with such passion that it overtook Zoya. She leaned into him and felt as if she was about to melt into his body.

Moments later, André's hand slid up under her top, and Zoya pushed up to meet his hand, but before she could understand what was happening, as many times before, André stopped.

"Zoya," he breathed heavily, pulling back, "Let's wait till I get back. Okay?" He gave Zoya a passionate look that pierced her. Unable to speak, Zoya nodded in response. "As soon as I get back, then…" André kissed her with such tenderness that Zoya believed him: their relationship would be transformed as soon as André returned to Pittsburgh at the end of the summer.

They decided to spend the day in Shadyside, which was a short walk from Oakland. Shadyside was home to the trendy Walnut Street and housed the most high-end stores in the city. Among them was Zoya's favorite, Benetton, which she adored. That the store in Les Hales she had visited on her first trip to Paris, in her dream, was nothing other than a Benetton, Zoya established after moving to America.

It happened at the Red, White and Blue thrift store, when Jessica pointed to a label on a sweater, and Zoya immediately recognized the white letters on a green background, which were exactly the same as those on the label of her pink sweater from Les Halles, the one she saw in her Parisian dream. Once she figured out the name of the store, Zoya immediately went to Shadyside to check whether the brand really existed.

Her doubts were completely dispelled as soon as she saw the Benetton store on Walnut Street — the decor was exactly the same as in her dream: bright white walls reflecting the sun, and a green sign with stylish white lettering. As much as

Zoya didn't want to accept that her teleportation to Paris could reflect reality, she was in awe of the Benetton brand.

For months now, Zoya had been dreaming of buying a piece of clothing from Benetton. But it remained a dream – she could not afford anything there. Asking her parents for thirty or forty dollars for a single shirt from Benetton was out of the question. It was a total waste of money, a completely unreasonable expense, especially considering the fact that her father had just found a job and her mother was so keen on buying a house. The Kassatkins had to save money, not spend it on Zoya's clothes from Benetton that she didn't really need. And of course, she could always get nice enough used clothes from the Red, White, and Blue thrift store or from Nate's, and maybe even switch over the price tag there to get a deeper discount.

Zoya and André walked along Walnut Street. When they passed the coveted Benetton, Zoya looked away to the other side of the street as she usually did, to avoid the temptation of going there, but André suddenly grabbed her hand and led her to the entrance.

"Come on, I've thought of something."

"What?" Zoya's heart started beating fast. She'd dreamt of going into the Benetton store for so long, and it was finally happening!

"You'll see." He smiled. "I think you'll like it."

They went inside, and André led her to a stack of women's shirts. He instantly pulled out an emerald-colored one from the pile and handed it to Zoya:

"Here, this is your size, isn't it?"

Zoya blushed. She hadn't expected André to know her size. Zoya was embarrassed that her breasts were small and seemed stuck on the smaller side of a B cup. A few months prior, Zoya had read in *Mademoiselle* magazine that breasts grew until the age of seventeen, and she waited for her size-B cups to finally transform into a C, but it hadn't happened yet.

André didn't notice Zoya's embarrassment. He trotted over to the rack of men's clothes, from where he confidently pulled out a T-shirt of the same emerald color in size XL. A salesgirl, a young woman with bouffant hair and plucked eyebrows, emerged from behind the cash register. She walked past Zoya, as if she hadn't noticed her, and turned to André, leaning against the counter and flirtatiously sticking out her hip.

"How can I help you?" she purred.

André looked at the woman in amazement, as if he did not immediately understand that she was speaking to him. Then he nodded at Zoya and pulled her to him. "My girl-friend and I are looking for matching T-shirts. I saw these, the green ones, I like the color, but maybe you have others? The main thing is that the color should be the same in men's and women's styles."

The salesgirl blushed and mumbled, "Of course, of course," and then disappeared without an explanation, as suddenly as she appeared.

Once inside the store that she adored, Zoya wanted to touch and try on everything, even socks. But she was embar-rassed by the unpleasant saleswoman and André's purposeful look. He unfolded both T-shirts and placed them next to each other on the counter, as Zoya observed his actions and didn't dare touch anything without André's permission.

"What do you think?" he asked.

"Are you going to buy these for us?" Zoya asked, still in disbelief that this was happening.

"Yes; look, you and I will have the same color T-shirts. As a memento."

Zoya knew that she should feel gratitude, and she should be happy over André's romantic gesture. But the desire to choose and try something on her own was so strong, that Zoya could not force a smile. She felt like crying. She had dreamt of buying clothes at this store for so long, had been so happy when she recognized Benetton when she saw it in Pittsburgh and realized that it was the same store from her first dream trip to Paris. The crushing disappointment about not being able to buy something there stayed with her. Now, when André was going to buy them matching shirts, asking for her opinion, but then choosing the color for them instead, she could not stay calm. A whole tide of emotion rose in her, and Zoya could barely control it.

But how could she share with André how she felt? His reality was so different from her own – an inheritance from his biological father and a wealthy step-father. Zoya had never told him about the lack of money and the suffering it was causing her and her parents. Never told the stories about the humiliating trips to Right Mart, nor complained about the freezing apartment that they could never heat through in the winter, nor had she mentioned the fact that her father had once had to work at a supermarket, following the advice of the awful Paul, whom Zoya could barely stand. André had no idea that Zoya bought all of her clothes either at thrift stores or at Nate's after hours of sifting through piles of clothes, looking for the best bargain. André had bigger problems – he had escaped from his mother and scary stepfather, was making his own way in America, and was working hard to prove himself. *And even if I told him, would he understand?*

"Don't you like them?" André stared at Zoya with undisguised surprise. He looked so confused that Zoya felt sorry for him. And then she felt sorry for herself.

"I … I do. I like them very, very much," responded Zoya, as tears welled up in her eyes. "It's just that you are leaving soon, and then, it will be all over!" Zoya stopped fighting tears and gave in to sobbing. She was glad to have found an explanation that André would find reasonable.

"Zoya, chérie, don't worry. I wanted to make you happy, so I thought you would like it if we had these matching T-shirts from your favorite store." His words made Zoya cry even harder, as she remembered that all of her clothes that carried the Benetton label actually came from a thrift store, bought with Jessica's help after hours and hours searching.

"Yes, I, yes, I love Benetton!" Zoya wept even harder, thinking about how badly she wished she could buy anything she wanted at Benetton rather than rely on André's choice.

"Perfect! I knew you'd be happy! I am going to go ahead and pay," André announced with relief and walked to the counter with a bounce in his step.

The salesgirl with plucked eyebrows gave André an ingratiating smile, as he approached the cash register. Zoya had been noticing that women often flirted with André: saleswomen, waitresses, even ordinary passersby. Women regularly asked him for directions. Some asked for a light, or to check the time. Others asked for his help to get something off a high shelf at a supermarket. Women noticed André. They liked him.

If the woman was particularly beautiful Zoya felt those old feelings of unworthiness creep back in. But mostly, she managed to push them back down. André had chosen her and she chose him. André reacted to the flirtations impeccably, was invariably polite and courteous and remained completely indifferent to a point that Zoya wondered if he even noticed the extraordinary amount of attention he was getting from women. *Or is it that he is so used to it that he doesn't even care anymore?*

Zoya was not surprised that the saleswoman wrapped André's purchase with particular care, and then, moving her finger along the crease line of the package, asked André where he came from, noticing his accent.

"Ah, France! Awesome!" she said dreamily, fixing her hair. Her tiny eyebrows flew all the way to her forehead. "I learned

French at school. *Voulez-vous couchez avec moi ce soir[2]?"* she hummed and giggled. "Is your girlfriend also from there?" The salesgirl asked, pointing at Zoya as if she were an appendage of André and couldn't answer the question herself.

"No, she is from the USSR." André always emphasized the fact that Zoya was born in the Soviet Union, despite the fact that the country no longer existed. André thought that Zoya should be proud of the fact that she was born and raised in such a unique place.

"The USSR?" The saleswoman furrowed her brow, and her face took on a confused expression. Then she laughed, thinking that he'd made a joke. "Ha, you are funny," she said. He did not correct her.

"Thank you."

"And thank you. Come and see me again! I'm here almost every day, well, except Monday."

Zoya was amazed at the insolence of this woman. *Is she hitting on him? Inviting him to come and see her, and right in front of me?* Zoya fumed inside. She herself had never taken the initiative with the opposite sex. She was too shy to openly express her interest in someone. *A woman must play hard to get. Especially when meeting someone for the first time!* Zoya was certain of that.

In response to the saleswoman's proposal, André smiled politely, took Zoya's hand and headed for the exit. Zoya turned around. The saleswoman was folding a sweater and purring to herself. Zoya could make out a faint *'Voulez-vous coucher avec moi se soir'* as the door closed behind them.

"So! Where do you wanna change?" asked André the second they were outside.

"Change what?"

"The clothes! So we can wear our new shirts!" André's

---

2.  Do you want to sleep with me tonight? (Fr)

eyes sparkled, as he said this, and he looked so young and eager, and not at all like the grown-up, serious and stressed-out André that Zoya was used to seeing in Pittsburgh.

"Great idea! I didn't think of that." Zoya jumped up and clapped her hands, happy to partake in the excitement.

"Yeah, I wanted to put them on in the store, but I figured the salesgirl was waaay too clingy." André smirked and tightened his grip on Zoya's hand.

"Did you notice that she was hitting on you?" Zoya asked shyly.

"Well, yeah." André shrugged.

"Oh, I see," said Zoya, although in fact she did not feel any clarity. She wanted to know how he felt about these flirtations, whether he was embarrassed or flattered. But Zoya was afraid to stay on the subject any further: *You never know, maybe he'll be offended, or he'll think I'm jealous.*

"So now we gotta find a place to change. I really want us to wear our matching T-shirts together." André bent down, pulled Zoya close to him and kissed her on the lips. She blushed with pleasure, and immediately thoughts of jealousy, of concerns over the sales clerk's flirtations and of other women disappeared, and all that remained was her love for André.

"I know where we can change, we can hide in this parking lot, there is a guard's booth, we can go behind it." Zoya pointed to a side street.

"Right on the street? Aren't you going to be embarrassed?"

"No; if you block me in, no one will see me." Zoya was surprised at her own ingenuity and led André along. They turned into the parking lot and came around the corner of the guard's booth. Surrounded by dense shrubbery, the booth was completely hidden from view.

"Here," said Zoya, stepping into a clearing.

"Let me go first," André squatted and took off his gray

Carnegie Mellon T-shirt, and Zoya marveled at the perfection of his body and his sculpted muscles. Zoya knew that André was very proud of his affiliation with the prestigious university and even bought a baseball cap with the CMU logo on it. He never got used to wearing it, and it was displayed in his room on the shelf above his desk. André pulled on the new Benetton shirt, ripping off the tag and they switched places.

Zoya half-expected André to watch her change. But he turned away, and didn't seem at all interested in watching her undress. Quickly, she took off her shirt and pulled on the green Benetton top. It smelled new and fresh, the unfamiliar to Zoya smell of new clothes. Clothes that she found at the thrift store smelled differently, old and musty. And Zoya always washed them before wearing. But the smell of a new T-shirt was refreshing and cheerful. *How wonderful!* Zoya thought as she inhaled.

"You look great!" André pulled Zoya to him and hugged her.

"Thank you! You do, too!" she said, pressing her body against his.

"Let me look at you," said André, loosening her grip and stepping back. "I wanted to watch you change, but I didn't want to gawk."

"Oh, really?" Zoya widened her eyes in amazement. *He thinks of everything*, she thought.

"Oh God!! You turn me on so much!" André's face turned red as he pressed her against him.

They spent the rest of the day enthralled by each other. Zoya and André strolled through Shadyside, then had lunch at 'Max and Irma's'. Zoya enjoyed the restaurant, which was sunny and beautiful. The waitress was a serious, older woman who did not flirt with André, but, on the contrary, was very attentive to Zoya, calling her a 'young lady'. Still uncomfortable placing an order, Zoya let André choose her meal, and he did not mind.

"Zoya, I'm leaving early Sunday morning. Tomorrow I'll be packing, and I need to buy presents for my uncle and cousins, but if you have time, stop by tomorrow night, okay?" said André, as he paid for the meal.

"Of course I will," Zoya promised and then her heart sank, as she remembered her plans to go to the nightclub with Evan on Saturday night. Evan, raves, dancing, it all seemed ridiculous to her now, because in real life, her one and only true love was only with André.

*Why would I go anywhere without him at all? I should stay home and dedicate myself fully to my wonderful boyfriend. And why did I ever call Evan back?* thought Zoya, *I'm not going anywhere tomorrow, and instead of dancing, I'll come by André's to see him off before he leaves. I don't need Evan in my life at all,* Zoya decided and was glad of it. She felt as if a heavy weight lifted off her shoulders. *And everything will be fine, André is right: the summer will go by quickly, it's just over three months, and we will be together as soon as he comes back. And then we'll start a real relationship!* Zoya remembered André's promise and blushed at the thought. They left the restaurant, holding hands.

"I'm going to the bus stop then," André said.

Zoya and André had an implicit agreement that they would not come too close to her house. They embraced, and Zoya's eyes filled with tears, despite the fact that a minute ago she was sure that their parting would go unnoticed.

"Zoé, please don't cry. I'll write you a letter every day, I promise. And you write to me, okay?"

"Okay." Zoya nodded, wiping her eyes.

André stroked her head, and then whispered, "And don't forget: we're going to get serious when I get back."

"Promise?" Zoya looked at him with tearful eyes, her face flushed. André kissed her on the cheek and then said, "Call me tomorrow, let me know when you can come over."

"See you tomorrow," Zoya whispered back.

At the usual time, she arrived home as if she'd been to

school. Her parents hadn't yet returned home from work and she had the afternoon all to herself. She breathed a sigh of relief and erased the message she'd left on the answering machine, warning them of her late arrival home, in case André wanted to spend the whole afternoon together.

She inspected herself in her new emerald-green Benetton T-shirt in the mirror that hung in the living room. Zoya had never bought clothes in that color before. She turned to the side and checked herself from the left, then the right. She decided that the color looked good on her. The emerald shade of green accentuated her eyes and made them a brighter brown. *Wow, how did André manage to choose such a beautiful color? He has great taste,* thought Zoya.

Suddenly, there was rustling on the stairwell. The next second, the front door opened and Zoya saw her parents. Not only did they come home much earlier than normal, they came home together. Zoya panicked, she tried to disappear into her room, but it was too late.

"Zoya, good, you are home. We found a house!" her mother announced, smiling brightly. "Papa and I just went to look at it; it's a dream come true! It's so beautiful, just a miracle!"

"A house?" Zoya stared at her parents in excitement.

"It's absolutely wonderful, all brick, and it costs fifty thousand dollars. We have to go to the bank, get a mortgage, and then the house is ours! I know it's meant to be." Zoya's mother looked dreamily somewhere at a distance.

"Ella, wait a minute, we may not get approved for the mortgage." Zoya's father shook his head. His shoulders drooped and he looked at his wife in resignation, as he did most of the time ever since moving to Pittsburgh. "I personally did not like the house all that much. It looks small."

"What do you mean, small? It's America, it's a regular house."

"I don't think we should rush into buying it. It's a big decision. We can find a better one."

"Peter, you're always like this. Too lazy to change things. I'm sick and tired of this apartment. I want to move out as soon as possible."

When it came to the new house, Zoya had only one concern: its exact location and whether she would have to take the school bus. Zoya heard that terrible things could happen on a school bus – and wanted to avoid riding it at all cost. She was just fine walking to school, even if it took a good twenty minutes each morning.

"Where is the house?" Zoya asked, trying to sound like she did not actually care much about the answer.

"Oh, it's in Greenfield, not far from here." Her mother waved her hand vaguely and looked away again.

"The location is terrible!" Her father remarked. "It's right across from the freeway exit, it's the worst. You walk out of the house, you run right into I-376, and there's a hell of a lot of noise from all that traffic."

"Peter! Why are you making this up?"

"What do you mean, I'm making it up? You saw for yourself that there's a highway nearby. I didn't build it. Only an idiot would buy a place in that location."

"Well, it might be the case, but who cares, we are meant to buy this house. It is adorable. And anyway, where else are we going to find a house of our own for that ridiculous amount of money?"

"Fifty thousand dollars is not a ridiculous amount of money to me. And anyway, throwing it away on some hovel is a big mistake."

"Peter, how can you? Why did you pretend to like it? I am now going to have to explain to Tatiana that we are backing out of the deal, and she's been so helpful! And I've already promised her that we're buying this house. She is counting on us for her commission."

"She should be ashamed of herself for offering us such crap. What kind of a real estate agent is she? Does she even care about her clients? She should be picking better places for us to see, not trying to shove her customers into barns where they'll suffer."

"Peter, but the house is objectively good!"

"Ella, objectively I won't live there. And I wouldn't advise you to live there either."

Zoya's father exhaled angrily and went into the bedroom, slamming the door behind him. Zoya had never seen him so upset and so forceful in his opinion. Neither one of her parents noticed Zoya's new outfit, and Zoya decided not to change. She popped a tape of The Simpsons into the VCR and took a seat in front of the TV to watch her favorite show.

# CHAPTER 7

The following morning Zoya got up early, even though it was a Saturday. She needed to see André again before he left. Zoya knew that he liked to get up late on weekends, so she never called him before nine o'clock. The time was determined by a book on etiquette that Zoya had read back in Moscow. According to the book, any time between the hours of nine in the evening and nine in the morning was considered 'private', so unless specifically requested, it was rude to disturb someone. Now, in America, Zoya followed that rule.

At exactly nine o'clock, Zoya dialed André's number. The phone rang, but no one answered. Zoya called back, and again no one answered. *He is probably still asleep,* Zoya sighed and sat down to do her homework. Every weekend, she set aside two to three hours for homework, especially at the end of a quarter, when she would normally have big exams. Just as she opened her algebra textbook, she remembered that she had missed school the day before. *What if we have an assignment due on Monday?* she thought with dread. *What if there's a quiz?* Zoya rushed to the phone and called Jessica.

"Yo!" Jessica answered the phone right away, sounding alert.

Zoya could hear her friend chewing. "Hey, umm, did we get like any assignments yesterday?" Except for French and art, they had almost all of their classes together.

"Nah, you didn't miss much; but why didn't you come to school yesterday? You didn't go to Nate's without me, did you?" Zoya heard Jessica slurp and imagined her drinking a coke.

"André is leaving soon, we were saying goodbye."

"You're crazy! You missed a whole day of school because of him?" Jessica yelped. She did not approve of Zoya's relationship with André and did not hide her disregard for Zoya's boyfriend.

"But it was a Friday, and I haven't skipped school in ages!!!"

"So what if it was a Friday? You could have said goodbye to him after school. I can't believe he's leaving."

"Oh, come on. So I didn't miss anything?"

"No. You wanna come over? We can do homework together. We covered a new chapter in algebra," Jessica offered. Zoya thought that she heard gloating in her friend's voice.

Zoya checked her watch. It was already after ten a.m. She thought that she should call André again and arrange a meeting. And then Zoya remembered that she had made plans with Evan to go to Pegasus. *But how am I going to go see André, study with Jessica and then be back in time to meet Evan and go to Pegasus?* Zoya panicked.

"Umm, I dunno; I have to go to André's to say goodbye to him."

"Ha? Didn't you just spend all day yesterday saying goodbye to him?" Jessica's voice full of irony. "How many good-byes are there?"

"He's leaving tomorrow for the whole summer!" Zoya pleaded.

Zoya rarely shared information with Jessica about André. Mostly, Jessica knew the basics: that they hadn't slept together yet, and that Zoya did not want him to leave for the summer. Jessica made no secret of the fact that she thought André's departure was a positive development. "There's no reason to get hung up on just one guy, especially at sixteen!" her friend asserted.

"You'd better come over and study, or you won't understand anything on Monday," Jessica insisted.

"I have to see André before he leaves," Zoya insisted.

"You can call him from here. I got a phone at my house, you know." Jessica mocked.

"Okay, you're right. I'll be right over. Like in about fifteen minutes."

"Cool! Mom's making pancakes!" Jessica remarked.

Every weekend, Jessica's mother prepared an elaborate breakfast, consisting of fluffy, thick pancakes with maple syrup. Zoya had never had maple syrup before trying it at Jessica's and now loved it.

"Oh! Pancakes! My favorite. I'm on my way!" After hanging up, she began to throw her books and notebooks into her backpack.

"Where are you going?" Zoya flinched, hearing her mother's voice.

"To Jessica's! To study!" For once she didn't have to lie about her plans, knowing that her mother approved of their friendship. And her father didn't pay much attention to Jessica. He often referred to her as 'your friend Sofie', in honor of Zoya's friend who had long ago moved to Israel from Moscow.

"Good for you, run along then," her mother said.

"Bye, Mama, I'll be back in the afternoon," Zoya blurted out, hoping that nothing else would keep her, and opened the front door, when the phone rang again. Without thinking, she grabbed the receiver.

"Zoya, hi. It's me, Evan," she heard a low voice. "Did you remember about the club?"

"Yeah, of course!" Zoya exhaled. She was glad that she had managed to answer the phone and that Evan wouldn't have to leave a message with her parents, causing a wave of worries and questions.

"Then I'll pick you up at five o'clock, okay?"

"Isn't that a little early?" Zoya tried to calculate the time to get everything done. The day was shaping up to be hectic.

"Umm, I was kinda thinking, maybe we go hang out somewhere before the club? Like, we could have dinner together?" Evan responded. His voice sounded shaky. Zoya immediately thought that it sounded like a date, but, as if reading her thoughts, Evan said: "Nikki will also be there."

"Cool! See you guys later then!" she said and hung up.

Zoya was in a great mood. Her day was about to be nothing short of spectacular. Zoya ran out of the house and headed for her friend's house. It was a short walk away, and in a few minutes the two friends were sitting in Jessica's kitchen with huge plates of pancakes in front of them. As usual, Jessica's mother entertained them with stories about the school where she taught Civics, and the girls listened in admiration. Then they sat down to study, and time flew by so fast that Zoya came to her senses only when it was a quarter to two.

"Oh! André! I completely forgot," Zoya cried out. "I need to call him!"

"Whatever," Jessica shrugged. "Why do you always run after him, like a lapdog?"

Zoya flinched at her friend's words, barely containing her indignation. "What do you mean, a lapdog?"

"Why you gotta run after him? You skipped school yesterday because of him. You never skip a day, except to go to Nate's, and we always plan it a month in advance. We check the schedule and everything, and now, bam, you don't show up for school, like it's no big deal. I don't even recognize you! And all because of some guy!" There was concern in Jessica's voice, and Zoya decided she wasn't going to be offended by her friend's bluntness.

"He's leaving! For more than three months!" Zoya cried out, suppressing tears.

"Exactly! He's leaving, but he could have stayed," said Jessica cruelly. "He knows how badly you want him to stay and he's leaving anyway."

"He doesn't know. And anyway, he has no choice, he has to take care of some stuff." Zoya tried to make the same argument as André, when he explained his departure, but it felt unconvincing.

"You haven't been yourself lately. Though I gotta say, the rave was fun! At least we had a good time." Jessica winked.

"Oh. I didn't know you could tell," Zoya widened her eyes in disbelief that all this time Jessica was aware of how upset she had been over André's departure.

"Of course I can tell. As soon as he told you he was going away for the summer, it was like a different Zoya. You turned into a real mess. Want a hug?" Jessica walked over and put her arms around her.

When Zoya first moved to America, she found the American habit of hugging ridiculous, even shocking. But now the gesture reassured her. It meant that Jessica was on her side, that her friend cared about her, and Zoya liked that. In Jessica's embrace, Zoya felt herself relax and exhaled in relief. Jessica continued:

"And then think about it. Maybe it's actually a good thing he's leaving. At least you'll be able to think clearly. 'Cause now, you're always going on and on about him. And you gotta give him space. It'll be good for you."

"That's not true!" Zoya looked indignantly at Jessica, but her friend continued inexorably:

"Look, why doesn't he come to you to say good-bye?"

"When? He's too busy! He's packing, and he has presents to buy." Zoya threw her hands up in frustration.

"And you are not busy? You're also studying, you have things to do, parents, and whatever, why don't you let him come to you for once. Maybe it's good that he's going away for the whole summer. Maybe you'll decide that you don't need him at all and that you're better off without him!" In response, Zoya chuckled:

"No way. Me? Decide that I don't want him? But we are perfect for each other."

"You're only sixteen years old, why are you so obsessed with one guy? You'll probably have twenty more Andrés in your life. Just like that. Or maybe even better!"

"I don't need anyone else! And he is perfect for me!" cried out Zoya.

"Oh, come on, Romeo and Juliet!" Jessica laughed. "All right, all right. Just please don't sulk all summer long, while he is in France being French and all that."

"I won't. And he's not French, he's Corsican," responded Zoya. Once she said it, the remark seemed so absurd to her that she let out a giggle, and suddenly both she and Jessica were laughing. Jessica doubled over:

"Corsican? Oh, I can't even!"

"Yes, Corsican," Zoya nodded, tears of laughter in her eyes.

"Okay, okay, this is crazy," Jessica stopped laughing first and winked at Zoya.

"But I really need to call André now. Is that cool?" Jessica nodded, and Zoya picked up the phone. There were long rings, but again no one answered.

"Don't they have an answering machine?" Jessica asked, raising her eyebrows.

"I don't think so. There's always someone at home, there's like a whole house full of people. It's weird, why doesn't anyone answer?" Zoya frowned. "In the morning he did not pick up the phone either. And when am I going to see him?" She felt panic grip her throat.

"Well, it's not a big deal, you said goodbye yesterday."

"I wanted to meet him today," Zoya whimpered.

"Umm, you gotta be tougher. Men need to be trained, that's what my mom always tells me." Jessica shrugged. "Matt apologized, asking me to forgive him after he left us at the rave the other night. He calls me twice a day. He gave me flowers the other day."

"Flowers!" Zoya exclaimed, impressed! André had never given her flowers.

Zoya returned home at around three pm. Despite not being able to reach André, she was pleased with her Saturday so far: she had done her homework and got to spend time with Jessica. Once at home, Zoya dialed André's number again. This time there was an answer, and Zoya heard Sybil's voice, who spoke with a French accent and Zoya suspected that she made it stronger on purpose:

"Oui, hello."

"Sibyl, it's Zoya. Is André home?"

"André? I don't know, let me check. I just got back, Mikey and I went to the Strip District. He was looking for some special olive oil." Sybil sighed heavily. The girl put down the receiver and Zoya could hear her footsteps, as Sibyl climbed the stairs to the second floor.

Mikey loved spending Saturday afternoons at the Strip District – a market in Pittsburgh's former industrial district adjacent to the river near Downtown. In the early twentieth century, it housed factories and warehouses, but now was full of shops and restaurants. There were several Italian stores in the Strip District where Mikey bought special ingredients for his culinary experiments. He could talk for hours about the virtues of parmesan with the salesman, and discuss what kind of flour to use for lasagna. Sibyl patiently accompanied him, though it was obvious that she was not interested.

There was a muffled conversation, then some voices and the sound of approaching footsteps.

"No, he's not here. Mikey said he'd gone out this morning to get presents for his uncle."

"Can you tell him that I called?" Zoya asked, trying to sound calm.

"Of course I can! But you are coming for dinner, aren't you? André said you were going to come over tonight."

"Yeah? He said that?" Zoya's eyes widened in surprise. She and André had no clear agreement on the time of when they would be meeting.

"Yeah, for dinner. Mikey wants to make something special to celebrate his departure, and André said you'd be there. The four of us will celebrate."

"Oh, what time?"

"I don't know." Sybil sighed again. "We just got back; Mikey's napping. And it usually takes him at least two hours to make dinner, so we'll probably sit down at eight."

"Eight? Okay." Zoya's heart sank, and she tried not to show her disappointment.

If she had known in advance about dinner at André's, then she would have canceled her plans to go to Pegasus with Evan. And now she had made overlapping arrangements. *Why did André not mention dinner to me? Does he think I have nothing else to do? That I sit around all day waiting for him to call?* Zoya was fuming on the inside. *I should be tougher on him!* Zoya heard Jessica's words in her head: "Why do you always run after him, like a lapdog?"

She felt rage boiling up. *Jessica is right! I've been trying to reach him all day and he didn't even bother to tell me he was expecting me for dinner tonight? It is him who is leaving, and he could have stayed! He is leaving me all alone to suffer.*

Zoya's excellent mood evaporated. She felt like crying right there and then. She wanted André to feel all of her pain and to fully acknowledge his guilt. Since the moment he had announced that he would spend the summer in France, Zoya bottled up her emotions and kept them to herself, stubbornly suppressing them. She had not shared her feelings with André directly, and now she felt like she was about to burst.

Zoya could no longer contain her hurt. She slammed her fist against the corner of the couch and felt piercing pain. Her amber bracelet, a gift from Yegor Vlasov, jammed into her wrist. She cried out in resentment. *Why couldn't André change his mind and stay in Pittsburgh for the summer?* If he decided to cancel his trip, and instead stroke her head, kiss her, and promise to always be there for her, she would forgive him right away. But André was out of reach, and Zoya had already promised to go to the club with Evan.

"You gotta be tougher. Men need to be trained." Jessica's words echoed in her head again.

*Enough is enough!* thought Zoya. *Jessica's got a point. I gotta be tougher. I'm going to the club with Evan, as planned, and it's André's own fault that he didn't invite me to dinner earlier.* Zoya wiped her tears, adjusted her bracelet and went into the bathroom to clean herself up.

# CHAPTER 8

At exactly five p.m., she saw Evan's car pull up to her house. Zoya was impressed by his punctuality. Evan was dressed in a long raver T-shirt and wide pants that fully covered his sneakers. Zoya had seen hundreds of skaters who wore similar outfits, and always thought that they looked unkempt. But Evan's clothes had been neatly ironed, his hair was slicked back and his glasses sparkled brightly. He looked impressive. Zoya got into his car and smelled Evan's cologne. She liked it. *If only André could pick me up like this,* thought Zoya.

Zoya found Nikki with another girl in the backseat – she thought she recognized her. Nikki held out her hand:

"I remember you! You were at the rave last week. My name is Nikki." The girl's palm felt warm and soft to the touch.

"And I'm Soup," said the other girl. "I don't remember you, but I took a lot of stuff, and that night's a blur." She chortled. Her voice was a little husky, and didn't quite match her very pretty face and delicate features.

"You tell her your normal name, why you gotta go by Soup?" Nikki shook her head in disapproval.

"Well yeah, my name is Kelly, but everybody knows me as Soup," said the girl. "That's 'cause I like soup," she clarified, "a whole lot."

Soup was wearing a black baseball cap, and her blond bangs protruded from underneath. Her eyes were a chestnut brown, and the combination of her dark eyes and blond bangs reminded Zoya of the model Cindy Crawford. Soup was very pretty. Zoya was glad Evan didn't come alone, but with these nice girls.

*So we're not on a date or anything, so nothing weird is going to happen,* Zoya thought with relief as they drove in the direction of Oakland. Suddenly, an idea flashed through her mind and she almost jumped up in excitement: *What if we all stopped by André's on the way to the club? Then I could say goodbye to him, and we could all go out dancing. And maybe have dinner. And André won't think I'm sitting around waiting for him, while he is having fun in France. I will show him that I have friends, and not just him!* The idea of stopping by André's seemed so genius to Zoya that she could barely sit still.

"Why don't we pass by the Beehive? We could hang out there, and then go to Pegasus at eight?" Evan looked over his shoulder briefly at them.

"Nah, I don't want to go to the Beehive, it's boring," Nikki responded, and Soup muttered:

"How about Wendy's? I'm feigning for some fries, just dying."

"Soup, are you stoned again? You're always craving fries," said Nikki. Kelly giggled in response.

"So where are we going?" Evan pulled over and looked at the girls questioningly.

"It's too early to go to Pegasus," Nikki reasoned. "Let's get her the French fries, or she won't shut up." Nikki gave Soup a look of mock disapproval. Her friend shrugged and silently adjusted her baseball cap.

"Let's go to Wendy's, then," Evan said.

"Do you guys wanna stop by my friends' house? They live in Oakland." Zoya suggested. She deliberately avoided mentioning André and the fact that they had a much closer relationship.

"Friends? Umm, okay." Evan looked at Zoya doubtfully.

"Yeah! Of course! Are there any cute guys there? I love meeting cute boys!" Nikki giggled, but Soup immediately reacted:

"Don't you get enough of them at work?"

"At work, it's different. And besides, I'm not allowed to talk to clients outside of work."

"Where do you work? I'm going to start a job at the library this summer." Zoya was happy to keep the conversation going.

"She works at a strip club," said Evan with a smirk.

"I am a dancer there," Nikki clarified. "And I gotta work tonight, by the way; I'll dance with ya'll for a bit at Pegasus and then Evan will drop me off. Isn't that right, hun?" Nikki patted his neck.

Evan nodded affirmatively. "Of course I will. We have a deal."

"Thanks, kitten. I have to be there at eleven. Schedule this week kinda sucks, but at least it's a Saturday night. I've already worked three Saturdays in a row, the girls at the club aren't super happy, so I gotta give up the Saturday night shift eventually," said Nikki.

"Where are we going? Where do your friends live?" Evan asked.

"Nearby, you need to turn onto South Bouquet, and then their house is right down the street."

"Cool, so it's right around here," Evan said, while Zoya listened intently to Nikki.

"And by the way, our club is very friendly, great team," continued Nikki. "Listen, Zoya, are you Russian? Evan told me, but you have no accent at all."

Zoya blushed, flattered by Nikki's words, and decided that she liked the girl even more. "I'm from Russia, yes." She already knew: there was no need to specify that she was from Moscow. Most Americans weren't interested in the city where she had grown up. Zoya thought that now Nikki would ask her when she had moved to America, and prepared to answer, but Nikki chirped animatedly:

"Oh, wow! So cool! And I have a client, he's also Russian. He is so generous. Only his name is horrible. His name is Igor!? Can you believe it?" Nikki laughed.

Zoya already knew that Americans associated the name Igor with the hunchbacked assistant from the movie *Frankenstein*.

"Yes, it's a regular name in Russia," said Zoya, trying to sound informative and pleasant.

"That's crazy! When I heard that his name was Igor, I just laughed. But he's very nice, he gives great tips! He's the best customer ever. Maybe he'll be there tonight."

"Listen, enough about your tips," Soup interjected. She had been silent up to that point, seemingly ignoring their conversation.

"Well, it's your fault. I tried to get you a job at the club. But you showed up to the interview stoned and fell asleep on the couch." Nikki shook her head. "I almost got fired because of you. They thought I was also smoking weed. But I wasn't. I can't lose that job! I need the money. I fixed my mother's house, and now I'm saving for my own apartment."

"Nikki, come on, will you please stop?" Soup pleaded.

"I was trying to help you. Where else are you gonna get that kind of money? Oh! By the way, Zoya, do you want to come work for us?"

"At the strip club?" Zoya liked the idea of making good money. "What do I have to do?"

"If you want, I'll tell my boss about you," Nikki promised.

"She's only sixteen years old, leave her alone," Evan interjected.

"Wait, what??? You're not eighteen yet?" Nikki gasped. "You gotta be eighteen. So you're just a baby. I thought you were older. We're twenty. Evan and I graduated high school together. I'm from Greensburg, too. We're childhood friends, aren't we, kitten?" Nikki patted Evan's neck again, while he muttered something incomprehensible in response.

"But maybe I can work there when I turn eighteen?" Zoya did not want to give up her dream so easily.

"No, you have to show ID."

"Oh no, but how much does it pay?"

"Well, look, you can make three thousand a month easily, it all depends on the schedule and how customers treat you. If they like you, you get tips. And it's an easy job: you dance, and that's it."

"Do you have to work at night?"

"They pay more at night, but you can get a daytime job. I'll ask today. Maybe they'll make an exception for you. Igor would really like you!" Nikki said.

And then a terrible thought pierced Zoya's imagination: *what if her parents knew Igor, as all Russian immigrants knew each other.* Zoya imagined how Igor would share that a Russian girl worked at a strip club, and how the news spread all over Squirrel Hill. And then her parents would find out and make a scene so terrible that Zoya would never recover from it, and accuse her of disgracing their entire family. They might never let her out of the house again.

"And Igor, what does he look like?" Zoya asked in a thin voice.

"He's kind of... Average height. Kind of cute. Blond hair. Blue eyes. Looks like Ivan Drago." Nikki giggled.

"So where's your friends' house?" Evan interrupted their conversation.

"It's right here. You can park on the street, right here,"

Zoya pointed to a space next to the familiar porch. Evan deftly turned the car around and slid into the space in front of the house.

"Oh, who are your friends? You never told us!" Nikki crooned as she fixed her hair.

"That's 'cause you've been rattling on and on about your club again," Evan said with a smirk.

"So what? I'm proud of my job!"

"You can't talk about anything else ever since you started working there."

"Come on, don't be jealous!" Nikki laughed.

"Jealous of what?" There was a sense of judgment in Evan's voice.

They got out of the car. Zoya walked up to the door and knocked. Evan, Nikki and Soup crowded behind her. Sibyl opened the door. She was wearing an apron and her hands were covered in flour. In spite of this, she managed to look glamorous. Sibyl smiled amiably, not at all embarrassed at the sight of her guests.

"Oh! Zoya! Hi!" She crooned, as she leaned in to give Zoya a kiss on the cheek.

"Hi, I'm Nikki. And this is my best friend Kelly," Nikki pushed Soup forward.

"My name is Evan," Zoya heard his voice from behind her. Evan stepped forward and shook Sibyl's hand.

"Nice to meet you. Sibyl." The Canadian flicked her long hair away from her face and smiled ingratiatingly. "I'm helping my boyfriend cook," Sybil remarked with a hint of belligerence in her voice as she looked at Nikki and Soup. "Come in and have a seat," Sybil pointed to the sofa by the window. "Only André is still not back," she said after a short pause, giving Zoya a meaningful look.

"And where is he?" Zoya's voice croaked. She tried her best not to sound concerned, but she felt her palms sweating and her heart fluttered.

"Umm, he left to get presents this morning and hasn't come back yet. You can wait here while I go to the kitchen to cut the tomatoes. Mikey, umm, that's my boyfriend, is so demanding," Sybil gave Nikki and Kelly a stern look.

"Thank you, Sybil!" Zoya plopped down on the couch and took a look around. Nikki and Soup sat down next to her, while Evan hovered by the window. She felt responsible for inviting Evan and his friends to André's house. Now that it turned out that they had nothing to do, Zoya agonized about their next move. But a second later, Soup saved the day.

"Umm, this sucks. Can we go get my French fries now? This is boring as hell," Soup moped.

"Yeah, for real, let's go," said Nikki jumped up and headed to the door. Evan followed, then Soup, while Zoya closed the procession, feeling incredibly relieved. She realized that she was glad that she didn't have to introduce Evan and André, and that deep-down, she didn't particularly want to see André at all.

They got into the Saab, argued for a while about which Wendy's to go to, then discussed the merits of fries from Wendy's compared to those from McDonald's, and finally rode off. Sitting on the front seat next to Evan, Zoya felt at peace with the world, silently happy that she had made new friends.

# CHAPTER 9

Zoya really liked Pegasus. The club was divided into two parts, the downstairs, with the bar, and the upstairs, where there was dancing. The music had a steady beat, which was easy to move to, and Zoya's body, as if on its own, followed the rhythm.

"They play mostly house music," Evan explained, "you like it?" Instead of an answer, Zoya nodded and smiled. "It's better upstairs, that's where you can dance and stuff," he added.

She spent several hours talking and dancing with Nikki and Soup. Evan also danced, though not as much as he had at the rave, but Zoya didn't mind. She liked simply being around him.

A few minutes before eleven, as he had promised, Evan dropped Nikki off at work, and then took Zoya home. Soup stayed behind.

"And how will she get home?" Zoya asked, feeling responsible for her new friend.

"She'll figure it out, she's a big girl." Evan shrugged. "She's a nomad, kinda, you know, a free spirit."

"What do you mean?" Zoya raised her eyebrows. She had

not met any free spirits before and was very curious to know more.

"Umm, kinda like a drifter. She might sleep over at Ike's tonight. He's this dude, says he's an African prince, lives nearby; she hangs with him from time to time."

"What do you mean, an actual African prince?"

"Umm, I dunno; I guess so. He's a DJ too, you'll see him around, he goes to raves. But mostly he's a dealer."

"A dealer of what?" A new, exotic and wondrous world full of raves, strip clubs, African princes and dealers was opening up to Zoya and she loved every minute of it.

"You know, like a drug dealer." Evan gave Zoya an incredulous look.

"But if he's a prince, what does he need money for? He must be rich already?" In her mind, princes didn't need to earn extra money.

"Good point!" Evan said and looked at Zoya with undisguised admiration. "I had never really thought about it. Maybe he is not a real prince?"

"So, Soup will go to Ike's tonight?"

"Yeah. He supplies her for free."

"Supplies what?"

"Well, like gives her free drugs. She doesn't complain, and why should I interfere?" Evan shrugged, showing that the conversation was over. "Anyway, I'll call you."

Evan stopped the car near her house. Zoya smiled as she got out. Although they had met only a week prior, Zoya felt at ease around Evan. As she opened the door to her apartment, Zoya checked the time: it was almost midnight. She gasped, as she thought of how she would explain her late arrival to her parents. But the lights in the living room were out, and Zoya tiptoed to her room. The apartment was very quiet. Without turning on the light, Zoya got into bed, but couldn't immediately fall asleep. Her ears still buzzed with the beat of the house music.

She turned on the light and reached for her diary. As she stared at a blank page, she thought of how drastically her life had changed in just one week. *I am so lucky to have met these nice ravers, Evan, Nikki, and Soup! So glad Jessica invited me to High Voltage!* Then Zoya remembered André and felt a now familiar heartache. *Will I make it through the whole summer without him?* The thought flickered through her mind and disappeared.

# CHAPTER 10

May 15, 1993

As promised, Monsieur Mbia hosted members of the Taylor Allderdice French Club at his house. He lived near the school, in a small house on a hill not far from Frick Park. The meeting was scheduled for two o'clock on Saturday afternoon, and Zoya spent the whole morning preparing. She changed her clothes several times, trying to look dressy, but casual, and then checked the book that she would bring along.

Monsieur Mbia asked them to share a book about France or one written by a French author. Zoya initially wanted to bring one of the novels by Marguerite Yourcenar, whom Monsieur Mbia had once mentioned to her, but she could not find anything at the library, so Zoya chose *The Little Prince* by Saint-Exupery.

*Of course, it could be considered a children's book,* Zoya thought, *but it's so kind and beautiful. Such wonderful illustrations and originally written in French.* Zoya had adored *The Little Prince,* ever since reading it with her mother when she was a child. Zoya was fascinated by the intrepid pilot Saint-

Exupery, who wrote the novel after crashing his plane in the Sahara and almost dying there.

Zoya lovingly examined the copy she would be taking to the meeting. She'd bought it in Paris earlier that year, at a store called FNAC. Once there, Zoya couldn't tear herself away from the bookshelves. There were so many amazing books in French that she wanted to buy, and even literature in Russian. But she only had enough money for one book, and she decided to buy this to read it in the original. Zoya happily leafed through the book with its familiar blue cover, bright yellow stars, and a picture of the prince himself, who was calling her to an obscure planet.

Walking up to Monsieur Mbia's door, Zoya bumped into Grisha Kantorovich. He was dressed as usual, in suit pants and a silk shirt. This time the shirt was decorated with bright Hawaiian flowers, which contrasted with Grisha's frowning face.

"Good afternoon." Kantorovich cleared his throat as he greeted Zoya.

"Hello," said Zoya, trying to control the inflection in her voice and to sound as neutral as possible.

"What, dear, you decided to reminisce about France?"

"Umm, yep, that's why we are meeting today, right?" Zoya responded cheerfully, knocking on the door and walking straight into the trap that Grisha had set out for her.

"Well, yes. Besides, who knows when you'll manage to get to France again? It's not cheap, that's for sure." A nasty smile crept across his face.

"I did not think about that," said Zoya, and only then realized what Kantorovich meant.

"That's right, better not to think about it! By the way, my mom promised me that we'll go to France together this summer. She's never been there, and as soon as she passes her medical exams, we'll go right away. To celebrate."

"That's great, Grisha, congratulations." On the inside,

Zoya seethed. "You know what my dad says about American doctors?" The feeling of imminent revenge made her feel giddy.

"What?" Grisha looked pleased.

"That doctors in America can't be decent people. That they're all bloodsuckers and murderers, and don't cure people, but only cripple and make money from people's suffering."

Grisha's cheeks turned beet red, and his face twisted in indignation. He clenched his fists and Zoya was about to move back.

"He also says that honest and good people can't deal with the American medical system and insurance companies charge people a ton of money and deny treatment to ordinary people. That–"

At that moment, the door opened, and she saw a beautiful woman on the threshold. It was a tall redhead. She looked as if she had a halo around her head, she was so bright and sparkly. The woman smiled and immediately turned to Zoya.

"And you must be Zoya? I've heard so much about you! Welcome!"

"Ahem, excuse me, my name is Grisha Kantorovich." The boy cleared his throat and threw a disgruntled look at Zoya. He extended his hand to the beautiful woman.

"Sure, sure, come in, guys." The woman gestured for them to enter, and then added: "Oh, I didn't introduce myself. I'm Evelyn Mbia. You may call me Madame Mbia, the French way." She giggled, delighted by her own joke, and sailed away into the back of the house, leaving the two of them alone at the entrance.

"I don't understand, who is she?" Kantorovich asked in Russian, throwing a confused look at Zoya. "What's going on? Who lives here?"

"What do you mean who is she? It's Monsieur Mbia's wife." Zoya rolled her eyes.

When Grisha spoke to her in Russian, Zoya found him even less tolerable than normal. The Russian language created the appearance of intimacy between them, which Zoya wanted to avoid at all cost.

"Wife? But she's white!" Grisha snorted contemptuously. "What, he couldn't find one of his own?"

Zoya got ready to parry, but did not have the time – she saw a familiar silhouette. An African woman with large glasses, wearing jeans and a simple black sweater. Zoya recognized her immediately. *It's Fatima! Fatima Mbia!* Zoya's heart leaped at the sight of the woman, who was sitting on the sofa in the corner of the living room, flipping through a photo album. It was as if an apparition from Zoya's dream suddenly came to life.

Fear gripped Zoya's throat, as she panicked: *Oh, it's really her! Should I talk to her? But what if she's just a regular person, not the one from the dream; she'll think I'm crazy, won't she? And then Monsieur Mbia will think I am nuts, and the whole school will know.* Zoya was paralyzed with anxiety. She badly wanted to ask Fatima about the dream, about the Templars, and the miraculous rescue from St. Anne's, but she needed to do so without giving herself away.

A minute later, a large group of other invitees arrived. It got noisy in the house. Zoya did not notice when their host appeared and called everyone to the table laid out on the spacious veranda. Madame Mbia announced they would be making fondue, producing a large pot of melted cheese and tiny fondue forks. Grisha threw a contemptuous look at the cheese, snorted that fondue was actually a Swiss dish and not authentically French at all, but then, smacking his lips, dipped bread into the melted cheese and even licked his fingers in the process.

The rest of the French Club members were busy chatting with each other and did not seem to notice his comments.

Zoya wondered if she were all alone in paying attention to what Kantorovich was doing and getting annoyed by him.

Conversation at the table was lively, the French Club members enthusiastically recalled the trip, and shared their plans for the summer. Zoya was silent. She had no plans for the summer other than going to raves and working at the library, and was still trying to figure out how to approach Fatima Mbia. She could see the silhouette sitting on the sofa out of the corner of her eye. A few minutes later, Evelyn Mbia sat next to Fatima.

Of the adults, only Monsieur Mbia was at the table with French Club members. He listened attentively to their conversations and took an active part in planning their trip to France the following year. At last, he invited them to share the books they had brought and to explain why they had chosen them and how.

"Let's start with you!" the teacher announced, turning to Zoya as soon as everyone placed their books on the table.

"Me? Oh, umm, I," said Zoya, feeling her cheeks flush in embarrassment. Squeezed into a corner farthest of the table from the teacher on purpose, she did not expect Monsieur Mbia to ask her to speak first. Kantorovich, sitting next to her, snickered dismissively. In front of him, lay a thick volume of Proust's *In Search of Lost Time*. Grisha lovingly stroked the book's spine as he looked at the room victoriously.

"Yes, Zoya, you can go first."

"Well...okay," Zoya hesitated. Saint-Exupery was one of her favorite authors, and she wanted to do him justice in her presentation. Zoya looked around the table and saw Monsieur Mbia's reassuring gaze. "I chose *The Little Prince*. A book I used to read as a child and remember well. It made me incredibly happy. For me, it will always be a symbol of a good and carefree time when I was little. I also really like the author of this book himself. He was a very brave and kind person. The personality of the author plays an important role, that only good people can write really good books. And Saint-Exupery is just such a person. I think he was a really good guy!"

"Zoya, thank you!" Monsieur Mbia nodded approvingly. "And now, Grégoire, it's your turn. Let's go clockwise." Grisha cleared his throat and picked up the volume of Proust.

"I selected this book to share with you." Kantorovich raised the book and shook it, to demonstrate its significance. "I believe the first thing one must do is to master the classics, to learn from great minds, the thoughts of geniuses who have been recognized as such. Marcel Proust is exactly the type of author we should all be reading."

"Grégoire, thank you. Did you like the book?" Monsieur Mbia adjusted his large square glasses.

"Umm, Monsieur Mbia, if you would excuse me, but my opinion about this book is irrelevant. It's a book of a genius." Grisha fidgeted in his seat and stared at his hands.

"Okay, Grégoire. How long did it take you to read it?"

"Well," Grisha suddenly blushed, "I haven't finished it quite yet. I just started reading it."

"Thank you, Grégoire, for sharing it with us. There are seven volumes in this edition, if I'm not mistaken?" Monsieur Mbia gave Grisha a gentle smile.

"Yes, seven." Kantorovich wiped sweat from his forehead, threw a frightened look at the teacher, but he had already turned to the next speaker.

Zoya, taking advantage of the moment, quietly got up from the table and snuck into the kitchen. She could hear the conversation between Fatima and Evelyn Mbia, who were still sitting on the living room sofa. Zoya pretended to look for the bathroom, while she was trying to muster up the courage to approach Fatima. She stood in the kitchen, right against the wall adjacent to the living room and eavesdropped on the conversation of the two women.

"Wow! Was it difficult?" Evelyn Mbia fluffed up her hair.

"No, not at all. It's not exactly easy, but you definitely can learn how to do past life regression."

"That is incredible! And you did your own as well?"

"Yes, of course! That's part of the training. Dolores Cannon facilitated mine."

"That woman you told me about earlier?"

"Yeah, that's the one."

"And what did you see?"

"It's a long story, but it was very interesting. It's kind of like a dream, but not really, because you are operating at different frequencies from sleep. And then whatever your higher consciousness shows you is what you see, and then you describe it, and the regression therapist explains it all to you. it can all be explained by the laws of physics."

"Wow. So how was it? You must have been scared, right?"

"At first, of course, it's a little scary. I mean, it's things we aren't used to experiencing. But I'm very happy with the results. I learned a lot about my parents and my grandmother. You know how my grandmother treated us, right?" Fatima sighed, and Zoya's mouth hung open in shock, as she remembered how in her dream Fatima had told her about the twin curse and how her grandmother in Cameroon did not want to accept her grandchildren.

"Yes, of course, David told me."

"Well, there you go, so I had to figure out where all this was coming from. And it turned out that in a previous life, David and I were also incarnated as siblings. And that our grandmother had been our half-sister in that past life. Our father married a second wife, and this little girl was born. My brother and I refused to accept her: we behaved terribly towards her, harassed her, and as a result we got into a karmic knot. That little girl became very ill and died very early. We felt no remorse and even openly gloated after her death. So in this present incarnation, David and I have to feel all the pain of our unwanted appearance in the family. And the instrument was our grandmother.

"But this is just incredible! Who would have known?" Evelyn cried out.

"Evie, we mustn't let them hear us or they will think we are doing some kind of sorcery here," Fatima whispered, and laughed.

"But if you're going to take on clients, you have to be open about this stuff, don't you?"

"Yes, but you have to choose your clients carefully, you know. We'll see how it goes."

The two women fell silent, and Zoya shifted in place, not knowing whether to wait for the conversation to continue or if she should go back to the veranda. The floor underneath her feet squeaked and Zoya froze, afraid of being discovered in her hiding spot. Then she heard:

"Evie, I think I'm going to go for a walk. I've been sitting here for way too long, I need to stretch my legs."

There was a rustling sound, and Zoya realized that Fatima had gotten up from the sofa and was heading in her direction. In a panic, Zoya immediately rushed to the door, slammed it and pretended to have just entered the kitchen.

Fatima threw a quick glance at Zoya, nodded in her direction, and headed for the front door. Zoya looked after her. The girl felt like she was under a spell from what she had just heard. *So it was all true? So there are past lives and we can find out what they are? So I was once Robert, and André was Johannes!* Zoya's heart fluttered and her palms were sweating, as she recalled her dream in Paris and Fatima's explanation.

*So what I'd seen in that dream was kinda like a past life regression,* Zoya thought. *And that means it was all real, and the burning! Those clues again, those strange visions. Why is everything so confusing? All so weird! How do I deal with that villain who pushed Johannes to betray me? Why can't I be normal?* Zoya stood in the kitchen fully absorbed in her thoughts, and did not hear how the door to the veranda opened and Grisha appeared next to her.

"Well, my dear, that wasn't bad, you got off easy with your fairy tale. Don't you read any real books?"

"What fairy tale?" Zoya had long forgotten about Saint Exupery and the *Little Prince*. She gave Kantorovich a distant look, reliving the events of Johannes' betrayal back in Paris. She could picture his eyes – the same eyes that André had, gray, slightly slanted. They were the eyes of a traitor, someone she needed to forgive, were she to have a future with André. Zoya remembered Fatima's words and shuddered.

"About the prince. Geez, some people have no shame!"

"What are you talking about?"

"That you were not prepared for the meeting. You should have brought a serious book, not a board book." Kantorovich huffed and raised his eyebrows.

"It's not a fairy tale, it's a philosophical book," Zoya said, doing her best to maintain an appeasing tone. She wanted the conversation with Kantorovich to end as quickly as possible, and for that, she needed to avoid a confrontation.

"No, it's a fairy tale. Do you understand anything at all about literature?" Grisha shrugged dismissively and pointed at the volume of Proust in his hand. "Here! This is real literature, not some nonsense."

"Look, just leave me alone." Zoya turned and rushed for the front door.

At that moment, Monsieur Mbia came up to her. "Zoé, you didn't even say goodbye. Did something happen?"

"No," she mumbled. Zoya could hardly hold back tears from the emotions of thinking about her past lives and Kantorovich's onslaught.

"Zoya, I really liked the book you brought today, and I liked your story very much. I think it was the most sincere story I've heard today. You did great, and I'm glad you shared a favorite book from your childhood."

"Do you mean that?" Zoya's breathing slowed down, and she looked up at the teacher. She didn't feel like crying any longer.

"Yes, of course. We love books not because of the number of pages or because someone else appreciated them, but because of the way they affect us. And you said exactly what many people don't realize, even at an older age. Bravo, Zoé."

"It was just a coincidence!" said Zoya, embarrassed by the teacher's compliment.

"I don't think so. Maybe you underestimate yourself. Thank you for coming. And think about what I just told you." Monsieur Mbia smiled, and Zoya saw the teacher's huge bright eyes, which gleamed for a moment behind his glasses.

# CHAPTER 11

Following André's departure, Zoya started regularly spending time with Evan. It happened gradually, so much so that Zoya did not notice how their calls and meetings became a routine. At first, she invited Jessica, but her friend was either busy with Matt, her boyfriend, or working at Sandcastle, a water park, and unavailable because of an unpredictable schedule. Matt had stopped going to raves, and Zoya suspected it was Jessica who forced him to quit after he left her and Zoya alone at High Voltage during an acid trip.

Evan called Zoya every day after work. Sometimes, in the evening, he would come to pick her up, and they would go out to a coffee shop. Evan was invariably polite, gallant, always opened the door for Zoya, and never hit on her. If it was a school night, Zoya returned home by 9 p.m. With just a few weeks of school remaining, she managed to continue getting good grades. On Friday and Saturday nights, they went out dancing. After being out, Zoya would tell her parents that she was staying at Jessica's, and would sneak into the apartment early in the morning. Evan managed to find clubs and raves every weekend, and by mid-June Zoya considered herself a true raver.

Except, there was only one difference between her and most of the other ravers: after the first rave she never did drugs again. As she soon learned, acid and ecstasy were practically mandatory attributes of the rave scene. A lot of what went on at these parties involved drugs. Even the seemingly harmless lollipops the ravers were sucking on helped them while they were on ecstasy. Some used Special K, a drug that gave them energy to dance. There were ravers who brought massage tools and helped each other by massaging the shoulders and neck – again, this was especially enjoyable while taking ecstasy. The more experienced ravers carefully planned their raves to spend their time as comfortably as possible. They gathered in groups and timed their ecstasy trips so that the peak was at one or two in the morning. That way, they were no longer 'peaking' in the morning and could return home at dawn. And the best DJs would play their sets after midnight also for that reason.

Zoya learned all of this gradually, from Soup and Nikki's stories and from Evan's occasional comments. This had no temptation for her – it was simply how others chose to spend their time at a rave. Evan's presence and the fact that he was always sober helped. For the first time in her life, Zoya felt like she belonged. She was accepted for who she was and was welcomed into the raver world with open arms.

Soon, ravers started to recognize her, and Zoya met many others, besides Evan, Nikki, and Soup. Zoya's heart leaped in excitement, when she saw groups of ravers dancing, sharing lollipops, and simply laughing. Ravers were sociable and friendly, and the slogan of PLUR made Zoya feel incredible love for everything around her! Raves were fun, and even more so, a way to connect to others, to meet kind and loving people. And an opportunity to dance all night to great music.

School was about to end for the summer, and Zoya was

counting the days, looking forward to going clubbing three or four times a week. To celebrate the end of the school year, Evan invited Zoya to a rave in Cleveland. She warned her mother ahead of time. They had just eaten breakfast, and Zoya was helping to clear the plates from the kitchen table. Thinking it the right moment, as her mother seemed distracted, Zoya noted casually:

"Umm, I'll be back by six in the morning."

"Aren't you ashamed of yourself?" her mother squeezed out, glaring at Zoya.

"Why should I be ashamed of myself?" Zoya shrugged.

"Are you going to be gone all night again?" Zoya's mother crossed her arms on her chest.

"What's the big deal? I'm only going dancing, there's nothing going on."

"What about that man? Is he going to be with you?"

"Yeah, his name is Evan, by the way."

"I don't care what his name is. Where did your Frenchman go?"

"André?"

"Yes, why isn't he here?"

"You didn't like him, why do you care?" Zoya retorted, but her eyes widened in surprise. She had been sure that her mother had long forgotten about André.

"Why wouldn't I like him? I liked him a lot. Where did he go?"

"He went to France."

"And you broke up?"

"No," Zoya muttered. At the mention of her boyfriend, Zoya flinched. Despite assurances to call her once a week, André had called her only once, in early June. Since his departure, she had received just two letters from her boyfriend, but not every day, as promised. Very quickly, Zoya also realized that she did not have time to write to him every day either.

"Why are you suddenly running around with a new guy?"

"He and I are just friends. You don't understand."

"Does Evan know about this? That you are just friends?" Her mother raised her eyebrows and looked at Zoya in mock surprise.

"Of course he does. We're friends, we have common interests, we're good together."

"I see. So you'll be home at six in the morning?"

"Yes!"

Ella Kassatkina turned around and left the kitchen, slamming the door. Zoya decided to pretend not to notice her mother's indignation, and did not run after her to apologize. Instead, she started getting ready for the rave. She decided to wear the green T-shirt that André had given her. Zoya looked at herself in the mirror, and suddenly tears came to her eyes.

*André!* The thought flashed through Zoya's mind. She imagined his handsome face, his dark gray eyes, and she felt uneasy. *Maybe I shouldn't go to this rave. Maybe Mama is right? But I like it there, I dance, and besides, what does she understand about real life? She doesn't know a thing about relationships!* Zoya turned in front of the mirror, and then suddenly decided to make an entry in her diary. The notebook she brought from Moscow was gathering dust in the top drawer of her desk. Zoya opened the diary and wrote:

*June 18th, 1993.*

*Today was the last day of school. I am now a Junior! I finished the year with honors.*

Zoya wondered what else to write. Her eyes darted left and right, and she was unable to focus. She sat for a minute, staring at the diary, nibbling the pen, and suddenly realized that her hand started moving on its own. Thoughts poured through it, as if bypassing her consciousness. The words quickly appeared on the page and formed into lines all on their own. After a few minutes of writing, she stopped, when half of a page was already filled with text.

*You must forgive André, let go of his betrayal when he was Johannes, and only then you can build a romantic relationship with him. In this incarnation, you must conquer your fear of love, allow yourself to love, and begin to love yourself without fear of loss. Courage in love. Discover this pure power within you and find the transformational power of light in your relationship.*

At the bottom of the paragraph was a caption: a heart and *'Your Guardian Angels'*.

Zoya stared at the page and then her hand added the word *Alum* under the caption *Your Guardian Angels*.

Her eyes skimmed the entry several times. Then she closed them and suddenly felt a current run through the top of her head. It was like a strong pulse that spilled over her entire body and gave her a pleasant, warm feeling. *What is going on with me?* Zoya thought. *I've lost my mind. That must be it. Why is someone named Alum writing to me in my diary? What kind of a name is that? How could I have invented it? And why am I writing instructions to myself in my journal all of a sudden? How is that even possible?*

As usual when situations arose for which she could find no explanation, Zoya decided to push them out of her mind and instead switched to a flurry of activity to stop herself from thinking too much. Zoya slammed the notebook shut and shoved the diary into a drawer. *I shouldn't have gotten into it at all, because Evan will be here soon; I should be getting ready for the rave, not doing silly things like writing in an old notebook! This stuff isn't real anyway.*

She shook her head with disdain. Persistent thoughts still swirled in her mind. *Fear of love? Whatever! That's ridiculous. How can anyone be afraid of love? I've already found my true love, that's André. Maybe I am hallucinating? Flashbacks? Can acid last that long? But it's been over a month. What if I'll have flashbacks all my life? I just wish all this weird stuff would go away and I can keep on dancing!*

With those thoughts, Zoya paced her room, gathering various necessities. She put a bottle of water, toilet paper, and cookies in her bag, then inspected it with satisfaction, proud of being so resourceful. Over the last few weeks of dancing, her leg muscles had gotten stronger and she felt tall and powerful as she looked at herself in the mirror. *I love dancing all the time! And it's better than aerobics!* She smiled at her own reflection, grabbed her bag, and rushed downstairs.

The punctual Evan was waiting for her outside. This time he was alone. Nikki had to be at work, and Soup didn't want to go to Cleveland without her. The drive took over two hours, and Zoya wondered what she and Evan would talk about that whole time. But time flew by unnoticed. He spoke about music, and even shared that until recently he had been a drummer in a band called 'Chick Flick', but then their lead singer moved away and the band broke up.

"But why didn't you tell me about it before?" Zoya sat up in surprise. Despite the fact that they had known each other for a little over a month, Zoya considered Evan a close friend now.

"What's there to tell? We used to have a gig at a club, we were doing great. But now it's over." Evan's shoulders sagged and he slumped in his seat.

"But maybe you can find another singer?"

"There are a lot of people who wanna sing with us," Evan shrugged, "but everything's gotta fall into place: the voice, the timbre, and they gotta have an ear for music. Do you know who our lead singer sounded like?"

"Who?"

"Bjork! The one from the Sugarcubes." Evan reached over and took a cassette from the glove compartment. "Here, have a listen!" Zoya heard a deep soprano voice with a slight treble, accentuated by soft undertones. The voice was a little raspy and beautiful.

"She'll be releasing a solo album soon! She rocks. That's the kind of singer I'd like to find for 'Chick Flick'. Can you sing?" Evan suddenly looked at Zoya attentively. She shifted in her seat, and felt a knot form in her stomach.

"Oh, no, no, no. Especially not like that, on stage! No way." She shook her head and looked away. Zoya was afraid of singing and could not imagine feeling so exposed.

"Come on, why don't you try, it would be so awesome if we could perform together: I'd play the drums and you'd sing. And we have a guitarist, a nice guy. We still practice, ya'know."

"Like you have actual rehearsals?" Zoya tried to change the subject from Evan's offer.

"Yeah. We used to do it twice a week. We even wanted to record a couple of songs and send them to a record company. Yeah, well, that's not happening now." Evan shifted gears. "I guess it wasn't meant to be," he added, as they merged on I-376. Zoya enjoyed watching him drive and she liked being around him – Evan was smart, kind, even funny. *But we are just friends, nothing can happen,* she stopped herself, remembering André.

"Maybe you'll still make it?" Zoya suggested. She was surprised by Evan's fatalism, which she had never seen in Americans before. She thought Americans were always positive, courageous people who believed in themselves and hoped for the best, and that only the Russians or the French gave up in despair at the smallest obstacle.

"I don't know, we had been with that girl for two years. Everything was going so well, we even had regulars coming to our gig. But she wanted to move to Florida. Can you believe that? And Chick Flick had already been invited to perform, like to open at a concert, and a local bar was asking us to have a Thursday night event. Look," Evan reached across and produced a neatly folded leaflet from the glove compartment.

"Oh, look at that! That's your name, Evan Kalina! And the singer!" Zoya marveled at the drawing of a girl with pink hair.

"Yes, I did the layout at work. No one has seen it yet. I'm into design, so there; do you like it?"

"I love it!"

"Yeah, I can design you stuff at work. Like a cassette cover or something."

"Cool! Thank you," Zoya answered. Evan was offering to do something interesting and exciting for her, which made her happy.

The Cleveland rave turned out to be almost identical to the raves she'd attended in Pittsburgh. Zoya even saw some of the same people, there were several rooms with different kinds of techno, and groups of ravers sat around, high on either acid or ecstasy, or both. There were also balloons with nitrous that ravers inhaled, and then laughed hysterically for several seconds before asking for more.

She could hear shouts of PLUR!; ravers hugged each other and enjoyed the music, admiring the rave and planning which other ones they would go to over the summer. Zoya and Evan drove back home to Pittsburgh at dawn. Zoya's legs ached pleasantly after many hours of dancing, her eyelids felt like they would close on their own from exhaustion, despite the rising sun that beamed right into her face. Zoya felt complete satisfaction - she finally found people close in spirit, true friends, who were kind, nice, and they had a common interest. Music, movement, dancing!

It wasn't until they were half-way to Pittsburgh that Zoya remembered Alexei Kulikov. *Oh, no, why didn't I think to stop by and say hello to Alexei, while I was in Cleveland?* Zoya thought. *I probably should have invited him to come along; we haven't seen each other in almost six months!* Zoya was upset with herself for a second, but then Evan put on the 'Chick Flick' tape, and soon she forgot about her childhood friend.

# CHAPTER 12

A s soon as the school year ended, Zoya started working at the library. Working there was the fulfillment of her childhood dream, which she did not realize she had until after Melissa told her about the job.

She spent her whole life surrounded by books. Zoya adored reading, and at times she felt like her apartment was more of a library than a home. Literature everywhere in their Moscow apartment, and it was books that her family moved to America. Not tables and chairs, not beds or linens, not the beautiful antique mirror, but books, hundreds of them.

All throughout her childhood, Zoya had heard from her mother that books were the most important thing in life, a source of knowledge that formed one's character and influenced a person in the most favorable way. Her parents had a personal relationship with a number of authors. Zoya's father adored Pushkin, and he and Zoya often discussed the 'Belkin Tales', which her father considered the author's best work. Her father's relationship with Dostoevsky was 'complicated', and he considered Leskov to be a true literary genius. Zoya was ready for the fabulous world of the library and anticipated the start of her new job with excitement.

But reality was different. Working at the library, except for the occasional conversation with Melissa, turned out to be tedious. Zoya had to sort through hundreds of books, organize them on a cart in alphabetical order or according to the Dewey decimal system, and then shelve them. Once that was done, she had to repeat the same thing over and over again until her three hours were up. If Zoya worked for more than three hours, which during the school year happened on weekends, she was entitled to a break, but only for fifteen minutes, just enough time to sit in the employees' lounge and flip through a magazine. Zoya's schedule overlapped with Tiffany's, the very girl whom Melissa disliked so much. Tiffany went to church every Sunday and read the Bible during her break. The girl claimed that she didn't need other books in her life.

"The Bible has everything! It is the only book one needs," Tiffany would say, if she saw Zoya reading *Mademoiselle* or *Seventeen* magazines during break, Zoya's favorite.

"But this is fun!" Zoya contradicted her coworker.

"Have you ever read the Bible?" Tiffany raised her eyebrows.

"No; I've started, but not all the way through." Zoya looked away in shame. The Kassatkins owned the Bible in Russian. It had been printed on very thin paper, and Zoya's father bought it at a black market in Moscow in the early 1980s, when it was forbidden to read religious literature. Once Zoya tried reading it, but she could not get through more than the first few pages. The font was very small, the pages seemed fragile, and she stopped reading after the genealogy of Adam.

"When you've read the whole Bible, and several times in a row, like I have, then you'll realize you don't need anything else! You could spend your whole life reading the Bible and you would still not fully understand it. It's God's work!" Tiffany smiled dreamily, and Zoya sighed, unable to picture herself reading the whole Bible back to back, and could forget about doing it more than once.

Their boss was Mrs. Specter, an elderly, stern woman with a neat haircut. There was another librarian, Rachel, a young woman who did not eat meat for ethical reasons. This was the first time Zoya had met someone who was a vegetarian out of pity for animals, and she found Rachel fascinating. One day, when a man came into the library and asked for information on hunting, Rachel refused to help him and rushed over to Mrs. Specter.

"Mrs. Specter, that man is a murderer, I can't deal with him! He is a hunter, a killer! He murders animals," Rachel screamed.

"Rachel, just give him the brochure," said Mrs. Specter, "we have to share information regardless of whether we agree with it."

"But then I'll be an accessory to murder of innocent deer! I donated $100 last year to the World Wildlife Fund!" Rachel's face turned red with indignation as her eyes filled with tears.

Zoya listened to the squabble and thought that a year ago her family could have definitely used the dues that Rachel had paid to defend deer, to have enough for food and rent.

Zoya was counting down the days until August 20th, when André was due back in Pittsburgh, so that their relationship would resume. The last letter from him arrived in early August, and Zoya did not answer it, since André was supposed to return soon after that. She'd considered checking with Jessica whether she'd made the right choice, but since her friend did not approve of André, Zoya decided against it, and kept it all to herself instead.

The day of André's arrival finally came! It was a Friday, and Zoya went to work in the morning. That day she was full of joy, and even the mundane responsibility of shelving books brought her pleasure. Zoya felt at peace with the world – a benevolent, happy place, where she belonged. After work, she had planned on going straight to André's house to pay him a visit. They had not seen each other all summer! Zoya was sure that André was just as eager to see her. She rushed to the payphone and dialed the number she knew by heart. Sibyl answered.

"Sybil! Hi!" Zoya yelled, and so loudly that some of the library patrons looked at her disapprovingly.

"Hello, hello!" answered Sybil. "He's back! Are you coming over!" She laughed.

"Oh, thank you! Don't tell him, I want it to be a surprise!"

"It's not gonna be a surprise, he can't wait to see you! He's been waiting for you and he called your house like five times already! Just come over!"

Zoya trembled when she heard Sybil's words. *André missed her, too! He also couldn't wait to see her!* All her doubts disappeared, she and André would be together, and nothing would prevent them from becoming a happy couple! In twenty minutes, Zoya was already standing on the familiar porch. Her heart fluttered as she hesitated, waiting to knock.

*I wonder what he'll look like now?* Zoya worried. *What if he's changed? And what if I won't like him anymore? It's been more than three months!* But then Zoya remembered that even a longer separation after she'd moved to America from Moscow had not affected her feelings toward André, and sighed. *We are destined to be together!*

No sooner had Zoya knocked, than the door opened and she found herself in André's arms.

"Hi!!! Zoé! How nice to see you! And you are wearing our T-shirt!" André's face lit up and his smile was so sincere and happy, that Zoya knew right away: *They would be together again and that's all that mattered.*

"André!!!" she yelped. She felt like crying and laughing all at once, as she threw herself on his chest.

"Don't cry, don't cry, I'm back." André held her close.

"How was your summer? How is your uncle? And your

mother?" Zoya asked, walking in, though she wasn't particularly interested in hearing about André's summer. What she wanted to hear was that he missed her and suffered every day without her.

"Don't even ask." André sighed heavily and his face darkened. Zoya was amazed at how quickly his expression changed.

"Did something bad happen?"

"I don't even know; nothing happened." André shrugged and led Zoya to the couch in the living room.

"What do you mean, nothing?"

"Nothing happened. I mean, I talked to my mother and stuff. But I wish I hadn't done it at all. She acted like nothing happened. She pretended I didn't have a fight with my stepfather. You know, she wouldn't even admit that he was poisoning me, that he was experimenting on me. At all! I told her I was doing well, that I was about to start my junior year at a prestigious university in America, in Pittsburgh, that my uncle was helping me, and she told me: 'My dear boy, you have hurt your father so much. He tried so hard and was so kind to you. But he's coming to Pittsburgh soon, he has a joint grant with the Upper Hill Psychiatric Institute, and that's so wonderful, because you'll see him!' Can you imagine? Calling that bastard my 'father' and thinking I'd agree to talk to him in Pittsburgh.

"That's terrible. So he's actually coming to Pittsburgh?" Zoya widened her eyes in fear. "Did you tell her what happened to you?"

"She refuses to listen to me. She only responds with: 'my dear boy' and 'you need to make up with your father' and then asks me when I'm going to change my last name back to de Vigny. She actually said that that monster is very worried about my 'psychological well-being'. What can I say in response to that? The bastard is supposedly *worried*! I told my uncle about it, he was shaking with anger."

"So you didn't make up?" Zoya tried to give her face a concerned expression, to show sympathy and compassion for André.

"My mother pretended that we never fought, so we couldn't exactly make up. But I'm not going to change my last name to the old one, I'm Orsini now, and I don't want anything to do with de Vigny." André slumped and sighed dejectedly.

Zoya wanted to hug him, to comfort him. She looked at André and suddenly had a vision of Johannes' face in front of her. The conversation between the Master Templar de Vigny and Johannes-André came to mind. How de Vigny incited Johannes to betray Robert, and Johannes had willingly gone along with the betrayal. He had lied to her, Zoya, or, rather, Robert, who had been her past incarnation, if Fatima were to be believed.

It all led to the execution of Robert, but it had been her soul, Zoya's. It was an experience she had undergone in a previous incarnation and remembered well. The entry in her diary about forgiveness and love came to mind. *I will look it up as soon as I get home,* Zoya thought, sitting next to André, sure that she had the same concerned and focused look on her face. This whirlwind of thoughts made Zoya feel dizzy. Immediately, she recalled what Fatima had told her: "You must forgive André, let go of that betrayal, and only then will you be able to build a romantic relationship with him."

"Zoé! Zoé!" She jumped at the sound of her name. "What are you doing? I'm telling you about my summer, and you're mumbling something. Aren't you listening to me?"

"Me? I'm not mumbling." Zoya, still half-immersed in her own thoughts, tried to pretend that she heard what André was telling her. "I'm listening to you."

"You're not listening, I know you even better than you know yourself." André smirked and shook his head. Zoya did not take the risk of lying to André any further, but she was reluctant to tell him about their past incarnations together.

"I was just thinking," she said and smiled, trying to sound pleasant and adorable.

"Umm, okay, I see. Maybe we should go hang out with Mikey and Sybil, because I haven't seen them all summer. And Rick's about to come home."

Zoya felt a lump form in her throat. Trying not to let the disappointment show, she nodded. She acknowledged he probably had jet lag and still wanted to see her, but she hoped for more time alone with André before they joined the others. It stung that he wanted to spend their first evening together in the whole summer mixing with everyone else too. Perhaps his feelings had changed? Or maybe he didn't know how to properly woo her? Thoughts of how Evan treated her crossed her mind.

"Okay, let's go," Zoya responded in a near whisper, trying to hide her disappointment. As always, she did her best to hide her emotions. Zoya was afraid to show her true feelings and preferred to pretend that André's actions had no impact on her. And suddenly an idea occurred to her: *what if I invited André to a rave? He would see how wonderful it was, and he would surely like it. And then he would realize that I have friends and a life of my own.* Zoya blurted out:

"André, why don't you and I go to a rave together? Tomorrow night?"

"A rave? Why?"

"Umm, we'll dance together. It's so much fun! I'll ask Evan to come pick you up," Zoya said. At the mention of Evan, André looked at Zoya questioningly, and squinted, as if trying to examine her face.

"Alright, let's just go see Mikey and Sybil now," he said after a short pause.

Zoya nodded and followed André. Mikey was in the kitchen, flipping something from one sizzling frying pan to another. The aroma was intense and Zoya couldn't help but take it in. Steam was rising from the boiling pot.

"Hey, bro! Trying to make some steak for your visit!" Mikey waved toward André and wiped the sweat off his forehead. He did not pay attention to Zoya nor acknowledge her presence in any way. Zoya was used to the fact that when men saw each other, they greeted one another first. Girls were like an inconspicuous appendix, and were addressed only after greetings between men had been completed. She stood to the side, trying not to disturb the conversation between Mikey and André.

Their exchange of pleasantries dragged on, and then Mikey got flustered, remembering that he had something to fry, and he patted André on the back and announced:

"Good to see you, bro! You haven't changed at all over the summer! I hope you won't study as much, 'cause last year you were into those books, we didn't see you at all while you were plowing away."

"Well, we'll see." André smiled and winked at Zoya. She was standing to the side, patiently waiting for the guys to finish talking.

"Okay, soon everything will be ready. I found a new recipe, this amazing sauce. You have to marinate the tomatoes beforehand and then salt them, it's unbelievable!" Mikey pinched and kissed his fingertips, smiling with pleasure.

"Thanks, man!" André said and then, turning to Zoya, suggested: "let's go sit over there."

"Sure," Zoya squealed and followed. They sat back down on the couch in the living room. From the kitchen, they could hear the clinking of pots, the clanking of metal.

"So you really want me to go to the rave with you?" André asked, as if their conversation did not just have an interlude in the kitchen.

"Of course I do!" Zoya tried to look as sincere as possible, but she could barely manage it. André's eyes were drilling straight through her.

"Then, tell me, when do these things happen? We can go next weekend? If you really want me to, of course." André smiled.

"Yes! Definitely! Yay!" Zoya clapped in excitement, once again feeling reassured.

Soon after, Mikey called them to the table. They had a wonderful dinner, spent time with Mikey and Sibyl, and then went for a walk. The weather had cooled, and Zoya walked proudly next to André, happy to be next to such an attractive guy, who was tall, handsome and smart. Soon she would start the eleventh grade, she had a great job at the library, and her boyfriend had finally returned from being away all summer.

# CHAPTER 13

As soon as she got home, Zoya immediately called Evan to share the news. She had not mentioned André to him all summer, justifying her silence by her boyfriend's absence. Now, Zoya felt an urge to make sure that André's first rave was a great experience, as wonderful as her own had been, and to preferably also take place at the Irish Center, which she considered the benchmark of rave culture.

"Evan, hi! Remember when we stopped by my friend's place in Oakland, but he wasn't home?"

"Umm, like back in May?"

"Yeah, with Nikki and Soup, we went to his house? Well, he was in France all summer, and now he's back, why don't we take him to a rave?"

"Why?"

"He's curious, he wants to go to a rave, and he doesn't have a car." Zoya thought her argument sounded convincing.

"The next big one is gonna be over Labor Day weekend. I heard Dieseldude would be spinning and also a DJ from Chicago. Hardcore!"

Hardcore techno sounded like accelerated house with low

bass notes which Zoya liked. Though the music was heavy and pushed too hard, Zoya preferred hardcore to jungle.

"Wow! So in two weeks? Isn't there anything before that?"

Labor Day fell on the first Monday in September, which also meant the beginning of the school year and the end of the summer, and Zoya did not want her wonderful summer to end. And she wanted André to experience a rave as soon as possible so that he could fall in love with the movement, just like she did.

"Umm, I guess not, but we can take your French friend there in two weeks, no biggie," Evan said without much enthusiasm.

"He's not really French, he's Corsican," Zoya noted casually.

"What's that?"

"Never mind! Thank you, Evan! How cool?! He will like it for sure. And maybe you guys will get to be good friends!" Zoya immediately lit up at the thought of introducing Evan and André. *Why didn't I think of it before, it's a great idea! Evan and I are great friends, which means we can all hang out together, and André will like Evan who is smart and well-mannered.*

Despite waiting for the rave, the next two weeks flew by quickly. Zoya worked at the library, where she was suddenly put on the schedule for six hours each day to fill in for Tiffany, who was away on a church retreat with her parents.

The girl explained that every year their church went to a retreat in the mountains of West Virginia, camped out in the woods, and then spent their days praying. According to Tiffany, it was her favorite time of the year, and that the Lord had specifically blessed their church and their retreat site in West Virginia for the retreats. Zoya wondered if there might have been some truth to Tiffany's words, and then tried to figure out: *did I meet Tiffany in a past life? Or Melissa, perhaps?* But there were no definite conclusions Zoya could draw.

Ever since she overheard Fatima talking to Monsieur

Mbia's wife, Zoya often thought of past lives and her possible other incarnations. Her fantasies turned her into different people, from an ancient Egyptian woman to a Russian peasant. At times, she imagined battles where she slaughtered her enemies and wore armor, but Zoya did not like to think about male incarnations, and quickly shunned these thoughts away. Despite her curiosity, Zoya did not do any additional research into her past lives, hoping that the strange ideas would eventually go away on their own.

Ever since his return, a certain unease had set between her and André, though Zoya couldn't figure out what it was. She tried her best to ignore it and occupied herself with preparing André for his first rave instead:

"You're so lucky! Your first rave will be on a long weekend and the best DJs are gonna be there! You'll see!" Zoya could already picture André dancing next to her, thanking her for the wonderful experience, and how from then on they would go to raves together, spending every weekend in each other's company.

"Zoya, I'm only going for you, I don't need this at all." André shook his head.

"You just don't know it yet, you'll understand; I didn't expect to like it so much either, but it's the best thing ever!"

"Okay, but only once! Alright?" André winked at her and hugged Zoya, pulling her to him before she went for the bus back home.

Junior year, which Zoya was about to start, was, according to Mrs. McNeal, the most important year of high school. Colleges paid attention to grades and student performance in the 11$^{th}$ grade, and Zoya had to continue to do well in school, while also getting serious about applying to colleges. The glory of Zoya Shapiro, who studied at Harvard, haunted her. Zoya dreamt of attending Harvard, aspiring to be like her successful namesake, though she kept her ambitions to herself.

On the day of the rave, Zoya agreed with Evan that he would pick her up first, and then they would get André together.

"You need to wear wide pants and a loose t-shirt for the rave," Zoya'd warned André ahead of time. "Ravers don't wear regular clothes". André attentively listened to Zoya's suggestions and nodded in agreement. For the rave, Zoya dressed as fashionably as possible. She bought a bright orange tank top that accentuated her breasts and brand new wide rave pants that she adored. Zoya spun in front of the mirror in her new outfit, checking herself from all sides, feeling very pleased with her appearance. She looked like a real raver. The only thing she was missing was a tiny back-pack that the ravers loved to carry and kept on while dancing.

At the agreed time, Zoya flew out of the house and saw Evan's car. He arrived exactly at 7 pm, as agreed. Once again, she felt gratitude for Evan's punctuality. If he ever promised something, he always delivered. Evan was silent and calm and attentively listened to her even if she was sharing a simple thought or was complaining about something. But if Zoya ever wondered if she liked Evan more than a friend, the thought of her relationship with André immediately held her back.

"Hi!!" Zoya giggled, opening the car door and plopping on the front seat next to Evan. Over the summer, Zoya had gotten used to being in his car, and felt right at home.

"Yo," Evan muttered. He looked grim.

"Can you believe it? The summer is almost over!" Zoya said. They'd been discussing this topic since July, and had both concluded that it was a shame the summer was ending.

"Yep, summer's over," Evan bowed his head dejectedly, looking like Eeyore, the glum donkey from Winnie the Pooh.

"But at least we had a great summer together! We danced our asses off!!!"

"Yeah, I guess so," Evan responded, and suddenly

grabbed her hand. "Zoya, listen, I need to tell you something."

"What?"

"Zoya, I'm sorry, but I don't know how to tell you everything, I…" Evan stammered.

"Evan, are you okay?" Zoya released her hand. *Oh … is he about to tell me he likes me? Not that! That's the last thing I need, now that André is back!*

"I need to talk to you!"

"Let's talk tomorrow? 'Cause we are going to a rave and we will dance! Hooray!!! Will Nikki be there? What about Soup?" Zoya tried her best to change the subject.

"Dunno. Probably." Evan pulled back and looked at Zoya with sad, droopy eyes.

"You remember we're picking up André on the way, right?"

"Yeah, I remember." Evan turned away.

"Do you know where to go? He lives in Oak–"

"Yes, I remember everything, don't worry," Evan interrupted Zoya.

They drove in silence. When they arrived at André's house, Evan abruptly stopped the car and froze in place.

"Let's go in." Zoya reached for the door handle.

"Where?"

"Let's go inside the house for a minute."

"No, you go in, I don't wanna be late. Grab your escort and let's get going."

"He's not my escort, he's…" Zoya stammered. The word 'escort' sounded so insulting, that Zoya could not figure out how to react.

"Who is he then? Your boyfriend? And what are we doing here anyway? Zoya, I don't understand anything at all!"

"Evan, please, because we agreed; we wanted to go dancing, we had such a good time all summer!" Zoya pleaded.

"That's right, everything was great all summer, and what

are we doing here now? Who is this dude and why are we picking him up exactly?"

Seeing Evan's reaction, she knew that bringing him to André's was a mistake. Her whole plan, which had seemed to her so logical, where she and Evan took André to his first rave and spent the night dancing together, was unraveling. Zoya did not know how to behave, and decided to pretend that she didn't understand Evan's indignation.

"But please? Let's pick him up, you promised?" Zoya remembered how Nikki always patted Evan on the back of his neck and almost did it, too, then decided it would be too intimate.

"Uh-huh," Evan frowned, and Zoya ceased the opportunity:

"Just hold on a second. I'll be right back!" She jumped out of the car, rushed to the porch and gently knocked on the door. Nobody answered. She knocked again and waited a minute. And again no one answered. Then Zoya touched the handle of the door – it was open. Zoya went inside. The house was quiet. She looked at her watch – it was exactly 7:30, and she and André agreed on this exact time. She decided to check his room, climbed the stairs and found the door of his bedroom locked. Zoya knocked.

"Hello, Zoé!" She heard André's voice.

"André, what are you doing?" Zoya entered and saw André sitting on the bed. He was almost naked with the exception of a bath towel wrapped around his waist. In front of him lay a huge textbook, open in the middle.

"Oh, I bought textbooks for the semester today. This one, the Physics one, is very interesting. There are these ..." André looked up excitedly at Zoya, and his voice faltered.

"But André! We agreed! We are going to a rave!" Zoya gritted her teeth.

"But it'll start late, you told me yourself. I thought that I still had a minute. Why are you upset?" André shrugged.

"I like to arrive at the start, and Evan too, because he is the one driving, he also doesn't like to be late, and then tonight there will be a cool DJ as an opening act, the set starts exactly at eight. It's some new guy, and no one knows him, but Evan says he's great. It's his friend, and if we are late, we will miss his set, and the friend will be offended. He needs our support!" Zoya rattled off explanations, as she nervously stared at André. The thought of Evan impatiently waiting in the car gnawed at her and she had a sinking feeling in the pit of her stomach.

"Okay, okay, I didn't think it was that serious. It's just some dance thing, not a dissertation defense!" André threw his hands up and got up from the bed. The towel slipped, nearly exposing him. Zoya's heartbeat accelerated. André was so handsome and desirable. She fought the urge to throw herself at him and drown in his arms – *how could she quarrel with someone who was her soulmate? He had a great reason for being late – he was reading a Physics textbook! André was so smart, so wonderful!* Sensing a change in her mood, André came closer and kissed her. He pressed his body against hers, and held her tight.

"I knew that you would forgive me!" He stroked her face, and she melted in his arms.

"But André, we should go, Evan is waiting."

"Who cares, don't you want to stay here with me? Forget Evan, let him disappear." André caressed her breasts. Zoya took a heavy breath. It was incredibly difficult to think, and if André offered her to stay on any other day, she would have definitely agreed. She'd dreamt of this very moment for so long. But the desire to dance was stronger! She wanted to go to the rave, the last rave of her fun summer. To see her friends, the people who had accepted her for who she was, and whom she liked so much.

"André, I can't. It's rude. Evan is waiting outside, and we

have tickets. Please, get ready, please?" Zoya bit her lip as she maneuvered out of André's embrace.

"That's too bad, but okay." As if by accident, André threw his towel completely off and turned to face Zoya. "I was just thinking, maybe it's time for us to try something new?" He winked at her.

"Um, try something new?" Zoya cleared her throat. *Is this really going to happen? So fast? Right now? But Evan is outside, how is that even possible?* Zoya's eyes darkened, and André laughed:

"Don't be afraid, I won't bite you!" He leaned in and gave her another passionate kiss. Zoya's whole body lit up from his touch, and it took all her willpower to separate from him.

"André, I'll wait for you downstairs, okay?" Zoya blushed and ran out of the room.

She did not understand what he wanted from her. Why couldn't he tell her directly what he had planned for the two of them? Two weeks had passed since his return from France, and they had barely seen each other. Not one mention about sex ... until now. *Why did he decide to tease me now? Or was he seriously going to sleep with me tonight if I agreed? Oh why is he behaving like this?* Zoya agonized.

She plopped on the sofa downstairs and waited for André. Sybil flashed by, kissed Zoya on the cheek, whispered: "Salut", and ran off somewhere deep into the house. She had been looking forward to this evening, so excited to introduce Evan and André and to bring her boyfriend to his first rave. Instead, Andre was behaving in a way she couldn't understand and Evan was also upset with her. Zoya wanted to abandon her plan and to go hide somewhere far away from everything.

"Zoya, what's wrong? Why did you run away?" André came down the stairs, smiling magnanimously. He was dressed in khaki slacks and a white T-shirt. Zoya could immediately tell that he would stick out like a sore thumb at the rave.

"Nothing's wrong. Let's go? Hope Evan is still waiting for us."

"Why are you so concerned with some dude? He can wait, whatever!" André shrugged and pouted.

"Evan is my friend."

"Yeah, friend, whatever!"

André exited the house first. The front door nearly slammed in Zoya's face. Tears of resentment filled her eyes, but she had to keep up with André, who was already halfway to the car. Seeing André, Evan got out and stood menacingly, his arms crossed, as if trying to have a face-off with the Frenchman. Both of the men seemed on edge and Zoya worried that her evening was about to get even more complicated. She ran up and chirped:

"So, here, André, Evan, meet each other! It's going to be great: the last rave of the summer, and it's in Pittsburgh." Immediately, she saw the calming effect her words had on the two guys.

Evan nodded, pretending to agree with her and André mumbled an enthusiastic comment about the upcoming party. Zoya sighed in relief. The idea of climbing in the back next to André crossed her mind, but she sat in the front next to Evan, as she had done all summer.

They drove in silence. Her heart fluttering in anticipation, Zoya thought of how she would show André off at the rave, introduce him to her friends, and explain the different types of techno and demonstrate her dance moves to him. They arrived at the Irish Center a little after eight, and found the space nearly empty.

"So, what do you think?" Zoya gleamed at André, as they stepped inside the first room and heard the pounding beats of techno. Zoya confidently made her way to the main room, where the DJ was warming up the early crowd. She felt a sense of elation and expected André to show his appreciation any minute about being at his first rave.

"I don't know, it's kind of dirty here," André yelled into her ear and frowned.

"If you get tired of the music, we can sit outside," said Zoya pointing to the slope where months earlier she and Evan had had their first conversation. "It's really cool here, this space is so nice and lots of room to dance."

"Dancing? No, thank you. I'll just stand if you don't mind." André threw a skeptical look around.

"Zoya! Hi!!!" Soup appeared and jumped up to give Zoya a hug. Immediately behind her was Nikki, wearing a tight pink t-shirt with sequins and bright blue pants trimmed with tinsel. On her head was a cap that had little light bulbs sewn into it. The lights, once turned on, blinked brightly in the dark.

"Look!" Nikki flipped a tiny switch on her cap, and it immediately started flashing yellow, red and green. "What do you think? I found this at Nate's! Isn't it awesome?"

"Oh, it's beautiful!" Zoya admired the cap and then rushed to hug her friends. "Just gorgeous! It looks great on you! Why are you so early?" Nikki, as a rule, if she didn't come with Evan, rarely showed up at raves before midnight.

"We're here with Ike, he wants to deal," Soup replied.

"Deal?" Zoya opened her eyes wide. The last thing she needed was for André to think that she was spending time with the drug crowd.

"Ya know!" Nikki threw a sideways glance at André.

"Oh."

Zoya looked at André. His face betrayed no emotion. The music was so loud, that Zoya assumed that he didn't hear Nikki's words.

At that moment, Soup screamed, "I already dropped! I'm about to peeeaaaak!!" Soup threw her hands up in excitement, as she rolled her eyes, leaving no doubt to what she was talking about. "I had such a great trip last week!! I think it's the same stuff! Caaan't wait!"

"Hey, Soup, let's go dance?" Nikki smiled and gently nudged her friend.

"Okay, Nikki! I can't stand in one place, I think I'm already feelin' it. It's so good, I need to move!" Soup spun around, showing exactly how good she felt. "Ike's stuff is the best! I think he'll do well. I gotta spread the word."

"Soup, come on." Zoya tried to stop Soup from revealing any more drug-related facts.

"Come on, Zoya, chill, everything is great! And soon Dieseldude will be performing. And how do you like hard-core?" Nikki smiled playfully and, turning at André, added: "Maybe your friend would like to try something too?"

"No, no, he doesn't want anything." Zoya felt her reality shifting. Everything was going wrong this evening, and she was trying with all her might to prevent a disaster from happening.

"Why, what do you have?" André grinned, turning to Nikki. If Zoya didn't know him and didn't feel his mood, she would have thought that he was actually interested in buying drugs.

"See, he is interested! Your friend wants to have a good time!" Nikki giggled and gave André a flirtatious look, "Soup, go find Ike."

"Great!" André agreed. He pushed his hair back.

"I'll be right back!" Soup immediately disappeared, followed by Nikki. Zoya and André stood alone, facing each other.

"Why don't we go sit outside, like you suggested. We need to talk," André said. His eyes narrowed into small slits, and Zoya felt frozen with fear. He was furious, Zoya knew this even before André spoke.

# CHAPTER 14

"Let's go outside, yes," Zoya mumbled, though she wanted to run away and hide from her boyfriend. A frightening premonition gripped her as she followed him.

"So this is why! This is why you've been lying to me all this time! How could you?" André hovered over her, like a monster who was about to take her life. Zoya involuntarily jerked back.

"I did not lie! What are you talking about? I wanted to show you, I wanted you to meet my friends. I wanted us to go to raves together!"

"What friends? Those junkies? Or that long-haired moron boyfriend of yours?"

"We're just friends!"

"Zoé, do you take me for an idiot? I'm not a boy, I'm nineteen years old, by the way. I've seen a lot in this world. You don't understand anything! You're a naive girl!" André's face contorted in anger.

"No! No! André, it's not like that, I don't want to do this!!!" A whole wave of indignation rose up in her, and Zoya knew that she would not be able to control it. All the emotions she had been trying so hard to contain, burst out in a terrible avalanche of rage. "It was you who lied to me, you didn't want to really be together from the start, it was just a joke to you, I knew it, I never believed you! You lied to me, you traitor!" Zoya could feel hysterical notes in her voice.

"I am a traitor? You're the one who got involved with some dude while I was away. You didn't even wait for me to come back. And you brought him to my house! How dare you? Damn junkie, you don't even know what you are doing! Are you sleeping with him in exchange for drugs?"

"What?? Evan is straightedge! No!"

"You told me you went to raves all summer with that moron."

"He's not a moron, he's my friend. We're just friends."

"You're right. I am the idiot, not him! You spent the whole summer with him while I thought about you every day and could barely stand being away from you." André raised his voice, too, and Zoya thought their altercation was starting to sound like her parents fighting.

"You're the one who left in the first place! You didn't want to be here this summer! You ran off to see your girlfriends in Lyon!"

"Zoé! What are you talking about?" A group of ravers walking by stared in their direction, but said nothing.

"All those girls, you told me about them. All the ones you'd had sex with!" Zoya didn't know where she was getting those terrible words, but they poured out of her uncontrollably.

"When did I tell you that? I never said anything like that."

"Yes you did, when we saw each other in Paris." The second she said it, Zoya realized that she had just referred to a conversation she'd had with André in her dream. The dream in which she saw the Templars and in which she was rescued from Saint Anne's by Fatima Mbia.

"Zoé, what's wrong with you? Did you maybe take something? Tell the truth. This friend of yours, did he get you hooked on drugs? Why did you do it? Please stop before it's too late."

"No, I don't take anything! Never! Neither does Evan! We only dance! André, please, I have to tell you one thing. You need to hear what I have to say, okay?" Zoya decided to play the last card.

"What? Are you going to tell me that Evan popped your cherry?" André clenched his fists again, and leaned forward, as if he was about to lunge at her.

"No!! How can you say that? I have something very important to tell you. Listen to me!"

"What is it?" André seemed to have calmed down.

"Remember, we talked about the Templars?" Zoya said and looked at André expectantly. A thought flashed through her mind: *she and André had never talked about the Templars either. That had been in a dream, too.*

"No, we never talked about the Templars. You confuse me with someone else, Zoé!" André's eyes narrowed into angry slits again.

"I am not confused, but you know about the Templars, don't you?"

"About the Templars? Well, yeah, of course I do, de Vigny bought an apartment right around their former fortress. Maman was against it, she didn't want to live in le Marais." André shrugged. "He convinced her we could get a bigger place there and the area was hip. Happy now? What about the Templars?"

"You liked them, right? Didn't you read about them?"

"Yes, de Vigny told me to, but I wasn't really into them myself."

"You and I have a connection, right, you told me yourself, don't we have a connection?" Zoya stared at André, as if begging him to agree.

"Yeah, we do. Or we did." André gave her a stern look.

"I think I found an explanation for our connection, I understood why we hit it off, and we felt as if we had known each other all our lives."

"Where did you find this explanation?"

"We knew each other in a past life! It's so simple!"

"Zoé! What are you talking about? It just so happened that we got to know each other, I liked you and you liked me. It's romantic. Why are you making up stories about past lives?"

"Don't you believe me?"

"Zoé, I'm sorry, but I can't believe in some nonsense about past lives! You're drugged out of your mind, like these friends of yours." André looked contemptuously around, as if Zoya was responsible for all the ravers at the Irish Center that night.

"It wasn't just us, de Vigny was there too! And that explains everything. We were all together, we were Templars! In a past incarnation!" Zoya tried to speak so as not to give away her excitement, but she was very nervous. Having kept this story from André for so long, now that she decided to tell it, she was in a rush to say everything to him before he might interrupt her.

"Zoé! How could you invent such a thing? What the hell is wrong with you?"

"I found a book! I'll show it to you. It's at my house. It's about Acre. And I had a dream about Acre, and in that dream you betrayed me." Zoya looked at André and was silent, watching his reaction.

"This is too much! How did I betray you? I told you that I had to go to France, I needed to figure things out with my mother. Maman is the most important woman in my life. Do you understand?"

"I understand! It all makes sense. It's like a past life, just a replay of our history when we were Templars. You betrayed me then. We were knights and there was a Master Templar, only it was de Vigny. Templars, we fought together, and my name was Robert, and yours was Johannes."

"Did you come up with names, too? Maybe you're schizo? Or you got multiple personalities?"

"I didn't make them up, I saw them in a dream. You had the same eyes, I recognized you."

"What, my eyes haven't changed since 1400?" André sneered.

"Since 1391, actually. Don't you believe me?"

"Are you nuts? How can I believe you? I'm a mathematician, a physicist, I don't believe in this nonsense. I believe in what I see. And what I see is that you're not right in the head."

"But the soul is immortal; why don't you believe it can transcend bodies? Think about it! What do you think happens to it after death?"

"I don't know, nobody knows that!"

"They do!! I recently talked to a woman who does regressive hypnosis. Her name is Fatima."

"Fatima who? What kind of hypnosis?"

Zoya noticed that two girls sitting nearby had stopped talking and were staring at them. She lowered her voice. "Regressive. You're immersed in alpha waves, as if you're partly in a dream: you communicate with your guardians, you see dreams, and information from past incarnations comes to you."

"Zoé! You're out of your mind. That's quackery. And what do you understand about alpha waves and physics? It's an exact science, not some nonsense."

She read the contempt in André's eyes. "No, no, you see, I had a dream, and I saw that we were together, I knew it beforehand! And then you came to Pittsburgh. So, in that dream I saw Fatima, and then she actually appeared later on, in real life. And she explained everything to me in my dream.

I knew about multidimensionality before. Remember my neighbor in Moscow, Inna Lvovna?"

"I remember Inna Lvovna, a very nice woman. But she never mentioned any of this nonsense. She was a normal person, her son too, the translator."

"Yes, yes, and a son, but that's not the point. Inna Lvovna used to tell me about temporal branches and travel through them and stuff like that. I didn't tell you, but I visited Paris in this sort of dream-state, back in 1989 and then again, earlier this year."

"What do you mean?" André pulled away, as Zoya involuntarily leaned in closer to shorten the distance between them.

"Well, it's a long story, but I switched places with my double Zoé. Inna Lvovna explained everything to me, and about quantum entanglement, too."

"Zoé! There is no such thing, no quantum entanglement."

"No, no, listen. Well, you and I used to be Templars, and I dreamed, or rather I saw Robert and Johannes talking, discussing the battle in Acre and the fact that the Templars were defeated there. I knew nothing about Acre at all, never even heard of it, and then I found this book. It found me! It fell on my head at the library. It wasn't even a library book. You know what I mean? It just came to me! As if the universe itself wanted me to find confirmation of that dream. It wasn't just a coincidence." Zoya was in a hurry, trying to share everything, but the more she spoke, the more confused she felt, and she could tell that her words sounded strange and unconvincing.

"Zoé, you're really something. You should become a writer. Really! I can't believe you." André shook his head and rolled his eyes.

"No, André! It's true, it was no accident that the book came to me. It was a sign that everything was true. Sometimes the universe gives us signs, our guardian angels communicate with us, plant information this way. They give us hints so that we can make good decisions. And we can draw our own conclusions."

André was silent. Zoya felt hopeful that she had managed to convince him she was right, and was closer to untying the karmic knot caused by Johannes' betrayal of Robert.

"Zoé…" André looked at her the way one looks at a sick dog. Zoya grew cold inside.

"Yes," she whispered, unable to move. Her voice trembled.

"Zoé, I'm sorry, but I don't think we should be seeing each other."

"André, how? Why?" Zoya's eyes filled with tears; she felt her hands become ice-cold and her toes stiffened. A feeling of impending doom shackled her whole body.

"Zoé, you're a junkie. I'm sure Evan got you hooked on acid. And I've told you many times that I can't take drugs. After all I went through with that bastard de Vigny, I can't risk being close to someone like you."

"So... so you don't love me?" Zoya was sobbing and couldn't stop. She knew that she looked ugly, her eyes were probably red and puffy, and her nose would look like a beet, but she didn't care.

"I don't know." His answer was the worst of all. It meant indifference.

"You don't know." Zoya howled. She wanted to postpone the inevitable – saying goodbye to André. In response, he only shook his head.

"André! Maybe there's something I can do? You came to the rave! Why?"

"Zoé, stop it. You don't have to keep lying to me and humiliating yourself. I'm sorry it ended this way. I was looking forward to being together. I thought so much of you, I wanted to be with you, but now I see that you're not who I thought you were. You are just a druggie." André sighed and looked at Zoya, taking a step backwards, away from her.

His gaze cut Zoya in half. She felt her breath catch, as if André had hit her in the solar plexus. Zoya remembered how Vlasov had once punched her in the gut, and thought that physical attack had been less painful than this.

"Goodbye," Zoya squeezed out of herself. She then turned around and ran as fast as she could, away from André.

# CHAPTER 15

Zoya ran straight into the main hall. Techno was blasting, walls were shaking, the ravers crowded around; some were talking, some were dancing, and there were groups of people sitting in the corners. Some of them were massaging each other, a tell-tale sign of a group that was 'rolling' on ecstasy. The rave was already in full swing. No one could see her face in the dark and Zoya was glad of it. Tears streamed down her cheeks, while a wild anger choked her. She had never felt such terrible, intense indignation at the injustice.

"How dare he? How could he?" Zoya squeezed her fists. *Was he really so loyal, intelligent, courageous? Or was he that way on another temporal branch, in a different reality altogether? How could André accuse me of being a druggie? How could he refuse to believe my story about the Templars and past lives?*

André, for whom she had waited so long, whom she considered to be her true love, had just dumped her. Zoya immediately blamed herself for not preparing for the conversation thoroughly enough. *I should have brought it up gently, not like this; what an idiot I am.*

As soon as Zoya remembered André's last words, the way

he had looked at her, how cruelly he expressed his disappointment, she wept. Zoya crammed herself into the most secluded corner of the room, away from the DJ and the groups of happy ravers, and let her tears flow. She curled up, convinced that she was all alone in the world.

"Hey, there she is!" Nikki appeared out of the darkness, followed by Soup. Nikki's cap was glittering with happy little light bulbs. "I told you we'd find her," she announced.

"Zoya! Hi! We've been looking for you for two hours and you were nowhere to be found!" Soup rushed to Zoya and stumbled when she saw Zoya's face: "Oh, what's wrong? Are you crying?"

"Of course she's crying, can't you tell!" Nikki sat down and hugged her. A gentle scent of perfume was coming from Nikki, and her hands were soft and warm. "Zoya, what's wrong with you? Who hurt you?"

"Ooh-ooh-ooh-ooh!" Zoya squeezed out and shook her head. She felt as soon as she opened her mouth, she would dissolve in her own grief.

"Let me guess, okay?"

"Uh-huh." Zoya gasped for air and tried to wipe away her tears.

"It was Evan! Did Evan hurt you?" Nikki stroked Zoya's hair, as one does with a small child.

Zoya shook her head. *Maybe he's disappointed in me too, and then I won't have any friends left!*

"No, it wouldn't be Evan," Nikki chuckled. "Because he likes you!"

"He does?" Zoya looked up at Nikki.

"Yeah, he's totally into you, but oops, I wasn't supposed to say anything!" Nikki put a finger to her lips as if shushing herself.

"For real"?

"Oh yeah, Evan's like totally in love with you. I can totally tell. And I know him – we went to kindergarten together."

"Oh, wow, Evan!" Hearing about Evan and his feelings for her felt good and pushed angry thoughts of André and his cruel behavior out of Zoya's mind.

"Yep. I wouldn't have said anything, but you were crying your heart out. I know it was that dumbass who hurt you, right? That narc? He's all uptight, wearing dad jeans like he's about to go golfing. I didn't like him right away. I could tell he was bad news right away." Nikki turned up her nose.

"He's a good guy, he didn't mean to." Zoya rushed to defend André.

"If he didn't mean to, why are you crying? What did he say to you?"

"He... he..." Zoya couldn't explain to Nikki what André had just said about drugs, nor could she share the story of the past lives, "I dunno." Zoya felt like she was about to burst into tears again.

"You don't need to say another word. I could tell by the look of him, dude was scared, we got our movement here, what we're about, the love, we're all cool, open to each other, and he freaked out. He wasn't ready for PLUR, that's all." Nikki raised her hands and moved them apart, as if she were about to hug the whole hall full of ravers.

"Not ready?" Zoya repeated. *Nikki had a point! André just wasn't ready for raves. And he wasn't ready for the joy and the beauty of simple companionship, either. All André wants is to study and pore over his textbooks.*

"Don't worry about him. Come on, let's go dance, the music is so good. This hardcore DJ is about to play a set! Forget that snitch."

"Okay." Zoya wiped away her tears and sniffled.

"We just gotta clean you up first, you're a mess." Nikki produced a cosmetic bag out of her raver backpack, and deftly pulled out a wet wipe, then a little mirror, followed by tiny jars of creams and mascara. Nikki touched up and smeared something on Zoya's face. Zoya felt a brush, then the soft touch of Nikki's finger. "There!"

Nikki put the mirror up for Zoya to see, and she barely recognized herself. Her face was completely different: the reflection looking back at her was that of a beautiful girl with heavy makeup. Her eyes, though puffy, had deep blue eyeliner making them look mysterious, her eyelashes were twice as long as usual, and there was a thick layer of powder on her cheeks and rouge on her cheekbones. *It's kind of like it's not really me anymore!* Zoya thought. *Maybe it's for the best! Who needs the real me?*

"Thank you!" she said. Nikki gave Zoya a hug, and then said, knowingly:

"See! And there's nothing to worry about, men come and go, who cares?" She held out her hand to Zoya. Soup, who had been sitting quietly in a corner, humming a song, shaking her head from side to side, got up after them. The three girls headed toward the hall, where the walls vibrated with low bass hum. The music pounded in Zoya's ears, and the rhythm made her whole body ache for movement.

"AHHHH!!! DJ Sun rocks! Check it out!" Nikki yelled into Zoya's ear. Zoya nodded in agreement. Nikki turned on the lights on her cap and ran up, positioning herself right in front of the DJ. She took a look around and started to move to the fast rhythm of the music. The bass was infectious, no one stood still.

A group of admirers immediately appeared around Nikki and formed a circle. Nikki twisted as if on a pole, squatted, and then rose, bent backwards, exposing her delicate tummy, then rose again and twirled like that for several minutes. Zoya had seen this dance several times and always marveled at how graceful and flexible Nikki was.

Soup danced beside them. She moved from side to side, bobbing her head, and looked aloof. Ike walked up to her. His perpetual sneer made Zoya feel uneasy and she cringed. He was tall and broad-shouldered. Ike wore striped oversized shirts that hung loosely over his wide pants and made him look like a Russian nest doll. Ike's hair was braided into tiny, playful braids.

Ike walked, jerked his head in tune of the music, but in reality was vigilantly surveying potential clientele. Noticing the girls, he nodded and smiled, then immediately turned away. Zoya knew that Ike was looking for customers. He walked up to Soup, took her by the forearm, and whispered something in her ear. Soup's face dropped, and she tried to free her arm. Someone clapped, Zoya turned to face Nikki, and she repeated her trademark number again, and by the time Zoya turned around again, Soup and Ike were gone.

Zoya began to dance and gave herself completely to the movement. Moments or maybe hours went by. Zoya thought about André, what had happened between them, and how she was going to live her life. *Was Nikki right? Is he not ready for raves? But André is so smart, so kind.* Then Zoya remembered how André had told her he didn't know if he loved her, and called her a junkie.

Tears welled up in her eyes again, but Zoya exhaled and stopped herself. The thought of past lives haunted her. *Was he right? Was it all just a dream and I told him about the Templars for nothing? But there were signs, and Fatima had been real! I should have talked to Fatima, why didn't I? Why am I always so afraid?* Zoya gnawed at herself. *Fatima would have helped me, and now all is lost!*

Someone's eyes were on her. Zoya turned and saw that Evan was dancing next to her. He nodded and smiled. Zoya felt at ease. *What a good guy. Maybe he does actually like me?* she thought. *And here I am, running after André, like a fool! A bird in the hand is better than two in the bush.* Zoya remembered the saying, though it had always seemed absurd to Zoya: *who wanted to hold a bird in their hands anyway? Shouldn't birds be free?*

Zoya looked at Evan – she had always found him handsome and pleasant. But now she paid particular attention to his appearance, to his glasses, to how nicely he was dressed, how stylish he looked tonight dressed like a real raver, how well he danced, and what a nice smile he had. *Reliable, manly, Evan is great!* thought Zoya. *And he has a car, always arrives on time, he's just cool. Why am I wasting time on André?*

Remembering André, Zoya again felt a lump form in her throat. The thought that they would never be together, that she would never feel his touch and speak to him, paralyzed her. Zoya sighed and forced a smile. Evan smiled back. They danced until the end of the set and then went out on the lawn. Zoya spent the rest of the night next to him – the considerate, polite Evan.

"So, ready to leave?" he asked. It was almost four o'clock in the morning, and people were starting to leave.

"Yeah, okay." Zoya sighed.

"Where did your buddy go?" Evan surveyed the space.

"Umm, I don't know. He left." Zoya did her best to look complacent.

"Left? How? Did someone give him a ride?" Evan raised his eyebrows. Zoya jumped up at his question – she had completely forgotten that André had gotten a ride to the rave with them. *How will he get home, and in the middle of the night?* Zoya panicked. *Poor André!*

"No clue. But I haven't seen him for a couple of hours. I guess he just left." Zoya shrugged.

"Did he take something?"

"Nah, that's out of the question. He must have gone home."

"Alright, then. As long as he hasn't passed out somewhere. You wanna go look for him?" Evan looked at her questioningly.

"No need; He'll manage. What does it matter? Let's just go." Zoya proceeded to the exit.

"Okay, let's go."

It was five in the morning when Zoya got home. As always, after raves, the first thing she did was to take a shower and wash her hair, then leave her rave clothes to soak in the bathtub. She now knew that if she didn't do this, she would wake up to the revolting smell of stale cigarettes.

After performing this ritual, she instantly fell asleep. Her legs were humming and the rhythm of the music was still echoing in her head. She dreamt of dancing, of ravers, of a DJ spinning. The lights on Nikki's cap flashed before her eyes. Evan appeared from somewhere and brushed his long hair.

Suddenly, Zoya twitched – dark gray eyes were staring directly at her. It was Johannes. Zoya recognized him at once. Johannes was mocking her. He squinted and his eyes became narrow slits. He spoke in the voice of Grisha Kantorovich: "Well, my dear, you wanted to lie to me? Are you going somewhere? No, dear, you have work to do." And then Kantorovich sailed away, and Zoya saw the terrible doctor.

She found herself in a cell in the Templar fortress, where de Vigny and Johannes were speaking. The doctor smirked and said, "That's it, that's it, that's exactly what I wanted. Now you will never catch me. You'll take lithium for the rest of your life. And acid. And Klonopin. You're bipolar and schizophrenic. All of the above! Junkie! You're too much, honey!" He cackled and blew out a candle. Zoya yelled out in horror and woke up to the sound of her own scream.

She sat up in bed. The clock showed eight o'clock, so she must have slept for only three hours. Her first thought was André. *Where is he? How is he? Did he make it home?* Zoya remembered his face, contorted in anger, his cruelty, his accusations. Suddenly, she was shivering.

Trying to warm herself, she put on woolen socks and a sweater, but it only made her feel worse. *Tea, I need hot tea!* In the kitchen, her parents were sitting at the table. Zoya's father was in the middle of brewing his never-ending Sunday tea.

Some time ago he had made the decision to drink only green tea, which, according to him, was the healthiest of all teas in the world and improved heart function. The tea had to be consumed scalding hot, and for this purpose Zoya's father put two kettles on at once and poured boiling water from one and then the other.

He was the only person in the family who fully understood the kettle system, and was stern and unforgiving if someone else committed an error, and poured water out of the wrong kettle or did not let the water 'boil properly'. If that happened, Zoya's father lectured the culprit about the dangers of unboiled water and reminded them that it was equal to poison and a breeding ground for bacteria. The kettle had to boil for several minutes for all the bacteria to die off and the water to become scalding, and only then could it be used for making tea. Zoya's father recently found loose leaf tea at a Japanese store, and now green boxes labeled 'Sencha' lined the windowsill.

"Good morning." Zoya cleared her throat as she walked into the kitchen. She tried her best to pretend like it was no big deal that she had come home in the wee hours, half-expecting a scene.

All summer she had made a consistent effort to get her parents used to her early morning arrivals. From time to time she thought that she had succeeded, but every now and then her mother would protest and complain that Zoya was 'totally out of control,' and her father would echo his wife. Zoya couldn't predict her mother's complaints. They could happen out of thin air.

Coming home earlier than expected, when her parents were still up, was the most dangerous. Her mother would look at the clock, sigh, then slam the door as she disappeared into the bedroom without saying a word. Zoya's father would rush after his wife, and the next day Zoya would be forced to ask her mother to forgive her. Zoya hated her mother's tantrums, and hated apologizing. *Why should I feel sorry for her? She throws tantrums when she's the one ignoring me. It's not like I'm doing anything wrong. What's wrong with going out to dance?* Zoya reasoned.

But this morning the parents were in good spirits.

"Zoya, good morning!" said Zoya's father.

Reaching for an empty mug, she cautiously looked in her mother's direction, expecting her to shout or somehow express her displeasure, but she was surprisingly calm. After a moment's pause, her mother announced:

"Zoya, Papa and I have been discussing something. And I think you should know, I'm going to look at a house for sale."

"Mama, you already looked at it, didn't you? Near the highway, right?" Zoya remembered her parents' conversation in the spring and how her father had flatly refused to buy the house that was across from the highway exit.

"Correct, but that was months ago. Now Tatiana found us another house."

"Who is Tatiana? Mama, why?" Zoya forgot all about having tea and sat down at the table.

"Tatiana is our agent. Because it's impossible to live in this apartment! We need a house, like real Americans!"

"But, Mama, we're already used to this place, and it's comfortable here. The school is close by and the library."

"I've already checked: it's maybe another ten minutes extra from the school, not a big deal."

"So I gotta walk for thirty minutes every day? It's only a twenty minute walk now." Zoya threw her hands up in exasperation.

"Zoya, don't exaggerate!"

"Where is it, this new house?" Zoya sighed, and thought that she noticed a smirk on her mother's face.

"It's in Greenfield, a great neighborhood."

"But how am I going to get to the library? To work?" The library was a five-minute walk from their apartment, while

Greenfield was across the bridge from the school. "I have to work until 8:00pm during the school year. They already put me on the schedule. How am I supposed to get home at night?"

"What are you worried about? Your father will give you a ride. Or you'll take the bus. And besides, you danced all summer long until midnight, so anything is possible!" Zoya's mother looked at her triumphantly and sniggered. Zoya felt her fingertips grow cold.

"Papa, can I have some tea, please?" Zoya shivered, and handed her father her mug.

"Sure!" Her father shifted his gaze to the tea kettles. Zoya knew that if the water was not at boiling point, her father would insist on waiting until it boiled again, but she was in luck. Steam was rising from the kettle. A few seconds later, Zoya had a mug of hot tea in front of her. She took a sip, trying not to burn herself and clasped the cup tightly, enjoying the heat.

"Okay, I'm off." Ella Kassatkina announced casually, throwing a meaningful look at her husband. "Today, Tatiana and I are doing the inspection. It's very important to check the house before you buy it."

"Wait, what do you mean?" Zoya rounded her eyes.

"I mean, I've already seen it, and I'm fine with it. Our offer has already been accepted, which is great. Tatiana said we just need to finish the inspection, but she assures me there won't be any problems. And then, we sign the contract."

"And Papa?"

"Your father doesn't care." Zoya's mother looked reproachfully in her father's direction.

"Papa?"

"I really couldn't care less." He shrugged. "Let them do what they want. The house is in a good location. I looked at a map."

"Papa, you haven't seen the actual house?" Zoya had

always thought that her parents, despite their bickering, were on the same page as far as important decisions and life events were concerned. It was she who was the black sheep of the family, excluded from important decisions. Seeing such deep differences between them struck Zoya.

"No, I said back in the spring that I would not go see any homes for sale. I don't care, and besides, my opinion doesn't interest anyone." Peter Kassatkin sighed.

"That's not true!" Zoya's mother huffed indignantly. "Anyway, I'm already late. Tatiana is waiting downstairs." She walked out of the kitchen, and a second later the front door slammed.

"So you really don't care?" Zoya asked her father, taking a seat next to him. "I thought you two would pick the house together."

"Your mother will do what she wants to do anyway. There's no point in looking at these houses. I checked one out: the ceilings are low, the walls are flimsy, not like our apartment in Moscow. It's like Vera and Simon's place, just awful. Since the 1950s, construction quality has been terrible in the US."

"But maybe this house will be better?" Zoya looked at her father hopefully.

"I doubt it." He shrugged. Noticing that Zoya was still warming her hands up on a mug of tea, her father frowned and narrowed his eyes:

"Why are you cold, Zoya? Do you have a fever?" He watched her intently.

"Papa, no, it's just, umm, I don't know." Zoya averted her eyes.

"Why don't you stop running to these 'knock-knock' parties." He smiled. Zoya adored the cute nickname her father gave to raves, after she described one to him.

"No, it's not the raves. I like dancing there."

"Well, then, where did your Vlasov go?" he asked after a pause.

"Vlasov? He stayed in Moscow, Papa." Zoya's heart sank as she answered her father – she was sure that he meant André, knowing his habit of using any name he remembered to refer to her friends.

"Well, not Vlasov, but the American who came by, drank tea here."

"Papa, that was a French guy. Actually, Corsican," Zoya said and then stopped. The thought of André felt like a sharp knife, cutting her inside.

"Yeah, so what happened to him? He was a nice young man."

"Nice? You didn't like him!"

"Why not? He was the best out of the bunch. Better than that lanky what's-his-name...?"

Zoya knew that her father was referring to Alexei Kulikov, but decided to pretend she didn't understand who he was talking about. "And this one, with the hair, is also unreliable. A man, but has long hair, like a woman. I don't like him." Her father shook his head to show disapproval. "He wouldn't last long in my old neighborhood, Domnikovka. They would have cut that hair off with a knife."

"Papa, how can you say that?" Zoya tried to sound upset, though she was amused. She imagined the cultured and polite Evan facing the bullies from Domnikovskaya Street, a rough neighborhood in the center of Moscow, where her father had spent his childhood and which he fondly remembered from time to time. But then Zoya thought of André, their last conversation, and the fact that it was all over between them. The corners of her mouth crept down all on their own. Zoya knew she was about to burst into tears again, just like last night at the rave.

"Did something happen?" Her father stared at Zoya.

"I guess. It's a long story." Zoya sighed. She could hardly

hold back the tears anymore. She again imagined André's face, contorted in anger. And his words accusing her of being a junkie. She pushed the mug of tea away from her.

"Papa, I'm going to lie down, I don't feel well," she squeezed out and hurried to turn away, so that her father did not see her tears.

"Zoya, have some more tea, you need something warm." Her father refilled the mug, which gave off steam. She half-turned, wrapped her hands around the mug again and felt the warmth soothe her. Her tears receded and she felt an unexpected rush of positivity. As painful as it was to think about André, she enjoyed chatting with her father.

"Thanks, Papa."

"And try, umm," her father stalled for a moment, "don't get hung up on them, those guys. That's my advice to you."

"Okay, Papa."

"Yeah, it's better to live, don't overthink it, don't waste your nerves on these things. I only realized it with age, but otherwise I would have saved so much time and energy. You don't have to get all worked up over relationships, especially when you are so young."

"I'm not."

"Good for you. Better focus on your studies, read interesting books, do things like that."

"Okay, Papa," promised Zoya, though she was not sure that she could force herself to switch to books or studying after what had happened between her and André.

Zoya went to her room. She needed to get ready for the new school year, but instead she sat down on her bed and burst into tears.

*Everything was lost. Everything.* And her relationship with André, instead of a beautiful, true love story, instead of becoming more serious, had just broken down over nothing. *I just wanted to show him one rave; to share it with him so we could go dancing together!* Zoya gnawed at herself. *Why did I drag him there? I should have waited, and things would have been different. And now it's over. He should have just stayed in France with his girlfriends.* Zoya vividly imagined André having fun in a group of chirping French girls, and was sickened by the thought.

Accepting the fact that André was no longer in her life was impossible. Although less than a year had passed since he had moved to Pittsburgh, and during that time they both had been so busy, she had gotten used to the idea of being in an intimate relationship with him. She and André had real feelings for each other, of that Zoya was certain. They were about to have sex, and, once that happened, she and André would have taken their relationship to the next level.

Zoya liked having André as her boyfriend. She was proud of him. In those rare moments when she and André went for a walk, when they sat at the Beehive cafe, Zoya enjoyed being around him. André always attracted a lot of attention and Zoya felt like that admiration reflected on her, too. By virtue of being next to someone so handsome and impressive, Zoya felt elevated in her social status. She also found André extremely attractive and felt pulled towards him, though André was never quite within reach.

He was too busy achieving, striving for something, struggling, the opposite of Jessica's boyfriend, Matt, whose only occupation was to hang around Jessica and take care of her. Matt even baked Jessica muffins and brought them over for breakfast one Saturday morning, when he found out that Jessica wasn't feeling well.

Anything like that was out of the question with André. If Zoya ever complained about not feeling well, the most André would do was to call and ask how she was doing. Zoya frowned as she remembered that André did not bring her one single gift from France, despite being away for over three months. *But then, what does it matter? We had a connection, a deep understanding, and a karmic bond!*

After their quarrel, Zoya felt empty. Weeks passed. Without André, or, rather, without the illusion of a relationship with him, Zoya suddenly found herself with a lot of free time on her hands. At first, she did not want to admit that she felt better alone. Gradually, Zoya started to realize that her thoughts of André and fantasies about their relationship had consumed a huge amount of her energy. Zoya had gotten used to constantly analyzing how André behaved, how he would feel, or how he would react to her actions. When André disappeared from her life, a vacuum formed in the place of her thoughts about him. For now, Zoya filled this void with homework. She studied with even more zeal than before.

She needed to do well on her SATs, and had to improve her English score. To raise it, Zoya had to learn hundreds of 'SAT' words. Many of them had Latin roots, and Zoya could guess their meaning, but others were completely unfamiliar. Memorizing them was the only way to learn them. Zoya, on Jessica's advice, made flashcards and spent hours memorizing SAT words. *Dearth. Peripatetic. Rancor. Bifurcate.* These words, as it seemed to Zoya, jumbled up in her head and were about to turn into mush, but then, gradually, she started to recognize them in texts and built up her vocabulary.

*Zoya Shapiro managed to get into Harvard,* she thought, *which means I can, too. I have to get a high SAT score and do something else to distinguish myself. There is no way she is better than me!* Zoya also wanted to prove Vera Shapiro wrong, and to show her competitor's mother that other Russian immigrants were also capable of achieving.

# CHAPTER 16

February 1994

"That's where I advise you to apply." Mrs. McNeal slid a sheet of paper to Zoya. On it, in her neat handwriting, were the names of six universities:

- *Georgetown*
- *Oberlin*
- *Columbia University*
- *University of Pennsylvania*
- *Carnegie Mellon*
- *University of Michigan*

Zoya scrutinized the list, and Mrs. McNeal watched silently. Harvard was not on it. Zoya sighed. After a short pause, the counselor continued:

"Think about whether you want to go to college in a big city or in the middle of nowhere, Zoya. Georgetown, Penn, Columbia are universities in big cities. Columbia is in New York City, Penn is in Philadelphia, and Georgetown is in Washington DC. Well, Carnegie Mellon you know. But if you want to live on campus in some rural area, I suggest you look at Oberlin or the University of Michigan. I'd recommend you go there and take a look at the campus and see if you like the university before you apply."

Mrs. McNeal tapped her pen on the sheet of paper, and Zoya thought of the practicalities of visiting university campuses. Going there with her parents was out of the question. Her father was busy at work, and her mother didn't drive. And there was one other obstacle – her parents had no idea that Zoya was thinking of applying to colleges outside of Pittsburgh. Another teacher walked in and called Mrs. McNeal.

"Please excuse me for a moment, I'll be right back," Mrs. McNeal turned to Zoya. Zoya was left alone sitting in the office.

Zoya knew her parents expected she would attend Carnegie Mellon and live at home, not on campus. She recalled her mother's conversation with Lydia, who had come to visit them at their new home with Alexei a few weeks ago, right after they moved into the house in Greenfield.

Their new house was not at all like Vera and Simon's, built in the Ranch style. The Kassatkins' house stood on a hill, and had large, cheerful windows. The rooms had high ceilings. It was built in the early 1900s and felt spacious. The house had a few strange things about it, like an incredibly beautiful, antique fireplace, but no kitchen. To be exact, there was a kitchen, but it had been constructed later, as an unheated annex. In the winter the space was incredibly cold.

When they first moved into their new home, it was the middle of December, and Zoya, having gotten used to the freezing apartment on Denniston Avenue, was not at all surprised to find their new house also uncomfortable in some ways.

Still, the Kassatkin family quickly settled into it, and Zoya's father even found some old boots and placed them near the kitchen door to wear in the cold space during the winter months. Zoya's mother adapted to cooking in the freezing kitchen wrapped in a downy shawl. And in spite of the fact that the kitchen was cold and uncomfortable, or maybe because of it, it soon became filled with dirty plates, peelings, uncollected crumbs, and the stove was covered with a layer of sticky slime, just like in all the previous Kassatkin residences.

Zoya liked the new home much better than their first American apartment. Back in February 1991, when Zoya first entered the drafty space with ice on the frames and white, hospital-like walls, she decided that life in America was a survival test. That by moving to America, the Kassatkins, as a family, unknowingly, had agreed to a whole string of difficulties and obstacles. In this house, however, this feeling gradually dissipated. Difficulties no longer seemed insurmountable, and America started to feel like home. Now, three years after moving to America, Zoya had almost forgotten her childhood apartment on Second Brestskaya Street in Moscow, the yard, the view from the kitchen window, and her wise neighbor Inna Lvovna.

"Oh, Ella, how lucky you are that Zoya will study right here and live with you," said Lydia. "Carnegie Mellon is a wonderful university, and you'll have your daughter at home. How perfect!"

"Yes, of course, it's wonderful," said Zoya's mother, despite the fact that she had not previously expressed much interest in where Zoya would go to college.

"And my Alexei... Carnegie Mellon would be perfect for him too. It's a wonderful university. But we don't have that in Cleveland, and I won't let my boy leave my side. He needs to stay right next to me, close to his Mama." Lydia looked fondly at Alexei, who was picking at a stuffed cabbage roll with his fork. This time, Lydia brought huge bags full of food, and Zoya suspected it was because she did not trust her mother's culinary abilities.

Ella Kassatkina was of the opinion that everything, including college attendance, had a way of working itself out on its own. She never spoke about college applications or enrollment with her daughter, but there was an implicit understanding that Zoya would apply to college 'when the time was right'.

There were several universities in Pittsburgh, and Carnegie Mellon was the best one in the city. And since Zoya was a good student, her mother thought she would easily get in, and so need not think of anything else. Zoya's father, on the other hand, realizing that his daughter was not particularly interested in science or chemistry and was never going to be an engineer, completely resigned from discussing her further education. Though he, also, had been sure that Zoya would attend college in Pittsburgh. Meanwhile, the prospect of staying at home after high school graduation suffocated Zoya. More than anything, she wanted to get away from her parents as soon as possible and start a new, more independent life.

There was another reason Zoya did not want to apply to Carnegie Mellon – André. Zoya, of course, would never admit to herself that she had crossed the university off her list, despite its stellar reputation, because she was afraid of running into her former boyfriend. After their break-up, she had come to hate Carnegie Mellon and everything associated with it. She shuddered at the sight of the university emblem on T-shirts and baseball hats, and found the combination of gray and burgundy, the colors of Carnegie Mellon, to be repulsive.

Hearing Mrs. McNeal's suggestion, Zoya at once knew that she wanted to go to college in a big city. Rural life, where the only attraction was the university itself, seemed absurd to her. *I'm from Moscow, I should live in a big city*, she thought. So Oberlin and the University of Michigan were crossed off the list. That left Georgetown, Columbia, and Penn. Zoya decided she was going to go to the library and look at the rankings of those universities. Her conversation with Mrs. McNeal was nearing an end, so Zoya dared to ask:

"Will they let me into Harvard?"

Asking the question that had been on her mind ever since she first met Zoya Shapiro, Zoya blushed, expecting Mrs. McNeal to laugh at her. But the counselor did not. Instead, she scrunched her nose, thinking. Then, after a brief pause, the woman responded:

"Zoya, I would say, your grades are fine, so keep up the good work. However, Harvard is unlikely to accept you, but I would advise you to look at Columbia and Penn. They are also very prestigious universities, some of the best in America. You need to get your SAT score up, of course."

"Thank you, Mrs. McNeal." She was grateful that the woman had taken her question seriously. Mrs. McNeal's words about Penn and Columbia struck a chord with her.

"And I'd also recommend that you do some volunteer work. You have to show that you're involved in meaningful extracurricular activities. That you are an active member of society, you take part in something exceptional, and you demonstrate leadership qualities. Admission committees pay a lot of attention to that. You have to stand out. Good grades and SATs aren't enough."

"I see, thank you, Mrs. McNeal." Zoya nodded.

Mrs. McNeal, was an experienced educator and had helped more than one generation of high school students, so Zoya understood the urgency of finding a volunteer position, something besides the French Club and her library job. *But what?* Some of her classmates volunteered at a local nursing home and spent time with the elderly reading them books. But where to start – where would she find a nursing home? And how to become a volunteer there?

The eleventh grade turned out to be very busy. There were so many classes that Zoya could barely cope with her homework, while also cramming for the SATs. Tests, quizzes, essays, and then her job at the library occupied her time.

Despite her busy schedule, Zoya managed to go to raves whenever they were taking place in Pittsburgh. Most of the time she went with Evan. After the botched introduction of Evan and André at the September rave and then her breakup, Zoya was too heartbroken to think about jumping into another relationship, and Evan did not make any effort to woo her. And so, Zoya and Evan continued being friends.

As months passed, Zoya thought of André less and less often. She avoided Oakland so as not to run into him. Even the Beehive, which she loved so much, became off limits. If Jessica suggested going to see Matt, whom she still dated, skateboarding on South Bouquet Street, Zoya would find an excuse not to go. She put the little tiger figurine, which André had given her back in Moscow, at the back of the shelf in the sideboard, blocking it with her mother's china service.

The only obstacle was French. Every time Zoya was in French Club, she involuntarily remembered André and their first meeting at the Kremlin Armory. She would see his face, and how he caught her, re-enacting their first conversation. Zoya would remember her trip to Paris, when she saw the two Templars, Johannes and Robert. Though this vision now seemed more like a nightmare.

*Why did I tell him everything?* Zoya agonized when she remembered the scene. *Why did I rush to do it? I should have just waited until the nightmares stopped like they did before! What did it matter what I imagined about those Templars? I could have lived in peace and not thought about this crazy stuff. And then André and I would still be together.*

# CHAPTER 17

arch 20th, 1994

As it was Sunday, Zoya decided to make the most of the day by studying for her physics exam. She felt an extraordinary burst of energy after being out with Evan on Friday evening to a great rave. Immediately after breakfast, she laid out her textbook and notebooks and beautifully wrote the date on the page. Then she proceeded to memorize two chapters. Physics was a subject Zoya did not understand, relying on her memory to pass it.

She was deep into the second chapter, when suddenly the doorbell rang.

*Maybe a neighbor?* Zoya thought. She still couldn't get used to the fact that they were living in a house, rather than an apartment. "Like real Americans," Zoya's father joked.

Zoya raced down the stairs and opened the front door. On the threshold stood Nikki. Her face was gaunt, her eyes were red, and mascara streaked down her face. Behind her, towered a grim-faced Evan.

"What happened?" Zoya shrieked and immediately looked around, afraid her parents would overhear, but remembered they weren't home.

"Come on, let's go," said Nikki.

"Where are we going? What happened?"

"It's Soup…" Nikki burst into tears.

"Nik, get in the car," muttered Evan. "Wait for us there."

Suppressing a sob, Nikki obediently ran down the stairs and disappeared into the familiar black Saab. Zoya looked at Evan questioningly.

"Listen, there is a problem with Soup. We'll tell you on the way. We gotta hurry, we wanted to grab you, 'cause you are friends with her."

"Of course," Zoya nodded, internally wondering whether she considered Soup her friend.

They seldom called each other, Soup led a nomadic lifestyle, lived with friends, had no home of her own, was nearly impossible to reach. If Zoya wanted to find Soup, she had to do it through Nikki. Zoya never discussed Soup's life or her dealings with Ike and drugs with her, so it felt as if there was something mysterious and sinister about her.

"Well, we thought you might care. They took her away the night before last." Evan sighed.

"Took her where?" Zoya opened her eyes wide.

"We'll tell you all about it. Let's go?" Evan nodded toward the car. "Are you ready?"

"Yeah, just a second, let me grab my stuff."

She rushed inside the house and hurried to the bathroom. Her heart was beating fast, and she felt out of breath, and her palms were suddenly clammy. Zoya looked at herself in the mirror, trying to calm herself, and held her breath. In her head, the terrible phrase pulsated: *they took her away.* She rinsed her face with cold water, exhaled, and only then went down out onto the street. Evan was already sitting behind the wheel, and Nikki was in the back, smoking, with the window rolled down.

"I didn't know you smoked," Zoya noted.

"I don't, not really, just when I am stressed." Nikki

shrugged and dragged on the cigarette. "I still can't calm down, you know? I found out ... I do not even know, she's all alone; what are we going to do?"

"Get in, let's go," Evan turned to Zoya. "They took her to the nuthouse, we just found out." Evan started the car and they drove off.

"What?" Zoya felt dizzy. *It can't be,* she thought. *Not that!* She pictured St. Anne's and how she'd been restrained to the bed, leaving her with wounds on her ankles and wrists. Images of the checkered floor, the interns, the barred windows, de Vigny and his awful smirk swam around her.

"Yeah, she's at Upper Hill Psych."

"How did that happen?" Zoya gasped.

"It was at that rave on Friday..." Nikki's voice quivered. "It was all my fault; I had to go to work so I left her by herself."

"It's not your fault, Nik, what are you talking about? Soup is a grown-up," Evan grumbled.

"Well, you know she can be a real idiot. I always told her not to mess with that creep. But she kept thinking that extra money wouldn't hurt."

"With Ike?" Zoya clarified, a sinking feeling in her stomach.

"Yeah, who else? We were all at the rave on Friday, and then I had to go do the night shift. Friday night, you know? Like the best night, customers are all generous. I was so glad they put me on the schedule, I didn't even think about her. If I had known this was going to happen, I never would have gone."

"That's enough now; tell the story," Evan ordered.

They had already passed Schenley Park, and Zoya realized they were on the way to Upper Hill Psych. It was a building one couldn't miss. The hospital was located in a high-rise on a hill on the North side of Oakland, towering over the neighborhood. Zoya turned to look back at Nikki.

"So," Nikki continued, curled up in the back seat, "I left for work, and Soup stayed at the rave. The creep promised her a ride. On Saturday afternoon, as usual, we'd agreed to meet up. I usually don't get up until about three in the afternoon, or 'round that, after my shift, you know, one thing after another, but Soup calls me, to wake me up." Nikki sighed again. "She didn't call me. That was a first; she always, always calls me, or sometimes she just comes to my place, but she didn't sleep over last week, she was somewhere else, so I thought maybe she stayed over there. I didn't even go looking for her right away. You know what I mean? It's all my fault! And this morning, I freaked out, 'cause I haven't heard from her, so I told Evan."

"Listen, you are just rambling," Evan said. "Anyway, Nikki called me this morning and said that Soup had disappeared. I checked with Ike straight away. Then we started calling hospitals and even morgues, and nothing, but we didn't think to call the nuthouse. But then Soup called, they let her, I dunno, I guess make a phone call, or whatever. We're on our way to check on her now."

"So, umm, she's at Upper Hill Psych?" Saying the name of the hospital out loud, Zoya immediately remembered the scary doctor and his disgusting face. It was as if de Vigny was looking at her and smirking. *Could it be him?* A wild thought flashed in her mind. *It can't be; it's all my imagination. There is no de Vigny here, and it's all nonsense. He stayed in Paris, and André is probably no longer in Pittsburgh, either,* Zoya reassured herself. But the face of the scary doctor was still in front of her eyes. Zoya could clearly picture the long nose, twisted lips, his shifty eyes.

"Hey, Zoya, why are you being all weird? Are you afraid, or what?" Evan glanced over.

"No-no, why?" Zoya stammered. Her fingertips went cold with fear. She wanted one thing: to jump out of the car and run away somewhere far away. They drove onto South

Bouquet Street, and Zoya realized that in just a few seconds they were going to pass by André's house. Her throat constricted, as her thoughts shifted to her ex-boyfriend.

She tried to look away, but an unknown force pulled her to look out the window. Zoya saw the familiar porch and noticed that a new gray chair had appeared on it. So ordinary, Zoya thought that she could be sitting in it if she hadn't been so rash and decided to take André with her to the rave. Bitterness, suppressed for months, now filled her whole being, and tears came to her eyes. She didn't try to fight them. Zoya cried out of self-pity, but her tears were also filled with compassion for Soup, whom they hadn't managed to protect.

Evan parked the car on a nearby street, and they headed toward the Upper Hill Psych building on foot. Zoya had only seen it from far away, and now, standing near it, she felt as if the tower could crush her. One step in the wrong direction, and the structure would collapse right on her head.

"Oh, it's so creepy here!" Nikki cried out, as if she had read Zoya's thoughts.

"Well, it's not a circus, alright?" said the disgruntled Evan. His eyes darted nervously from side to side. They approached the door and paused. Evan huffed nervously and stepped inside first, followed by Nikki. Zoya closed the procession.

Once inside, she felt dizzy. On the floor there were squares, the same black and white ones that were exactly like the squares in the ward at St. Anne's. Zoya remembered moving chess pieces across these squares in a state of a delirium, as she was trying to crawl into bed there. *What if it's the same here? What if I was really here and not at St. Anne's? What if it hadn't been a dream?* She began to panic.

As she looked around, Zoya half-expected the orderlies to appear out of nowhere, tie her up, and send her to the Upper Hill Psych ward. Of course, then de Vigny would arrive, prescribe her lithium and Klonopin, and tell her she was very lucky to be his patient.

"We are here to see Kelly Weiden," Nikki said, and Zoya opened her eyes in surprise. She had been so distracted by the black and white floor that they had reached the reception without her noticing.

It took a second before she remembered that Soup's real name was Kelly. This was the first time she had heard Soup's last name though, and she wondered about its origin. *Probably German*, Zoya decided. Evan, who stood to the side, was humming a tune that sounded a lot like Bjork's Human Behavior.

*I just imagined all that stuff, it was the stupid squares on the floor. There is no way that de Vigny could be here*, Zoya reassured herself. She frowned, surveying the lobby, while the receptionist issued them visitor passes. To contain her feeling of unease, Zoya started reading the bulletin board hanging next to the reception. There were instructions on visiting hours, announcements of courses, and advertisements of a psychotherapy center. On seeing a pink flier Zoya jumped up.

*We are looking for volunteers!*
    *Come join us!*
    *Our new Children's Play Psychotherapy Center*
    *urgently needs volunteers! Flexible hours*
    *Call Elizabeth at 412-555-0600.*

Zoya grabbed a pen that was on the counter and wrote the number on the palm of her hand. *This is exactly what I need for my college applications. A volunteer opportunity! And working with kids! How wonderful!* Zoya's heart leaped. *Tomorrow I'll call Elizabeth and make an appointment.*

Completely immersed in her plan, she was only half paying attention as the three of them were escorted into the waiting room. The space looked comfortable, with several sofas and stacks of magazines. There were practically no other visitors.

"Good thing we made it on time: visiting hours are almost over. I told you we should have come sooner," said Nikki, plopping on the sofa that stood by the wall.

"You've been too busy crying, so we couldn't leave earlier!" Evan retorted, sitting down next to her.

"Why isn't Soup coming out? I don't understand why it's taking her so long!" Nikki fidgeted, cocking her head. "Maybe they didn't tell her we are here?"

"Nah, come on, she's gonna be right out, just give it a minute," Evan said expertly, as if he'd spent his whole life visiting patients at a mental hospital.

Nikki sighed. "I'm just worried about her being alone in there."

"You should have thought of that sooner," said Evan, and then stopped short.

Soup floated into the waiting room. Dressed in oversized pants, tied at the waist, that hung awkwardly on her tiny body. Her T-shirt was an obscure, muddy yellow color.

"Hey, guys!" Soup grinned as if they'd met at a rave, and not in the waiting room of Pittsburgh's largest mental hospital.

"Soup, how are you? What happened to you?"

"I'm fine; the food here is so good!" Soup smacked her lips. "They have these amazing rolls, I ate three for breakfast. Cinnamon!"

"What rolls?" Nikki looked at Soup with bewilderment.

"You know, cinnamon rolls, with glaze or whatever."

"Soup, are you insane? You need to get out of here as soon as possible!"

"What for?"

"What for? You don't have insurance. Who's gonna pay for all this, have you thought about that?"

"No, why?"

"What do you mean why? Did you sign something when you came here?"

"I don't remember; I was walking around after the rave, and it turned out I was actually walking down a ramp to the highway. I was singing and I don't remember anything else. I was tripping my head off!!" Soup giggled. "I think Ike gave me some real strong stuff, I took it and then bam! I couldn't remember nothin', maybe I took a second hit, but I dunno. I was so wasted! You wouldn't believe it, Nikki!"

"I believe it. Oh why did I leave you by yourself?"

"It's okay. Don't worry about it."

Soup wasn't paying any attention to Evan and Zoya. Facing Nikki, she began to describe, vividly, how she had left the rave and walked along the highway at night. And how she was then stopped by a police car, and how the officer asked her what she was doing. Soup thought the police vehicle was a rave car, and the siren was a special musical accompaniment to her trip, and started dancing.

"And then he brought me here, wished me to 'get my head back together' and I said to him, 'my head is together!'" Soup laughed as she put her hands up to her head and tapped. "See! It's together now, too! They gave me something, and some clean clothes, so here I am. Resting. I like it very much."

"What about your ID? Or proof of insurance?" Nikki frowned.

"I don't remember; I think I had something on me."

"Soup, you're over eighteen, right?"

"Of course I am! I'm twenty!" Soup raised her thumb coquettishly.

"So you're here as an adult. And that means they are gonna charge you for treatment," said Nikki, frowning.

"Charge for what? They didn't ask me for anything."

"Soup, are you stupid?" Evan jumped in. He looked so stern that Soup stopped smiling.

"Wait, why are you being like that?" She fussed and looked around anxiously.

"You gotta understand, this isn't a joke. The hospital, the whole system. Haven't you ever been to a doctor?"

"Nah, like maybe when I was five. Who needs to see a doctor?"

"Okay, listen, I know how this system works." Evan said, looking at Soup gravely. "My mother was a hippie, and then she became like a full-blown alcoholic, and ended up at a rehab." Evan turned at Nikki, who nodded in response. "We got a bill for like four thousand dollars. You know? And we didn't have that kind of money. My mother was paying it off for like two years, crying every time, and blaming herself that she couldn't deal with drinking on her own. And she swore she'd never touch the bottle again. That's how she got cured."

"How long was she there for?" Soup asked, shrugging. "'Cause for me, it's been like only a day or so, and I love it here."

"I don't remember, it was a long time ago. I'm just saying, it's not free."

"Alright, I'll think about it, but I like it here so much! And the nurses are so nice." Soup looked up dreamily. "Actually, I'm fine here. And there's a TV."

"Soup, what are you talking about? I have a TV at home, you can come and watch it at my place," Nikki yelped. "This is a mental hospital, you can't like stay here for a long time, or you'll end up crazy for real."

"We'll see," Soup responded vaguely. Then she stood up, smoothed her shirt, and, turning away, mumbled: "I gotta go, see ya!"

"Soup, we got another five minutes," Nikki bolted upright, looking incredulously at the others, then down at her watch.

"They're about to serve hot cocoa! Swiss Miss!" Soup smiled cheerfully and rushed back into the hospital ward.

Evan, Nikki and Zoya looked after her in amazement.

"Look, I think they must have drugged her, she isn't herself," Nikki declared.

"Yeah, something's up. Cinnamon rolls? Swiss Miss? TV?" Evan shrugged.

"What do we do now?" Nikki asked.

"I don't know." Evan frowned, as he rose from the couch.

All three walked out of the hospital in silence. Once more, Zoya noticed the black and white squares on the lobby floor, but no longer thought of de Vigny and his experiments. She was thinking of the peculiar changes in Soup's behavior.

"I can drop in on her later this week," Nikki said, "before work."

"I can't during the week," Evan hummed. "Is she gonna be back to normal you think?"

"Of course, she can't stay like this, can she? It's like she's been brainwashed!"

"Yeah, it's like she's a different person. And she's only been here for like twenty-four hours."

"I'll go and see her tomorrow," Nikki promised.

"Zoya, can you come visit Soup over the weekend? If she's still here?" asked Evan. Zoya nodded in response.

"Okay, cool, so we'll come back soon. You keep me posted, Nikki, okay?"

"Yeah, of course I will. But I'm hoping to get her out of here tomorrow or the day after. I think I can change her mind." Nikki attempted a smile.

When she got home, Zoya copied the phone number from the ad onto a piece of paper, and then sat down to her physics textbook. The events of the afternoon seemed like a dream. Zoya tried to immerse herself in her studies again, but all she could think of was how she would call Elizabeth and become a volunteer, and then have an exciting activity for her college applications.

The very next day, after school, she called the hospital. A

friendly woman answered and then immediately complimented Zoya on her great judgment and good will, told her that being a volunteer at the children's Center was going to be the 'best experience ever', and asked her to come in for orientation. Then the woman apologized for the fact that Zoya would not receive a salary for her work, and promised to give her food vouchers for the hospital cafeteria and bus passes.

Zoya decided that this type of compensation was fabulous and quietly congratulated herself for noticing the ad at Upper Hill Psych. She could already picture how great her volunteer job at the Upper Hill Psych would look on her college application, and how she would be immediately accepted into the best college because of this experience.

*I can take the bus here, and the library is close by*, Zoya decided, as she hung up the phone. Since she did not work at the library on Thursdays, she would volunteer at the hospital on those afternoons.

Later that week, right after school, Zoya rushed to the 61C bus stop in the direction of Oakland. She felt like a pioneer conquering a new world. On the way to the hospital, Zoya remembered Soup and thought that since she was heading to Upper Hill Psych anyway, she should also check on her friend. But the thought of having to visit alone made Zoya panic. *No, I can't do that. They wouldn't let me in, I'm not even eighteen. And what's there to talk to her about?*

She felt embarrassed about not visiting Soup, but then consoled herself thinking that helping children was more important, and that her volunteer hours would count toward her admission to a prestigious college. *And Soup was fine yesterday. She probably doesn't want to see me anyway*, Zoya thought as she approached the building. Just then, she pictured Soup in her strange outfit, and felt uneasy. Worry about Soup, who was so helpless and seemed so naive, pressed on Zoya's mind. *Although, it is her own fault for getting here; there's nothing I can actually do!* Zoya reassured herself, entering the lobby.

This time, the checkered floor stopped her only for a moment. *I've got a job to do. I finally got a good volunteer position, and the rest doesn't matter. It's just some nonsense,* Zoya thought as she took the elevator to the third floor, to the office of the play center.

# CHAPTER 18

arch 24th, 1994

Zoya walked down the corridor of the third floor, searching for the office, when her attention was drawn to a door decorated with several drawings. There were bright yellow suns and ships, a few spirals, trees, houses and smiling clouds, all drawn by unsteady children's hands. A large sign read 'Children's Play Psychotherapy Center'. Zoya stared at the door for a minute, mustering the courage to knock. She realized the drawings had been pasted in such a way so that they blocked the small window in the door.

*Ingenious*, she thought and knocked. The door swung inwards and Zoya stepped in. She saw a brightly lit room, bursting at the seams with papers. They were stuffed into innumerable folders, crammed into two boxes and also laid in various piles on the floor. In the middle of the room stood a woman, holding a folder of yet more papers in her hands.

"Good afternoon," Zoya croaked, trying to sound polite.

"Zoya! Did I say your name right? It's Russian, right? I think you mentioned it. My name is Mrs. Finn, Elizabeth Finn." The tall, dapper woman with bright blue eyes dropped the folder on the floor and extended her hand to Zoya. "I speak Russian, took it in college."

"Oh, wow!" Zoya opened her eyes wide in amazement.

"Yes!" Elizabeth smiled brightly at Zoya. "I went to Pitt! I almost majored in Soviet studies," she grinned, "but then changed my mind, thank God! And the Soviet Union collapsed, so that would have been a disaster!"

"Oh, yes." Zoya nodded, not sure how to react, but trying to appear likable.

"In the end, I got a psychology degree, and then a master's, and now, here we are! I won a grant! And now I have this project. A therapeutic playroom for kids." Elizabeth proudly surveyed the space, not at all concerned by the messiness of the room. "I am so lucky, this project is part of my research on the effects of art therapy on children and their mental health. It's just a pilot, not that large, and I just opened it. So just setting everything up. And you are the first one to respond to my ad!" Elizabeth tilted her head slightly to the right and smiled at Zoya.

Zoya couldn't yet tell if she liked this woman. Elizabeth looked no more than thirty, she was dressed beautifully and elegantly – in tight black pants and a smart sweater, from under which the collar of a white shirt sparkled.

"Let me show you the place and what needs to be done," Elizabeth said, "this room is our reception area. Or it will be, once you sort all these papers." The woman pointed at the stacks on the floor. "So that will be your first assignment," Elizabeth said and Zoya felt a note of challenge in the woman's voice.

"Okay," Zoya responded.

"You see, we need to arrange all the papers in these folders and move them to the office." Elizabeth pointed to a door leading to a tiny room. Zoya saw two bookshelves with a stack of neatly inscribed folders on the bottom shelf, a desk and a chair.

"That is my office," Elizabeth proudly noted. "And this room…" The woman opened a second door that Zoya had not yet noticed, "This the Playroom". Zoya saw a large, bright space, with tiny multi-colored chairs and tables, which reminded her of 'Goldilocks and the Three Bears'. On the tables, there were neatly arranged pencils, stacks of note-books, coloring books, and paint sets. Zoya gasped, unable to contain her excitement.

"Do you like it? I bought it all. Decorated everything myself," said Elizabeth.

"It's so beautiful!" Zoya responded, wide-eyed.

"Yes, this is the place where therapy takes place. It's a magical space! I'm really happy with what I've done here," Elizabeth said with undisguised pride. "So once the papers are sorted, your job will be to put toys and art supplies away in here and to keep everything in order. You have to pick up everything neatly, to organize it so that everything for the next group of children will be just as beautiful. And, of course, make sure that all the drawings are signed, and then bring everything to my office. Then I sort out all the materials for analysis."

"Okay," Zoya nodded vigorously.

"It's very important, analysis of the drawings is the most important thing for the grant." Elizabeth raised her eyebrows, as if checking whether Zoya understood the importance of the work. "My husband helped me secure the funding!" She added suddenly, and then she flashed a bright diamond on her left ring finger. Zoya, normally oblivious to wedding rings, felt like she could not take her eyes off the bright stone.

"Ah, if it hadn't been for Scott, nothing would have worked out. The grant is just for two years, so in December I have to submit my first report, show the results, to extend the whole thing, or they'll just shut me down. Two years is noth-ing!" Elizabeth sighed and gave the papers on the floor a skeptical look.

In Zoya's experience, two years was plenty – everything had changed in Zoya's life in two years, counting from the winter of 1991 to the winter of 1993, but she did not dare contradict Elizabeth. She enjoyed listening to this woman, and was furtively examining her boss, whom she now found very pretty and smart. The more Elizabeth spoke, gesticulating, explaining, the more beautiful she appeared to Zoya. *She must really like what she does,* Zoya decided. *I wish I someday have a job like this, that I really love,* she thought wistfully.

"And how exactly do you sign the drawings?" Zoya dared to ask after a short pause.

"I'm so glad you asked that question!" Elizabeth gave Zoya an encouraging smile, "Sign on the back: first name, last name, age, and a code. The code can be found on the folder, it's a special number, then we use it to enter the information into the database."

"Into a database?" Zoya gasped in shock.

"Yes, of course, there is also a database. We fill it in separately. All the drawings will be recorded, and then we'll reclassify everything the children draw by special numbers. I have the nicest programmer from Carnegie Mellon, he is also an intern, who is helping me set it all up. He's a very talented young man, would you like me to introduce you?" Elizabeth suddenly perked up.

"Yes, okay," Zoya froze at the mention of Carnegie Mellon. *Could it be André? But André isn't a programmer, and such a coincidence is hardly possible...*

"Yes, he is a very nice guy, and I don't think he has a girlfriend. Do you have a boyfriend?"

"No," Zoya swallowed, feeling the shame at somehow lacking.

"No boyfriend? But you are so cute! Just adorable. I'll make sure I introduce the two of you. I'm so glad I came up with this idea. I love setting people up! I introduced my best friend to her husband, and my cousin is about to get married to someone she met through me! I got a gift!"

"What's his name?" Zoya ventured to ask.

"Whose?"

"Umm, the programmer's."

"Oh, of course; his name is Ben. He's a great guy. Smart and talented, he will earn good money in the future and be able to provide for his family!" Elizabeth listed the qualities of the CMU student.

"Thank you!" Zoya nodded, trying to make her voice sound appropriately enthusiastic.

"Great! Then it's settled. You're here on Thursdays, right? I'll get Ben to come in next Thursday. And you'll just sort of run into each other. Well, we can say goodbye for today; thank you, I'll see you next week!" Elizabeth stopped chatting and buried her face in a pile of papers.

"Thank you, goodbye." Zoya was about to leave, but then she remembered the food vouchers and bus fare that Elizabeth had promised her over the phone. "Oh, excuse me, please, how can I get the vouchers?" Zoya blushed, embarrassed to ask Elizabeth for compensation for her time, after the woman had been so welcoming already.

"Oh! How could I forget, I'm so silly!" Elizabeth shook her head in disapproval at her own forgetfulness. "Of course! I should have given them to you at once; next time, please ask me beforehand, remind me. I forget everything. And my husband tells me I need a secretary! Ha ha, can you imagine, I need a secretary because I can't keep everything in my head!"

Out of one of the folders, Elizabeth produced an envelope and handed Zoya one meal ticket, followed by a bus voucher. Then Elizabeth scratched her head, rummaged through the papers, and handed Zoya the whole envelope.

"Here you go!" she announced. "I'd better give it to you right away, so I won't forget next time. That's until the end of the month. In April, please remind me to issue vouchers for the following month."

Zoya accepted the envelope, trying not to give away the trembling in her hands. By her calculations, there was an equivalent of over $100 there: at least ten bus vouchers and about twenty meal coupons for the hospital cafeteria. Five dollars each. It was a fortune. Zoya thought frantically about how exactly to redeem the meal vouchers. *I could come to the hospital several times a day, but then I'd have to use the bus vouchers, or I could bring one of my friends to join me?*

"Thank you so much!" Zoya said, clutching the envelope in her hand.

"Thank you! It was very nice to meet you! See you next week!" Elizabeth smiled and turned away.

As she left the office, Zoya heard the rustling of papers. She shut the door tightly behind her and rushed downstairs, anxious to count the vouchers Elizabeth had just given her. Sailing through the lobby, she briefly noticed the floor again, and dashed out into the street.

There, stepping to the side of the entrance, Zoya pulled out an envelope and began going through the papers. There was a free bus pass for the rest of the month and twenty meal coupons. Zoya stared at them for a moment. *I shouldn't have left the hospital, could've redeemed at least one of them now,* she thought. *Guess I'll save them for next time!* She stuffed the envelope in her bag and headed for the bus.

As she was about to cross the road in front of the hospital, Zoya noticed a black Cadillac pulling up to the main entrance. Behind the wheel, sat a man in a cap. He looked like a professional chauffeur. *Just like in the movies,* Zoya thought as she stared at the car. The driver got out, and Zoya realized she had seen him before. This man had driven her and André around in Paris. *It can't be,* Zoya shivered. *I never saw André in Paris, that had been a dream. This driver must be a different person. I couldn't have seen him before!*

Zoya squinted, trying to get a better look at the chauffeur, when she saw a gray-haired man climbing unhurriedly out of the back seat of the car. Tall and imposing. An ugly nose hung over his upper lip, disfiguring his face. It was de Vigny.

As he stepped out of the car, Zoya recognized his gray suit and a pink tie. The terrible doctor said something to the driver, who nodded, and de Vigny, now there was no doubt in Zoya's mind that it was him, proceeded inside the hospital. Zoya hadn't moved during the entire interaction. She felt beads of perspiration on her forehead and her hands trembled. Her first urge was to run, to flee without a second thought, to go far away, to leave everything behind forever, to never come to Upper Hill Psych again.

Then a second thought pierced Zoya's consciousness. *André! I must warn him! He probably doesn't know about his stepfather's arrival. And now that dreadful man is here. What if de Vigny is here to hurt André?* Zoya's mind raced. A second later, she was darting in the direction of South Bouquet Street.

She raced down the hill, crossed Fifth Avenue, barely waiting for the traffic light; then, ignoring honking cars, dashed across Forbes Avenue and sped down South Bouquet Street to André's house. Zoya did not think about the last time they'd seen each other, the fight, about how André broke up with her, and about how she had suffered since. She was guided by one thing: the desire to warn André of the impending danger.

Zoya knocked on André's door, expecting Sybil to answer as she always did, and prepared to be questioned, but there was no response. Zoya knocked again, then yanked the knob, hoping the door was unlocked, but in vain. Zoya looked at her watch and sighed. It was only five o'clock. *André is probably still at a lecture or at work. Or tutoring his students. What do I do?*

She sat down on the gray chair that stood on the porch, and found it surprisingly comfortable. *I wonder if it was André who got it? Or Sybil? Or Mikey? Or Rick? Mikey isn't that orga-nized, or maybe it was a new girlfriend of André's?* At this thought, Zoya jumped up. Up until that moment, she had only mourned the loss of her relationship with André, but had not considered the possibility of him being with someone else.

*Of course, of course he has someone. That's right, he was always getting hit on by girls, even at the store!* Zoya remembered how the saleswoman at Benetton had flirted with André and how he had responded to that woman as if he was used to that kind of attention. And how the women on the street gave him wistful looks. *He must have forgotten about me a long time ago! This chair is proof of that! I'm sure he has a new girlfriend already. Maybe she put a chair here, already acting as if she owns the place.*

Hatred of André's new imaginary girlfriend instantly seized Zoya. She leaped off the porch, as if bitten by a snake. *What am I even doing here? Let him deal with de Vigny himself! And why did I even come here?* Zoya furtively looked around. The street was empty. *Good thing no one saw me. I'm going home.* She stomped up South Bouquet Street.

Midway up the street, Zoya remembered the envelope with the bus coupons and meal vouchers and fumbled for them in her bag. The happiness over Elizabeth's generosity had gone. Instead, she felt incredibly sad, and tears started streaming down her face all on their own. Zoya tried to stop them, but failed.

She cried about her lost relationship with André, about the fact that Soup was in a mental hospital, and about having to volunteer at that very hospital, and having to organize chil-dren's drawings into folders, and to help Elizabeth with some grant program, and about the huge ring on the woman's finger, and about being introduced to a programmer from Carnegie Mellon who was going to be a great breadwinner someday.

At the very mental hospital she'd run into the terrible de

Vigny. The man who, if she were to believe her dream, had condemned her to death in a past life, and she could do nothing about it. Her karmic knot with André would remain tied, and she had missed her chance to forgive André and ruined the only relationship she might ever have. And de Vigny would sneer and mock her again and threaten André, but now she didn't care, because André had betrayed her and had gotten involved with some girl who had bought him a new chair and put it on his porch. She badly needed the volunteer position at Upper Hill, because it was the only chance to stand out among the other applicants and to get into Harvard, as Zoya Shapiro had done before her.

Wallowing in her suffering, Zoya walked up South Bouquet Street. She was almost to the intersection with Forbes Avenue, where she could catch a bus home. The thought of beating Zoya Shapiro had given her a surge of strength — it was the energy of anger. Tears dried up all on their own, and she was filled with determination.

*So be it, I'll prove to everyone that I can do everything on my own. Get into Harvard, and meet Ben from Carnegie Mellon, and whatever, I can do anything, and the volunteer job is great, and there is nothing to cry about. And de Vigny... What about de Vigny? I'm not his patient!* Zoya turned the corner and bumped into someone.

"Oh, excuse me, please." Without raising her eyes, Zoya tried to walk around him, but he blocked her way. She looked up and saw André. A smirk wandered across his face.

"Hi, Zoé," he said. Zoya was silent in response. She could not breathe.

"Hey, what's up? Won't you look at me?" André was no longer smirking, but looked at Zoya in surprise. "Why are you crying? Zoé, did something happen?"

"No." Zoya forced a smile.

"You're not? I can see your face is covered in tears."

"It's not, I just washed it," lied Zoya.

"Where?"

"I don't know, leave me alone," Zoya snarled.

In response, André laughed. "I see, and what are you doing here?"

"Taking a walk. Why?"

"A walk? What about school? And your job?"

"You know about my job?"

"Of course I do."

"Oh."

"You told me yourself, didn't you?" André smirked again. Zoya had told him, of course, about how Melissa had gotten her the job, but she didn't expect him to remember.

"You didn't care." Zoya shrugged.

"No, I cared. I've seen you there. I go to the library sometimes." André looked at her with his dark gray eyes, and she felt like she was drowning. Terrified of her emotions, Zoya looked away and stared at the sidewalk.

"Zoé, can you hear me?"

"Yes."

"I went into the library, and I saw you there."

"When?"

"A while ago."

"Why didn't you say hello?" Zoya asked, though she knew the answer: André would never come up to her first.

"I was in a hurry," André answered. "How are you doing?"

"Me?" Zoya looked at André and suddenly burst into tears again. The tears that had been suppressed by anger at Zoya Shapiro suddenly flowed, so much so that Zoya felt as if she would completely dissolve in them. André was silent. He stood silently. A look of boredom crossed his face. "I'm alright," she muttered.

"Cool," André responded.

"André, where did you get the chair?" Zoya asked, wiping away her tears.

"What chair?"

"The armchair! You got a new chair. The gray one on your porch."

"Oh, that one? Mikey and I found it on the street, on trash day. Mikey thought it looked cool, so we dragged it over and wanted to put it in the living room, but Sybil said no. She said it was dirty and from the street. We had to leave it on the porch. But now we're used to it; sometimes I sit outside. It feels good."

"So you just found it! I thought that..." Zoya hesitated.

"What did you think?" André asked and pierced Zoya with his eyes. In response, Zoya sighed. Speaking with André was painful and uncomfortable. *I should just leave*, Zoya thought, but then she remembered de Vigny.

"André, actually I have something to tell you. It's important; I think I've seen de Vigny," she said, rounding her eyes.

"What do you mean?"

"Just now. I wanted to warn you, that's why I was here, in the neighborhood." She thought that her words sounded unconvincing and ingratiating, and tried to be as firm as possible.

"You think you saw de Vigny? Here? In Pittsburgh?"

"Yes, outside the hospital. Near Upper Hill Psych." André frowned at the mention of the hospital, but she pretended not to notice his reaction.

"Zoé, how did you know it was him?"

"I recognized him at once: he was wearing a gray suit, and he had a car with a chauffeur, like in Paris."

"A car? How do you know about the car in Paris? You've never seen it!"

"What do you mean, I've never seen it? I've..." Zoya stumped.

Zoya bit her lip, realizing her mistake in sharing too much – she'd just made a reference to something that she had seen in a dream. She'd never seen de Vigny in real life. All of her interactions with the scary doctor had taken place in a dream, or in a parallel timeline, or in a past life, depending on whether it was Inna Lvovna or Fatima Ndoku who explained it. And in this, real life, in which Zoya was with André, she had never met de Vigny. André was right. She couldn't know what his terrifying stepfather looked like. Certainly couldn't have recognized him on the street.

"Zoé," André looked at her with pity, "I'm worried about you. Even now. I still care about you. Tell me the truth, are you being treated at Upper Hill Psych? If that's the case, I'm all for it! I'm happy for you, if you've stopped taking all that crap and started taking care of your mental health."

"Taking care of my mental health?" Zoya gasped.

"You came to tell me you're starting a new life, didn't you? Are you in rehab?"

"No, I came to warn you that your stepfather's in Pittsburgh. You mentioned he might be coming here, remember? I thought you should know that he's *here*. I just saw him on the street outside Upper Hill Psych."

"I care about you, you don't have to lie to me, Zoé."

"So you don't believe me?"

"Zoé, how can I believe your stories? And it's not the first time. First you told me about some Templars, and now you've even invented de Vigny on the streets of Pittsburgh. Though this latest story is kind of ingenious, I gotta give it to you." André shook his head ruefully and sighed.

"But I didn't make it up, it's true."

"Zoé, do you even hear yourself? He isn't coming here, that was just something my mother invented to make me come back. You should be careful with your stories."

"But Alexei believed me. And he even helped me!" Zoya objected. "And so did Vlasov!"

"Who are those guys? Your friends? The druggies?"

"My Moscow friends."

"Whatever." André shrugged. "And the long-haired loser, he also believes you?"

"Who?" Zoya frowned.

"The one who goes to raves with you."

"Evan?" Zoya blushed with indignation.

"I can't keep track of all your gigolos."

"Gigolos? Evan is my friend. And no, I didn't tell him about past lives."

"Why is that?"

"Because he and I probably don't have the kind of connection that you and I had. So there was no need to bring it up." Zoya clenched her fists.

"Oh yeah, and what kind of a connection do you have with him?"

"We're friends,"

"Yeah, friends." André huffed. "I see. And anyway, I'm going to France in May."

"Oh, okay."

"Yeah, I'm gonna be gone the whole summer. I need to make things right with Maman."

"But that's what you were going to do last summer."

"Yeah." André gave her a foggy look. "Zoé, I have to go. Stay clean, keep up the good work!"

Without waiting for an answer, he turned around and walked down South Bouquet Street in the direction of his house. Zoya was frozen in place. As André disappeared from sight, she felt as if a black cloud swallowed her whole being.

Somehow, she made it back home. Once there, she surreptitiously slipped up to the second floor, bypassing the living room, and retreated into her bedroom. There, in the safety of her own space, Zoya got into bed and huddled under the blanket, curled up in a ball. *Sleep is the answer. I need to sleep to forget everything*, Zoya thought.

But sleep did not come. Instead, she saw André's angry eyes. The same dark gray eyes that pierced through her being.

Eyes that blinked and became the eyes of the traitor Johannes. One wrong move, and, Zoya could tell, she would sink into a wormhole. Johannes would condemn her to death again, and she would die, get burned at the stake, and relive Robert's torture and death all over.

*I need to act, to do something!* Zoya jumped out of bed and rushed to her desk, propelled out of her stupor. She took out her diary and opened it to a new page. Zoya stared at it for a moment, and then started to write. Her hand began to move across the page all on its own. Words appeared on the page, and Zoya read with amazement:

*Zoya, stay calm. Don't react to André's antics, he's not a threat to you.*
  *You are stronger, but you still have to grow.*
  *Get on with your studies and your work. Alum*

As she reread the words in her diary, Zoya frowned. *There he is again. This Alum guy.* She was about to put the diary away, but reached for the page again, and the next entry appeared:

*Ask your father about Grandpa Kassatkin.*
  *It's time to find out the truth.*

This entry was unsigned. For some time, Zoya stared at the page. She felt her panicked state recede, while her breathing returned to normal. Zoya got up and moved around the room. She felt good, even happy. Thoughts of André, the confusion that their meeting had caused, had disappeared. In their place, a new feeling appeared: optimism about the future.

*I guess I should actually ask Papa about Grandpa Kassatkin,* Zoya determined. She hadn't thought about the mystery surrounding her grandfather in months, ever since she had shared it with Alexei, but now felt a strong urge to get to the bottom of the story. Zoya sat back on her bed, immersed in her thoughts, when she heard her father's voice:

"Zoya, Zoya, where are you? Are you hungry?" Immediately followed by the sound of footsteps on the stairs. The next moment, her door opened and her father appeared on the threshold.

"Yes, I am kinda hungry, Papa." Zoya sighed. Now that she saw her father, the idea of asking him about Grandpa Kassatkin seemed much more difficult than it had been in her head. *There must have been a dark secret behind his story,* Zoya thought.

"I'll heat up some buckwheat for you." Her father looked at Zoya carefully.

"Okay, Papa," Zoya hurried out of the room past her father, trying not to look him in the eye.

"Zoya, what's going on?" Zoya's father followed her down the stairs.

"Nothing, Papa, I'm fine, I'm just tired." Zoya mumbled, as she walked through the living room.

Her father sighed. "I can tell you're hiding something."

"I'm not hiding anything, Papa." Zoya plopped down at the kitchen table. *Maybe I should just ask, what's the big deal? Why am I dragging this out?* she thought, and suddenly blurted out:

"Papa, can you tell me about Grandpa?"

"About my father?"

"Yes!" Zoya stared straight at her father, feeling relieved she finally dared to ask this question that had been in the back of her mind for so long.

"Of course I can tell you, why not? I've been meaning to for a long time. You definitely need to know the history of your ancestors, of your family." Her father smiled and pulled up a chair.

"Uh-huh," Zoya nodded. *If he thinks I need to know my family history, why did he hide Grandpa's story from me?* she thought, but tried to keep the expression on her face neutral.

"You see, kiddo…" Zoya's father began.

He had not called Zoya 'kiddo' since time immemorial, and the word sounded ingratiating, but Zoya was too interested in hearing her grandfather's story to react. "Your grandfather was a remarkable man, though I don't remember him very well. He went up to Northern Russia to work when I was only three years old." Her father looked at her expressively.

"He wanted us, your grandmother and me, to come with him, but my mother didn't want to leave Moscow. She was very afraid of losing her residency permit. You know, right after the war, if you left the city, there was no telling if you could ever come back to live in Moscow later. And up North, where he worked, it was the new frontier, barracks, life was hard."

Zoya's father shook his head. "It was probably the wrong decision, but Grandfather Kassatkin sent my mother almost all of his salary and planned to return home to Moscow quickly."

"Papa, he went to Severodvinsk, right?" Zoya watched her father carefully.

"Yes, to Severodvinsk, Zoya. How did you know that?" her father asked, but then responded to his own question: "Oh yes, there was that photo. How do you remember everything? Well done! And then he stayed there, he only came to see us once or twice a year, when he had leave."

"Did your grandfather ever tell you about Severodvinsk?"

"Not much; but I remember he said the sun never set there in the summer, that it was like another planet. Only it wasn't until 1957 that the town was called Severodvinsk. Before that it was called Molotovsk, and it was a military town, it had always been that way. My father worked there at an atomic submarines plant. It was a top-secret facility, you know."

Zoya's father searched her face for signs of understanding, and Zoya nodded in comprehension.

"Working there was a dream-come-true for your grandfather. He considered it a great honor to serve his country that way. He came from a family of peasants, and was a self-made man. He graduated from a top university in Moscow and was a military engineer."

"How interesting, Papa!" Zoya gasped. Up until that moment, in her mind all of her relatives were generations after generations of Muscovites. She tried to picture her grandfather as a child, a little peasant boy conquering Moscow and liked the image that she'd quickly formed in her mind.

"Yes, a different time," her father said and raised his index finger up, as if pointing to the sky. "Come on, let me heat you some food." He walked to the stove.

"Papa, but what happened to Grandpa after? Why did he disappear?" Zoya probed.

"We don't know exactly, Zoya," Peter said, as he put buckwheat in a pan and turned on the stove. He refused to use the microwave, claiming that it gave off radiation. "Your grandfather tested nuclear submarines. One day, he was just gone. We stopped hearing from him. The photo you found, the last letter that we received from him, that was it. My mother, she tried everything, asking questions, sending petitions, letters, looking for him, trying to figure out what happened to Grandpa. She wanted to go to Severodvinsk to look for him, but you needed a permit. So she couldn't even go to the town where he'd worked."

"But he couldn't have just disappeared, could he?"

"Of course not. I think he was killed during one of the tests."

"Killed? But that was after 1945!" It never occurred to Zoya that her grandfather might have died after World War II. In her mind, military men, soldiers, front-line men, were killed in action up until the end of WWII, in May 1945, and then, once the war was over, came peacetime.

"Yes, I think he was killed. That's the only explanation. But no one told us anything, so we don't know for sure. And they wouldn't even sign his death certificate. And without it my mom couldn't get a pension. And after Grandpa disappeared, things got very tough for us, for me and my mother. We could barely make ends meet on her miserable salary." Zoya's father sighed.

"Papa, why didn't you tell me any of this before?"

"What's there to tell?" Her father's shoulders drooped, as he stirred the buckwheat.

"But you couldn't find out why he was missing? What really happened to him?" Zoya threw her hands up in frustration.

"Yes, it was the USSR, that's how things were done. Severodvinsk was a top-secret location, all information was classified, where would I go to figure anything out?"

"Why didn't you tell me anything? Back in Moscow, when I found the photo?"

"I wanted to, but your mother and I were afraid they wouldn't let us out of the country. If you remember, Zoya, leaving the USSR was no simple matter, we needed a special permit and they checked all relatives, all connections, and especially one's parents. If your parents were alive, they needed to sign a permit, allowing you to leave. My father used to have access to classified information, and I never got his death certificate. So, technically speaking, he could have been alive. Imagine that."

"Oh, Papa! But maybe he isn't dead?" Zoya looked at her father in amazement.

"Zoya, I don't think so. I am fairly certain he's been dead since 1957."

"But then Grandpa Kassatkin was a hero, if he was killed performing these nuclear tests, right?" Zoya widened her eyes. She wanted to find a silver lining to the story.

"Eh, I guess so. Only no one will ever know anything about him." Zoya's father shrugged, as he put a steaming bowl of buckwheat in front of Zoya.

"Papa, I'll find out everything there is about him, I definitely will!" Zoya jumped up in excitement.

"Kiddo, I am sorry, but I don't think that's going to happen. We live in America. How will you ever figure this stuff out?"

"You'll see, Papa, I'll find a way." Zoya promised, as she dug into her buckwheat.

# CHAPTER 19

arch 27th, 1994

On Sunday morning, Zoya got a call from Evan, suggesting they visit Soup together. After running into de Vigny at Upper Hill Psych, Zoya was hesitant to go, but she felt too guilty to refuse. *What will Evan think of me if I don't go? I need to be a good friend to Soup,* Zoya thought. So exactly at 12pm, Zoya was getting into punctual Evan's car. Nikki wasn't there.

"She's at work." Evan sighed, when he noticed Zoya turning to the back seat, where Nikki usually sat. Evan's sad and a slightly wistful expression reminded Zoya of the Donkey Eeyore.

Zoya was not about to give in to Evan's despondency. In her pocket, she fumbled for the food vouchers she had received from Elizabeth the previous Thursday. She was determined to cash them in and share them with Evan.

Fifteen minutes later, they were already entering the Upper Hill Psych building. Zoya tried not to look at the squares on the chessboard floor, but felt a little dizzy as they walked down the corridor towards the reception. The wait was not long, and soon they were in the already familiar waiting area, greeting Soup.

"Wassup? Where's Nikki?" Soup asked. She looked cheerful and carefree.

"Working," muttered Evan.

"Oh, well, tell her I said hi; and I'm here watching TV, 'Ricky Lake'! I love it. It's so cool. And her guests, they are so funny." Soup sat down on the couch.

"Listen, Kelly, when are they gonna let you out? You seem fine." Evan looked doubtfully at Soup, who was sitting cross-legged. For the first time since they met, Zoya realized that Soup wasn't a natural blonde as she saw brown roots growing in.

"I don't wanna go anywhere! Why should I? They are feeding me soooo well! I can have chocolate pudding any time I want! It's so good! We should sell it at the raves; next time we go, I'll definitely do that. We could make so much money! It's the best."

"Kelly, you have to get out of here first." Evan again looked at his friend with disapproval.

"I get to be here for free! Didn't I tell you? And I sleep great, I'm doing real well."

"How are you here for free?" Evan shook his head. "I've never heard of a free hospital!"

"It turns out that there's a special study being done here, and I qualify under..." Soup thought for a second and furrowed her brow. "Under the pa-ra-me-ters," she proudly uttered after a pause. "I signed everything, and they won't charge me a penny, but I had to take some stuff and let them draw my blood a few times, and like whatever. I get free treatment, and I'm like at a spa." Soup looked fondly at the pale yellow walls of the waiting room.

"Soup, what study is that?" Evan looked around anxiously.

"'Who cares, just some study, I am contributin' to society

and stuff." Soup was playing with her hair, while avoiding eye contact.

"You said they gave you something to sign? I'll take a look, okay?" Evan insisted.

"Yeah, I've got a booklet, I'll get it for you." Soup cheerfully retreated from the waiting room.

A terrible premonition crept into Zoya's mind. She remembered that in her dream, de Vigny had mentioned a research study he had been planning on doing in Pittsburgh. *Could it be his study? But there is no way, that would be too much of a coincidence,* Zoya worried as she waited for Soup.

"There!" Soup, bouncing happily, ran up to the couch and handed Evan a pink booklet with white letters that read:

*Hormonal imbalance and personality disorders in young women, ages 13-20*

Beneath the inscription was a stylized image of a woman's face in profile.

"I told you, you wouldn't understand a thing: some kind of hormonal imbalance, personality, whatever. All nonsense," remarked Soup, watching Evan, who was leafing through the booklet, snickering perplexedly. Zoya's pulse quickened and her forehead was covered in sweat.

"Do you understand anything? Take a look." Evan handed the brochure to Zoya. On the first page, she read:

*A joint research study between St. Anne's Hospital in Paris and the Upper Hill Psychiatric Institute and Clinic, conducted by Dr. Mirani, a leading psychiatrist from Pittsburgh, and Dr. Jean-Marie de Vigny, a well-known French expert in teenage personality disorders.*

. . .

Zoya's hands started shaking. She forced herself to turn the page and saw a picture of an older woman with short hair, the very Dr. Mirani. Underneath her photo was a photo of de Vigny, his face solemn. The bulb of his nose hung over his twisted lips. The room suddenly spun, and the next second Zoya was on the floor, gasping for air.

"Zoya, Zoya, are you okay? What's wrong with you?" Evan leaned over and was patting Zoya's cheeks, while Soup looked at her in surprise, perched on the couch.

"Oh, wow." Zoya tried to sit up, but the room moved again, and she thought she was going to lose consciousness.

"Hold on to me," Evan said. "That's it, lean forward, don't be afraid." Zoya clung to Evan and cautiously lifted herself up. Pink spirals floated in front of her eyes, but the warmth of Evan's hands had a calming effect on her. She pulled herself up and sat back on the couch, leaning on him, and exhaled.

"Zoya, are you okay?"

"I don't know…I felt dizzy. The air here is so strange."

"Yes, it's stuffy," said Evan and threw a skeptical look around the room. "Listen, Soup, we're gonna get going, okay?"

"Go ahead, yeah. Take the booklet, see if anyone can use it. I was told they need more patients. But like they gotta meet the pa-ra-me-ters," said Soup, carefully annunciating the word.

Evan held out his hand to Zoya, and she stood up carefully. Standing was much harder than sitting, and she felt dizzy again, but Evan deftly took her by the arm and they left the room.

"Zoya, what's the matter? You're still not going to tell me?" He studied her face.

"I just don't feel well, that's all," Zoya lied.

"Maybe you're just creeped out? Last time you were all

weird too. I know how you feel, this place is freaking me out, I've seen 'One Flew Over the Cuckoo's Nest' and all that. Don't worry, Soup's not in any danger, she's fine."

"Evan, you don't understand, she's not fine." As they walked out of the building, Zoya felt a rush of strength. "Evan, I have to tell you everything, but you probably won't believe me. That doctor in the picture... He's a very scary man."

"What picture?"

"In the booklet, didn't you notice?"

"No, where?" Evan opened the brochure, and Zoya, afraid to see de Vigny's face again, quickly averted her eyes. "Umm, yeah, he does look kinda ugly, and the other one, Mirani, also kind of looks like a freak." Evan hummed, examining the brochure.

"I know; just trust me: he's a very scary man, and we can't let Soup be treated by him. We have to save her before it's too late."

"But, umm, she's kinda doing well, don't you think? And she signed some papers, I mean, come on, Soup's twenty years old, she's not a child."

"She's in danger. We have to get her out of there, Evan. That doctor will put her on all sorts of drugs, and then... then, actually, maybe she'll..." Zoya bit her lip.

She remembered how de Vigny had mocked her, how her hands and ankles were scarred by restraints on the bed at St. Anne's, how dizzy and nauseous she had been from Klonopin and lithium, both of which de Vigny considered harmless.

Though it had all been in a dream, the memory of de Vigny terrified Zoya. And then she thought of André, de Vigny's own step-son, whom the psychiatrist had forcibly kept in a mental hospital in order to get his inheritance. That had not been in a dream, but actually happened to André. The thought of him felt like a punch to her stomach. It pained her to think that she had lost him forever and that their relationship was over. Tears came to her eyes, and Zoya stopped talking to try to calm herself.

"Zoya, are you okay?" Evan looked at her affectionately. Zoya turned red with shame. *Maybe he still likes me, maybe Nikki was right, and I'm acting like this with him, it's not nice.*

"I'm just thinking about Soup, how to save her." Zoya tried to give her voice a neutral expression.

Evan shrugged. "If anyone can get Soup out of there, it's Nikki. She won't listen to anyone, but Nik."

"So let's tell Nikki everything, then." Zoya felt her heart racing. Evan's calm demeanor was starting to annoy her. *Does he not understand how much danger Soup is in?*

"Sure, as soon as she's back from work, I'll tell her."

"What time does she finish work? Maybe we can pick her up?" Zoya urged Evan, anxious to find a resolution to Soup's problem as quickly as possible.

"Nikki? Umm," Evan scratched his head. "I don't know for sure, guess we can stop by there. Though I kinda hate that place."

"Oh, yeah," Zoya looked up at Evan. She had not given much thought to Nikki's job at a strip club, but now was curious to see the establishment. "So, can we go over there now?" Zoya smiled, but Evan pursed his lips.

"Umm, I guess so, but I really don't wanna go in there; maybe you can go in without me?"

"Sure!" promised Zoya. Her heart fluttered at the thought of going inside of a seedy strip club. They drove in silence. Roads in downtown Pittsburgh were empty on a Sunday, and soon they parked on a narrow street on the edge of downtown.

"See that door? Where it says 'Rick's' there?" Evan pointed to a squat, long, windowless building that looked like a barrack. "There's gonna be a bouncer at the door, ask for Nikki, tell her you're her sister and it's urgent."

"Okay." Zoya got out of the car and straightened her

pants. She fixed her hair and confidently crossed the road. Next to the building, she could hear the hum of music. Zoya yanked the door handle, but the door wouldn't open. She pulled again, but again, no success. Zoya stepped back and only then noticed a bell, but didn't have time to press it. A tall bald man appeared right next to her and murmured in a lascivious voice:

"Baby, this must be your first time here, right? My name is Tim, I come here a lot. I am a regular. You just ask for Tim, okay, pussycat?"

Zoya was about to jump back and run to the car, but the door opened, letting them in, and she hesitantly followed Tim inside. It took a few seconds for Zoya's eyes to adjust to the darkness. Loud music rumbled at a distance. Tim disappeared, and Zoya found herself face-to-face with the bouncer, a huge man in a leather vest. His hairy arms were covered with tattoos. Zoya had to crane her neck to look at him, he was so huge.

"You here for a job?" The man looked at Zoya doubtfully.

"No, I need Nikki."

"Who's Nikki?"

"My sister, she works here," Zoya said, trying to sound confident.

"We ain't got no Nikki here, we only got nicknames."

"Nicknames?" Zoya felt like she was about to cry.

"You know what, little girl," the bouncer folded his arms across his chest and glared at Zoya, "you'd better get out of here, you don't belong here. Just go before something bad happens to you."

"Please, I really need to see her; a friend of ours is in trouble, Nikki is the only one who can help."

The man grumbled, and then threw a scornful look at Zoya:

"Dammit, I know people say I am too kind for my own good, my grandmother was right: at heart, I'm just a teddy bear. Stay here," he barked at Zoya and left. A few minutes later, the bouncer returned, with an annoyed look on his face. Nikki pattered right behind him. She rushed to Zoya and pulled her into a corner.

"Zoya, what are you doing here? I thought Tony was gonna kill me. I don't have much time, I gotta get back on stage, but then my shift's over soon."

"Nikki, we were just over to see, umm, Kelly." Zoya remembered Soup's real name just in time. "She told us that she signed some papers and now she's going to..." Zoya cleared her throat, "she's gonna be like a guinea pig. Staying at Upper Hill Psych for free, but in exchange they are gonna do experiments on her."

"What? No way!"

"Yeah, and she wants to stay there. She doesn't want to be discharged." Zoya opened her eyes wide.

"What do you mean, she doesn't wanna be discharged?" Nikki jumped up in surprise.

"Says she likes it there." Zoya clenched her hands, wishing she could just grab Nikki and go. "Evan and I thought maybe you could change her mind."

"I can try." Nikki nodded and looked over at Tony the bouncer. Then she kissed Zoya on the cheek and smiled. "Thanks for coming to see me." She glanced at the bouncer one more time, and he in turn shook his head in mock disapproval.

"So are you going to talk to her?" Zoya clarified. She wanted Nikki to rush to Upper Hill Psych to convince Soup to leave.

"Sure. I might stop by after my shift today or another day. But Soup's a tough girl. If you knew what kind of crap she takes at raves, you wouldn't worry so much."

"Thanks, Nikki," Zoya muttered, frustrated.

"You're up!" They heard the bouncer's bark and the next

second, Nikki fluttered away. Zoya walked out of the club and was immediately blinded by daylight.

"How was it? Did you have a chance to talk?" Evan asked, as Zoya sat down in the car.

"Yeah, she said she was going to stop by the hospital, but that Soup takes all sorts of drugs at raves, so we shouldn't worry."

"Ahem," Evan cleared his throat, "she's right about that, by the way. Okay, let's go. Nikki's a serious girl, she'll talk to Soup and set her straight. Just give her time."

"Yeah." Zoya nodded and sighed.

"You wanna stop by the Beehive?" Evan suggested. "Haven't been there in a while."

"The Beehive?" Zoya imagined running into André there, and the very thought of it made her feel sick to her stomach. "No, let's go home, I have homework to do."

"Suit yourself," said Evan with a tone of disappointment in his voice.

# CHAPTER 20

After visiting Soup, then seeing Nikki at the strip club, Zoya tried to focus on school. As soon as she got home, she ignored all thoughts of the unfortunate Soup and the terrible de Vigny, who was about to use the girl as a guinea pig.

In class, on Thursday, she watched the clock. Counting down the hours until she would go back to Upper Hill Psych for her volunteer job. *Do I really have to go back to that awful place? What if I run into de Vigny again?* she agonized. *Maybe I should look for another volunteer job.* She remembered the vouchers that Elizabeth had given her and felt obligated to go. *She paid me for the whole month, I can't just leave. She needs volunteers, or she'll lose her grant.* Zoya sighed.

Trying to ignore the fluttering in her stomach, Zoya entered the hospital lobby. She walked cautiously to the elevator and saw an arrow pointing to the cafeteria. Zoya quickly glanced at her watch: still fifteen minutes before she was supposed to be at the Children's center, so she followed the arrow. As she fumbled for the vouchers in her pocket, she felt proud of herself for remembering to bring them from home.

The walls of the hospital cafeteria were painted pale green. Square white tables filled the space. In the back, she noticed a middle-aged woman, who stood behind the counter and fixed Zoya with an unfriendly stare.

"Excuse me, please, I have these." Zoya produced several crumpled food vouchers from her pocket.

"Lunch is until half past one, it's already over," the woman grumbled.

"Is there anything I could get with these?" Zoya insisted, scanning the cafeteria with a hopeful look.

"Whatever's on the counter." The woman vaguely waved her hand to the side where Zoya saw a tray, filled with chips and cookies, wrapped in plastic. "Dinner starts at five." The woman shrugged and looked away.

"Okay," Zoya responded with a sigh. Her dreams of eating a salad, delicious chicken, and fruit were crushed.

"Oh, you can also get Pepsi or Fanta," said the woman.

"Thank you, I see," answered Zoya. Spending food vouchers was proving more difficult than she had anticipated. *Do I wait for dinner? But I'll be done by four thirty, does it make sense to hang around this place for another thirty minutes?* Zoya walked dejectedly to the elevator.

Absorbed in her thoughts, she paid little attention to what was happening around her. She pushed the 'call' button, and at that moment heard rustling behind her back. Zoya turned around. Behind her stood de Vigny. He was dressed in a gray suit that beautifully complemented his gray hair. Zoya froze in place. She felt her heart would stop beating altogether. Her fingertips went cold.

He paid her no attention and was muttering something under his nose. The elevator arrived unexpectedly fast, no time to think of an escape. Once the doors opened, de Vigny stepped inside. Zoya, frozen with terror, stood and watched. And then she entered. With trembling hands, she pressed the button for the third floor and stood to the side, trying not to breathe. Continuing to mutter something to himself, de Vigny pressed the button for the tenth floor. He did not look at Zoya.

The seconds it took to reach the third floor seemed like an eternity. Time stretched out, and Zoya felt throbbing in her temples from the exertion to keep from collapsing. At last, the elevator doors opened and Zoya stepped out. *I guess I was worried for nothing.* She sighed in relief. As she exited, she heard de Vigny's baritone:

"See you later, Zoé."

Zoya spun on her heels. The doors were closing, but she caught a glimpse of a smirk on de Vigny's face. Zoya darted down the hall, away from the elevator, from the frightening man. She could still see his face, his sinister grin. His words, which were an unveiled threat, rang in her ears.

"Zoya, no need to rush, you're right on time." Elizabeth emerged from the shadows of the corridor and, smiling merrily, opened the door to the center.

"Oh, it's you... I'm here..." Zoya gasped for air. *Did that really happen? Or did I just make it all up?* Zoya thought, trying to reassure herself. *He was silent the whole time, maybe he didn't say anything to me? Just a daydream and he wasn't really there?*

Elizabeth jerked Zoya out of her rumination. "I'm very glad to see you, Zoya; I asked Ben to come over today." The woman leaned closer and whispered conspiratorially, "The cute one". Elizabeth then stepped back and gave her an appraising look. Zoya nodded vigorously in response, trying to demonstrate full understanding and gratitude at the same time.

"Okay, Zoya, he should be here any minute, but meanwhile you can get started sorting these." Elizabeth pointed to a pile of drawings.

Zoya began sorting the papers into folders, labeling them, putting away drawing supplies, and thoughts of de Vigny receded into the background. Zoya enjoyed looking at children's drawings, and she marveled at the beautiful colors the kids used for their projects. *If only I'd had crayons as a child,* thought Zoya, putting a set of sixty-four back into the box. *How much room for imagination!*

"Good afternoon, Miss Fine," Zoya heard a young man's voice.

"Ah, call me Elizabeth, please, as we agreed," chuckled her boss. "And here's Zoya, our volunteer. Zoya, this is Ben."

Zoya turned around. Standing in front of her was a sturdy redheaded guy. His face was densely freckled. He was wearing a baseball hat and a T-shirt, both decorated with the Carnegie Mellon University logo.

"Hey, nice to meet you." The guy extended his hand to her and grinned. His hand was warm, his handshake firm, and his smile was sincere. *He is cute!* Zoya thought, despite the CMU logos that brought back memories of André.

"Nice to meet you, too," Zoya said.

"Well, I'm really glad you guys met. Ben is helping out with the database, he's doing amazing work! High tech!" Elizabeth said, smiling broadly.

"Oh, it's nothing." Ben shrugged, his cheeks reddening slightly, so that the color of his skin blended with the freckles.

"All the same, I am very grateful to you." Elizabeth smiled again and retreated to her office. Zoya heard the rustling of papers.

"What's your major? Are you pre-med?" Ben asked Zoya after a short pause. She looked at him in surprise.

"I don't have a major."

"Oh, you're a freshman?"

"No, I am a junior," Zoya responded.

"How can you be a junior without a major? I thought you were pre-med or something, since it's a hospital." Ben looked at Zoya, and she noticed that his eyes were an amazing shade to amber-yellow. *Wow, like a tiger's!* she thought. *I wonder if they change color in the sun?* "Oh, wait a second. Do you mean you're a junior in high school?" Ben frowned.

"Yes! I go to Allderdice!" Zoya smiled brightly, expecting a question about her accent, which usually followed.

"Well, alright, cool. I've got work to do, so I'll see you around." Ben started humming as he turned on the computer.

Zoya nodded, trying her best not to show her disappointment. *I guess he thinks he's too good for me. So what if I am still in high school? So what that he can program? Alexei Kulikov can also code, and he's about to go to Carnegie Mellon!*

She threw a curious glance at the redheaded student, but he was completely absorbed in his work and paid her no mind.

That afternoon, Zoya returned home in a terrible mood. Her parents weren't home, so she ran up to her room and closed the door shut, grateful to be alone. Everything in her life was going wrong: de Vigny was after her, but she wasn't sure if he really was, or perhaps he was a phantom that she had created; her relationship with André was over, and all because she had weird dreams and was dumb enough to share them with him; and the redheaded guy Ben ignored her because she was still in high school.

On top of all that, Soup was at Upper Hill Psych and refused to leave, and pretty soon her brain would turn into mush because of the drugs de Vigny was giving her. No one would be able to help the girl, and Zoya could do nothing about it. No one, not Evan, not Nikki, believed Zoya or was doing anything to help get Soup out of the hospital.

Zoya opened her textbook, she had so much homework that her head was about to explode. But then she remembered that spring break was around the corner, and slammed the textbook shut.

Instead of doing homework, she would first eat dinner and watch The Simpsons, her favorite show. She had been recording The Simpsons and had a tape ready. In the middle of rewinding to the start of an episode, suddenly the phone rang.

"Zoya, hi." She immediately recognized Evan's voice. Zoya liked the way Evan pronounced her name, gently accentuating the letter 'o'.

"Hey!" Zoya jumped, elated. She was glad to hear from Evan.

"I talked to Nikki, we're going to West Virginia on Sunday."

Zoya imagined that they would all go to a fun party together, and how she would have a great spring break. "To a rave? Cool! I'm…"

"No, not a rave; we're gonna see Soup's grandma."

"What grandma?" Somehow, Zoya could not picture Soup having any relatives, let alone an actual grandmother. Soup existed in a vacuum, she floated in space, like a dandelion, blown by the wind across the field, and she certainly could not have roots and relatives.

"Like, a regular grandma. But she's super rich, like a millionaire. Lives in Morgantown, and Nikki knows her. Apparently, Soup's grandma can pull some strings and get her out of Upper Hill. So we're going over there on Sunday. I'll pick you up at nine. Get ready. We have to go there and come right back. I've got stuff to do later."

"Okay, all right." Evan did not leave her any room to refuse. Zoya had heard of Morgantown, but she didn't know exactly where it was or how long it would take to get there. Still, there was a whole week of spring break ahead of her, and aside from her work at the library and a few hours of volunteering at the hospital, Zoya was completely free.

# CHAPTER 21

April 3, 1994

On Sunday, exactly at nine in the morning, Zoya heard a knock on the door. It was Evan. Yet again, Zoya was impressed by his punctuality.

"So, are you ready?" Evan adjusted his baseball cap. Zoya had never seen him wear one before. She suspected he left his head uncovered on purpose to flaunt his long hair.

"Yes, just a second." Zoya shouted to her parents: "I'm going for a ride, I'll be back in the evening". Without waiting for an answer, she slammed the door and ran downstairs to the car.

"Hi!" Nikki got out of the front seat and moved to the back. "You ride shotgun, I'm gonna take a nap. I'm tired!"

"Yeah, a nap!" Evan grunted grudgingly.

"Well, I worked till three in the morning today, so many customers. On the night before Easter, none of the girls wanted to work – they say it's bad luck. What do I care? I don't believe in bad omens. Money is money!" Nikki yawned and stretched. "Anyway, Zoya, thank you for stopping by my job last week. You were great!"

Zoya blushed with pleasure. The beautiful Nikki herself praised her!

"Remember, I was there, too!" Evan grumbled.

"Of course, of course, kitten." Nikki patted Evan on the neck, as she usually did. "Anyway, I went to check on Soup the very next day, and I know what you mean. She's totally brainwashed, like she doesn't wanna leave, and says they give her all kinds of meds and she loves them. And that she's tripping from them better than from acid, and some doc told her she won't regret nothing."

"Wait, wait, what doctor? She didn't tell us anything about a doctor," said Zoya, with a sinking feeling in her stomach. *Did de Vigny already sink his claws into Soup? Are we too late?*

"This dude, from the brochure." Nikki took a booklet from her pocket with a description of the study and handed it to Zoya. "That's the doc, Soup's crazy about him. She says he's good-looking and that the doc tells her she's *super lucky* to be in his study, 'cause she got in, or some bull like that." Nikki pointed to de Vigny's photo but Zoya looked away. She remembered that de Vigny used exactly the same words when he had been treating her at St. Anne's and chuckled:

"That's what he always says."

"Wait, you know him?" Nikki's ears perked up.

"I heard about him, from this girl at school, she was his patient too," Zoya lied, surprised at how easy it was to hide the truth, "then she went crazy."

"I'm not surprised. He really is freaky, and just look at his face!" Nikki poked at the brochure. "I think Soup's in love with him."

"How's that?"

"She told me that he promised to take her to Paris and show her France, but only if she would be a 'good girl' and 'help him in his research'. Ugh, that's disgusting."

"Nikki, will you stop talking about that doctor, you've

been talking about him for two days." Evan adjusted his glasses.

"That's cause he's a total jerk. Evan! I'm scared, I don't get how Soup could get into such a mess. We need to hurry up and get to her grandma. She can help get Soup out. Her grandma's real cool, she's a millionaire. I got to visit with Soup once and she's like a mogul. Owns half of West Virginia!" Nikki spread her arms wide.

"Come on, Nik," Evan shook his head. "There is no way she's a millionaire, but whatever, Soup's grandma is the only hope we got. Do you even remember how to get there?" He looked doubtfully in the rearview mirror.

Nikki winked back at him. "What do you think? I remember everything!"

They chatted during the ride and time flew by very quickly.

"Right here, this exit." Nikki pointed at a sign as they were nearing their destination. "There's supposed to be a forest nearby, Coopers Rock, that's the name. Soup told me she was always wandering around the mountains there, sometimes even running off into the night."

"Nikki, which way do we turn?" Evan's voice cracked, and Zoya had a sinking feeling in her stomach. *What if we get lost in a forest? Or there's no grandmother and we wasted a whole trip and Soup will be stuck at Upper Hill Psych forever?*

"Yeah, kitten, you see here, go up, and then you'll see a turn." Nikki pointed confidently, and Zoya calmed down a little.

"Okay." Evan muttered. He had been driving for over two hours, and Zoya suspected he was getting fed up with the journey.

"Yeah, straight ahead, then there should be a sign, and then you make a right. After that, I remember everything."

The next thirty minutes seemed like an eternity. They drove along the slopes, turned, then went up and down a hill, but there was no sign. After turning several times and circling back and forth, their car ended up in exactly the same place where they had previously turned to Coopers Rock.

"Well, then, I guess we're lost! It was a stupid idea to come here, and end up in the middle of nowhere." Evan pulled over and sighed, a dejected expression on his face.

"No, we'll find someone and ask for directions!" Nikki rolled the window down and looked out.

"Who are you gonna find here? A deer?" Evan chuckled.

"Up ahead, there's a church, look." Nikki pointed, and, though the church itself was not visible, they could see a neat cross, towering above the forest.

"Oh wow, a church!" Evan started the car and turned onto the road.

Nikki was silent, nervously biting at her nails. No one spoke. Zoya tried not to think. Within a minute, they had rounded the hill and were in a church parking lot. The church was a tall, spartan structure. Clean, straight lines and a peak on which the very cross was emblazoned. The parking lot was packed.

"It's Sunday service," Evan tapped his hands on the steering wheel.

"Yeah, it's Easter Sunday today! But it's eleven o'clock, the service is probably over." Nikki looked around. "I'll ask someone where we can find Soup's grandma, everyone knows each other here."

"Yeah, okay." Evan nodded.

It was the first time that Evan agreed with Nikki and didn't bicker with her, like he had been doing during the whole trip to West Virginia. As if on cue, the church doors opened and partitioners poured out onto the parking lot. Most of those leaving the church were women in colorful dresses, but there were also a few men.

"Oh, look how crowded it is," Nikki remarked. "Maybe we should have gone to the service, too."

"Nikki, don't get distracted; who you wanna ask?" Evan frowned, as he stared at the congregation.

"Look, there's a nice-looking mother; maybe her?" Nikki pointed at a full-figured woman, dragging a crying toddler.

"No, look, the kid with her looks upset, I don't know if she'll wanna talk to us." Evan sighed. Zoya thought that she heard notes of despair in his voice.

"How about that one? Look, such a friendly lady." Nikki pointed at a gray-haired, rail-thin woman in a pink suit with a matching pink hat.

"Exactly! Why don't you go over to her? Or Zoya?" Evan asked.

"Why not you? The old ladies love you!" Nikki giggled.

"Nik, come on, enough of this." Evan blushed.

"Enough of what?" Zoya stared at Evan, wide-eyed.

"Evan, can I please?" Nikki giggled again, and Evan turned completely crimson.

"Alright, but only very quickly. Grandma is already walking over to her car."

"It's just that Evan got an offer from one Greensburg widow. She asked him to become her, well, a sort of like a gigolo. Ya know, like the movie, with Richard Gere?"

"Whatever." Evan huffed and got out of the car. Taking off his baseball hat, he headed for the pink old lady. In less than a minute, the woman smiled and took Evan under her arm.

"I told you," Nikki said, "old ladies love him!"

The older woman adjusted her hat, while Evan listened politely, and then waved toward the car where Nikki and Zoya were sitting. The pink-attired old woman nodded, and then forcefully dragged Evan in the direction of the church.

"Oh, Zoya, that doesn't look good!" Nikki jumped out of the car, Zoya followed. They ran after the pink grandmother and Evan, who was about to disappear inside of the building.

Zoya heard a raspy voice. "Martha is here, I just saw her; she won't survive this, she won't survive this!"

"What am I not going to survive? Or are you talking about some other Martha?" A tall elderly woman dressed in a beige dress with a booming voice came out of the church and walked up to the pink old lady and Evan. Gold rings dotted Martha's fingers and earrings with large diamonds sparkled in her ears. Her swarthy face was wrinkled, as if she had spent her life in the sun or sunbathing in salons.

"Martha, please don't get upset; this young man here, he's got news of your Kelly." The woman shook her head. "That Kelly, I remember, she has been a difficult child since she was a baby, I'm not surprised," wailed the rosy old lady.

"Where's my little girl?" Martha rumbled, hovering over Evan. She was shorter than he was, but appeared enormous in her anger. Standing right at the church entrance, the two older women and Evan were an odd bunch.

"She... she... Can we talk to you?" Evan stammered, as he turned to Martha.

"What have you done to my little girl?" The fierce old woman looked at Evan as if she was ready to sizzle him with her gaze.

"It's not his fault," Zoya unexpectedly interjected. "We came to call you, because Sou..." Zoya paused. "Kelly needs help, and we'd like to talk to you. We're her friends. We all love her very much."

The fearsome old woman turned her attention to Zoya who involuntarily stepped back. The woman's eyes felt cruel.

"Okay, come with me." Martha thundered and nodded her head to indicate where to go. Zoya, Nikki, and Evan obeyed. The pink old woman remained standing at the entrance of the church. They heard her muttering:

"I meant well Martha, I brought ... I did not know."

Martha did not answer her. She led the group to a black Cadillac and confidently opened the car, which was unlocked. As if anticipating their questions, the woman grumbled:

"Everyone here knows my car 'round here. They wouldn't dare! Get in, let's go," she ordered.

Nikki and Zoya stood in stunned silence, and exchanged a look, but Evan was the first to find the power of speech:

"I'm sorry, Mrs. Weiden, I don't wanna leave my car here, can we follow you?"

"Ya'll can call me Martha," said the woman. She threw an appraising look at the group, and muttered through her teeth, "just a bunch of brats. Okay, y'all follow me, but you gotta keep up. And this one will go in my car." She nodded at Zoya. A knot formed in Zoya's stomach, but she dared not disobey the formidable woman, and carefully opened the door of the Cadillac. She was about to get in, but the passenger seat was littered with wrappers and papers.

"Oh, I ain't used to no passengers," Martha huffed, as she tossed the trash onto the back seat. Zoya sat, trying to show that she was kindly predisposed toward this strange woman. Martha started the car and right away honked, signaling for Evan to follow. She was holding the steering wheel with one hand and a lit cigarette, which appeared, as if by magic, in the other.

"Not offering, I see you don't smoke," Martha stated. "It's not far from here. Where you come from?" She turned, and this time Zoya thought that the woman's eyes did not seem cruel, but tired.

"I'm from Russia," Zoya answered, hoping the conversation would not lead to a discussion about the USSR, nuclear weapons, traitorous Russians, or Ivan Drago, the fictional boxing champion from Rocky IV.

Martha remained silent, and then nodded. "I see. And we are German."

At this point, the conversation broke off. Zoya expected the woman to ask her about Soup, about what had happened to her, but Martha drove in silence. As promised, the drive was short, and after a couple of minutes they made a sharp turn uphill. Zoya remembered passing this very turn several times with Evan and Nikki, but it had been covered by thick trees and Zoya had not noticed any signs. After making the turn, Martha stopped to check if Evan had caught up with her. When she saw his Saab, she smirked in approval.

"Oh yeah, he's alright." The Cadillac climbed up a steep hill and came to a clearing. A stunning view of the forest and mountains appeared.

"There you go," the woman pointed to a white sign on which Zoya read: "Weiden Enterprises." The Cadillac turned left, this time onto an unpaved road, which led them to a large trailer park. The car came to a stop.

"Is this all yours?" Zoya gasped, surprised at her own audacity.

"What d'ya think?" Martha Weiden smugly met Zoya's gaze.

*I wonder what kind of an enterprise this is,* Zoya thought. In her three years in America, she had never met anyone like Martha Weiden.

"All this belongs to me!" Martha pointed at a point in the distance, it was unclear if she meant the trailers, the residents, or the whole mountain.

The place reminded Zoya of the dacha near Leningrad, where she and her parents vacationed in the late 1980s. She noticed a variety of household items, drying laundry, children scurrying about. Then a rooster, bending his neck beautifully, came out from around the corner.

"This here is George, we use him for fightin'," Martha remarked, observing the rooster lovingly.

Zoya counted about fifty trailers, a whole village. Their car was parked near the largest one, which boasted a porch. Neat curtains with a floral pattern hung on the windows.

"Come right in," Martha commanded. And just then Zoya jumped. She had completely lost sight of Evan. *What if they left me? Turned around and drove back? I'll be here all alone with this woman.* Zoya tried to peek surreptitiously around, but Martha saw right through her.

"Don't you worry, they are right there." She pointed toward the entrance to the trailer park, and Zoya saw Evan's Saab emerge in the clearing. Zoya sighed in relief, and Martha barked, waving at the car.

"Come on, this way!"

They entered the trailer, where Martha ordered them to sit on a mustard-colored couch. The woman then poured herself a glass of Jim Beam and chuckled with relief:

"My fuel." She quickly downed the first glass and poured herself another. "Bourbon is the greatest American invention. Keeps the whole country going. And it's from around here, from Kentucky! By the way, Bourbon was invented by German immigrants. My granddaddy knew them." Martha twirled the glass in her hand and sat down in an armchair across from the group.

Zoya felt dizzy from the smell of alcohol on Martha's breath that she could sense even from across the room. Her stomach grumbled and her mouth felt parched, but she dared not ask for water. Evan and Nikki were now squeezed in next to her, equally hypnotized by the old woman.

"Which one of you is going to tell me what happened to my little girl? Ah! I remember you," she pointed her crooked index finger at Nikki. "Kelly brought you. So you couldn't find our place on your own, ha?"

Nikki shook her head.

"That's just how I like it," the old woman nodded happily. "I don't need no strangers comin' round here. I got a good thing going here." Martha took another sip of the Bourbon.

Zoya shifted in her seat. *I guess I should say something, she's waiting.* Zoya cleared her throat, and the old woman nodded at her approvingly.

"Oh, come on, there are brave people in the USSR. You're from the USSR, ain't you?" The woman sniggered.

"Yes, I was born there," Zoya sighed, "but it's called Russia now. And about Kelly, I…"

"Come on, come on, don't drag it out."

"So, Kelly was admitted to a mental hospital. We don't know the full details, but they took her away after a party. She's been there for…" Zoya counted in her mind, "a few weeks now."

"A mental hospital! My Kelly! That's why my little girl didn't come home for Easter. I been waitin' for her! My little girl always comes to home for Easter and Christmas." Martha sighed. "And sometimes on her birthday, my little darling."

Zoya's face dropped, and she felt tears in her eyes, as she imagined the iron Martha waiting for the unpredictable Soup to return, only to be disappointed.

"But, Mrs. Weiden, Kelly's in trouble; she doesn't want to be discharged from the hospital. This doctor, he's French, came to Pittsburgh to do research. He got Kelly to sign all these papers agreeing to take part in his study. Now she is stuck there. She says that she really likes it at the mental hospital and doesn't wanna leave. We brought a brochure." Zoya produced the pink booklet, proud of her resourcefulness, and Martha grabbed it with her bony fingers.

"French, you say?" Martha shook her head disapprovingly, flipping through the pages. "I don't like no French. Cowards and cheaters, that's what they are."

"Yes, he's French, and he is a very dangerous man, he's capable of anything," Zoya said, picturing de Vigny's twisted face as he threatened her in the elevator of Upper Hill hospital.

"Well, we'll find a solution for this Frenchie," Martha said. Her face took on a focused expression, as she picked up the phone, which was on the table near her chair, and punched in the numbers. "Frederick, come over here, quick," she said and dropped the receiver.

She picked up the Bourbon and took a sip, surveying the

group. If she was agitated, she did not show it, and sat expressionless, like the sphinx. Nikki looked out the window, Evan sat in silence, while Zoya tried to shake off the dizziness from thirst and the smell of alcohol.

"Fred will be right up," Martha remarked after a few minutes, pouring herself another glass of Bourbon. It was her third in less than thirty minutes, but the woman showed no sign of being intoxicated. "Frederick is my lawyer," Martha explained casually. "I gotta have the best. The most loyal. I found him around here, right in the trailer park; he was a smart kid, I paid for his university and law school, now he works for me. He's the best I could find. Loyal."

Martha looked critically around the room and suddenly yelled, "Nikki, that's your name, ain't it? Come on, get your friends something to drink. There's Kool-Aid in the fridge."

Zoya hated Kool-Aid – the colored sugary powder that dissolved in water – but she was so thirsty that she would settle for anything. Nikki jumped up and rushed to the refrigerator. From there she pulled out a jug of the purple liquid. Zoya determined that it was grape-flavored Kool-Aid, her least favorite. Nikki had just poured the purple concoction into glasses when a rail-thin, balding man of an uncertain age appeared at the door.

"I got here as soon as I could, Mrs. Weiden; I'm very, very sorry to keep you waiting," he said.

"Fred, I got somethin' for you," Martha interrupted. "These kids tell me they took my Kelly to a mental hospital in Pittsburgh. She signed over some papers and they are keeping her there," Martha looked at Zoya: "Do you know the name of the place?"

"Yes, of course, it's the Upper Hill Psychiatric Institute and Clinic, in Oakland," Zoya blurted out.

"Got that?" Martha raised her eyebrow at Fred, who immediately nodded. "Some doc, a Frenchman." Martha held up her index finger. "Got my girl, and she agreed to have him do experiments on her. I think it gotta do with my money, Fred. I can smell it. Make some inquiries, will ya? Maybe through your people in Pittsburgh?"

"Sure, Mrs. Weiden. How much time have I got?"

"You got none, my boy." Martha narrowed her eyes.

"I got it. I got it. I'm on my way there now."

"I know you won't let me down. Get my Kelly out."

"What about the doc?" Frederic asked, squinting and darting his eyes in the direction of the couch to Zoya, Nikki, and Evan.

"The kids are fine." Martha glared in their direction, taking Zoya's breath away. "Get rid of him." Martha gritted her teeth like a tigress on the verge of a kill.

The nimble Frederick scurried out of the trailer as quickly as he'd appeared. Martha glanced at the group and announced:

"Well, I'll thank y'all separately when my Kelly is back home. Thank you for coming and letting me know." Martha checked her watch and then got up from her chair. "I have to go to Easter lunch now, I'm already late."

Zoya, Nikki, and Evan rose from the couch at the same time, like a well-rehearsed circus troupe.

"Goodbye, Mrs. Weiden," said Nikki. Evan walked out of the trailer in silence. Zoya followed him out, having first collected the glasses with the unfinished Kool-Aid and taken them to the sink. They raced to the car.

"Evan, do you know which way to go to get out of here?" Zoya whispered.

"We'll figure it out; the main thing is to get in the car and go." Evan pulled the car off the brake, the wheels squealing as he turned around.

"Come on, don't freak out," Nikki laughed. "It's my second time here and I'm used to it."

"You should have warned us that her grandmother is all creepy, she's like the mafia, for real," Evan mumbled.

"She's a regular person, just got a lotta money." Nikki shrugged.

"And where did she get so much money? She prolly killed someone," Evan cried out.

"Come on! Soup said that her granny's second husband was some rich dude: like he raced cars or something, or won something at a casino or the lottery, I don't remember, but that her grandma took all the money and bought the land."

"Did she kill him? The second husband?" Evan looked back for a second.

"No! Come on!" Nikki huffed.

"So why does she live in a trailer?"

"I dunno; maybe she likes it, so cozy." Nikki sighed.

"Yeah, sure, cozy." Evan mocked. "Didn't you hear what she told that Fred guy?" He kept adjusting his hair, which he had gathered in a ponytail, and twisted his baseball hat back and forth.

"I don't understand what she meant by 'get rid of,'" Zoya chimed in.

"Yeah, exactly. That's what I'm talking about!" Evan shook his head. "Who says stuff like that??"

"She probably just said it for show, I don't think she means any harm," Nikki objected.

*It would be kinda cool if Martha could get rid of de Vigny*, Zoya thought. *It wouldn't be so bad if the doc disappeared forever.* She would have much rather preferred a future without the doctor. Zoya thought of all the suffering de Vigny had caused, how he had tormented her double, Zoé, mocking her when she had been his patient at St. Anne's. Now he would torture Soup and turn her brain into mush. *I met André because of him, and that whole story was because of him. If it hadn't been for de Vigny, I wouldn't have wasted so much time on André. I kept thinking it was true love, but ended up suffering for four whole years instead. Pathetic!* Zoya frowned.

"Hey, Nikki, did Soup ever mention that her grandma was

connected to the mafia? Or that she's into whatever the hell she's into?" Evan's continued to interrogate Nikki and interrupted Zoya's musings.

"No, of course not, she always told me that the whole trailer park was afraid of her grandma. But I kinda thought she was exaggerating. How could I believe a thing like that?" Nikki threw up her hands.

"Well, didn't you notice anything weird when you first met the hag?" Evan insisted.

"Nah, I just noticed that she drinks a lot." Nikki sniggered. "But I mean, that happens."

"That's for sure. It does," Evan sighed. "Reminds me of my ma before the rehab."

Zoya tuned Evan and Nikki out and immersed herself in thoughts about the world free of de Vigny.

# CHAPTER 22

April 10, 1994

Exactly one week after their trip to West Virginia, Zoya was at home. The evening before, she and Evan had gone to a rave, and she got up very late. Spring break was almost over, so she had to get ready for school. Mentally preparing for the last quarter of the school year, Zoya looked at the stack of textbooks and sighed. The chemistry textbook stuck out as if mocking her. Chemistry was her most challenging subject, and, despite her father's efforts to pass on his love of the subject to her, she hated it. Formulas merged into one enormous honeycomb-like pattern, and atomic weight and valence made her feel sick to her stomach.

The doorbell rang, and Zoya happily rushed to open it – anything to find a reason to get out of reading her textbook. On the threshold, stood a frail man in a black suit. His appearance resembled that of an undertaker. She recognized Mrs. Weiden's scrawny lawyer, Fred. The same one who had been ordered to get rid of de Vigny. Zoya noticed that his hair was neatly slicked to the side.

"Good afternoon," the man said and handed over an envelope.

"Good afternoon," Zoya swallowed.

"It's from Mrs. Weiden. With best wishes." Fred nodded, which, Zoya guessed, was his way of expressing appreciation on behalf of Mrs. Weiden, and scurried down the stairs without uttering another word.

After a moment, she closed the door. Back inside, she plopped on the couch and, with trembling hands, opened the envelope. Five one-hundred-dollar bills fell out. There was nothing else in the envelope – no note, no card. She slipped the money into her pocket and anxiously looked around the room even though her parents weren't at home. Zoya rushed to call Evan.

He immediately picked up the phone, as if he'd been waiting for her call. "Hey, did that guy come to see you?" Evan asked in a half-whisper. "I can't talk loudly, my ma's right here."

"Yes! How did he know my address?" Zoya's voice trembled.

"I dunno."

"You didn't tell him, did you?"

"No, of course not; he didn't talk to me at all."

"Did he give you something?"

"Yeah, listen, can we meet?"

"When?" Zoya was no longer thinking about school, chemistry, she needed to see Evan.

"I'll be right over." Evan hung up without setting a time.

Zoya checked her watch. It was two in the afternoon. The drive from Greensburg would take about forty minutes, so she had time to read her chemistry textbook. Zoya tried to focus on her homework, but her head was spinning from what had happened. *What did that man want? What's the money for?*

Zoya glanced restlessly at her watch, trying to anticipate

when Evan would show up. Suddenly, she grabbed her diary and began to write. Her hand moved across the page of its own accord. A few seconds later, the entry appeared:

*Hide the money, you'll need it soon. Soup is fine, and it's thanks to you. You did the right thing. Don't worry about de Vigny.*
   *Alum*

Zoya looked at the page in horror. *Alum again! What is happening!?* She felt panic rise. *The right thing? I didn't even do that much! And how can I not worry about de Vigny?*

And then, Zoya remembered her doppelgänger, the girl Zoé, whom she had tried to get out of St. Anne's in Paris. She could clearly picture Zoé lying on the bed and refusing to move, while she, Zoya, tried in vain to persuade her to run. *Was that what would happen to Soup, too? Then I did the right thing by warning Martha Weiden.*

Staring at the page, she thought: *But who is Alum? I wish I could ask Inna Lvovna.* She sighed, remembering her wise neighbor from Moscow, her energetic son Vlad, and their kitchen where they'd spent so much time chatting. There was no one like Inna Lvovna among the immigrants from the former Soviet Union, no volumes of Brockhaus and Ephron, no homemade Khourabia cookies, no stories about temporal branches and quantum entanglement. Their current neighbors loved discussing vegetable gardens and whether planting red currant shrubs in Pittsburgh was a good idea and how best to control the growth of raspberries on the property.

Suddenly, Zoya's pen moved again, and the following entry appeared:

. . .

*Alum is your guardian angel.*

*Oh, wow!* she thought. *A guardian angel!* Zoya imagined a beautiful angel with wings, as Michelangelo portrayed him. *Could Alum be a handsome young man like that?*

Zoya tried to imagine that a beautiful guardian angel, named Alum, would visit her, and how she would meet him in real life, rather than through written messages in her diary. She was still staring lovingly at Alum's message a few minutes later, when there was a knock on the door. Zoya went tumbling downstairs. Evan was standing on the doorstep.

"Hey," Evan muttered. "Are you ready to go?"

Zoya nodded and followed him to the car. They drove through Schenley Park in the direction of Oakland, and only when they turned on South Bouquet Street did Zoya ask where they were headed.

"To the Beehive, we'll talk there," said Evan and fell silent again.

Zoya did not dare contradict him. She hadn't been to the Beehive since before her fight with André. *I just hope he isn't there*, Zoya thought, her heart fluttering. *Not like I really care, I have more important things to do.* The terrible de Vigny came to mind and she wondered if André had seen his step-father in Pittsburgh. *Maybe now he'll believe me?*

Not much had changed at the coffee shop during her absence. The place was dark, groups of outcasts and misfits lounged around, and the same tattooed Isaac worked behind the counter.

"Long time no see," Isaac smirked, as he greeted Zoya. He was wiping a glass with a dirty rag. Zoya cleared her throat in surprise. Up until that moment, she had been sure that Isaac had not been aware of her existence.

"Hi," Zoya responded, averting her eyes.

"The usual? Mocha?" Isaac raised his eyebrows. Zoya nodded. *How did he remember?*

Evan picked a table in the darkest corner of the coffee shop.

"So?" Zoya asked, stirring her drink. She hadn't had a mocha since the last time she'd been there, and salivated at the thought of the delicious combination of chocolate and coffee.

"Get this! Nikki called me today, she woke me up: and it turned out she'd just gotten back from West Virginia," Evan said.

"What?" Zoya gasped.

"Yeah, the old witch and her side-kick, they came by Nikki's house on Monday. Took her with them, went straight to Upper Hill Psych, and then Nikki and Fred, I guess they kinda kidnapped Soup outta there. I don't know how they did it, but they got her out of that place."

"What?" Zoya's eyes widened in shock.

"Yeah. Nikki said that Soup was in a bad way, already on something, some kinda pills, she could hardly stand up. They had to like carry her out of there, or whatever."

Zoya shuddered, remembering her own experience at St. Anne's and how shaky and dizzy she had felt from Klonopin and lithium. And how de Vigny had mocked her. The scene of her own miraculous escape from the Parisian mental hospital came to mind. *Maybe it hadn't been a dream?* Zoya thought, but her thoughts were interrupted by Evan.

"Nikki said that Frederick was super smart, that now Upper Hill has to pay them compensation for violation of some rights or whatever."

"Really?" Zoya had never heard of hospitals paying anything. The way she saw it, hospitals only collected money and certainly didn't pay patients back.

"Yeah, they've already settled, it was real fast. So Soup is gonna be alright."

"That's great!" Zoya clapped her hands.

"Except, Soup's got a different problem. Her grandma won't let her off the mountain. Locked her in her trailer." Evan shrugged. "Nikki said that Soup's grandma is mad at her, and worried about her future."

"I see," Zoya replied, thinking that if she had been in Soup's place, she wouldn't have left such a distinguished grandmother, but would have stayed close by and helped her manage Weiden Enterprises.

"So we're never gonna see Kelly now. But maybe it's for the best, because she got mixed up with that Ike dude," Evan said. "Good thing she didn't get busted by the cops for selling or anything more serious."

"Yeah," Zoya nodded. "And what about that doctor?" He had been on her mind constantly. Images of the scary de Vigny taunting her, scowling, threatening her from the elevator spun in her head nonstop.

"I dunno, Nikki didn't say anything about the doctor." Evan shrugged.

"Nothing at all?" She raised her eyebrows in surprise.

"Zoya, who cares? Soup's fine. That's all that matters! By the way, what did Frederick give you?" Evan switched to a whisper.

"An envelope," Zoya admitted.

"With the money, right? Do you think they want something from us in return?"

"I don't know." Zoya shuddered at the idea that the money was a down payment for future services. "Should we give it back?" Zoya suggested, cringing inside. She badly wanted to keep the money, and had already thought of spending it on a bus ticket and the hotel to visit the University of Pennsylvania, as recommended by Mrs. McNeal.

"Nah, I gotta get my clutch fixed; I was just at the mechanic's the other day." Evan shook his head. "I really need that money now."

"And Nikki? Maybe she knows something?"

"Nikki didn't say anything about the money; but she's been there a long time, they must have given her a ton of cash."

"Fine; then we can keep the money, right?"

"Right!" Evan nodded.

"Listen, Evan, if you find out anything about the doctor, you let me know, okay?"

"Don't worry so much." Evan shook his head, but smiled. She felt confident that he would do his best to find out about de Vigny.

"Thank you," said Zoya and looked at Evan with gratitude.

At that moment, she felt someone's eyes on her. It was as if a hole was being drilled in the back of her head. When she turned around, she saw André standing near the counter. He looked away as soon as Zoya turned around, but she knew that he had just witnessed the intimacy of her conversation with Evan. She blushed with embarrassment. She didn't know what was worse: the fact that André had seen her with Evan and would now be sure that their relationship was romantic after all; or the fact that her friendship with Evan was taking a new turn, that there really was something deeper in their relationship than friendship, but she, Zoya, would not let that feeling develop now, because it would confirm André's suspicions.

"Zoya, what's up?" Evan raised his eyebrows questioningly.

"Oh, I just thought I saw someone I used to know." Zoya replied. *I'll never come here again*, Zoya decided. *I don't wanna risk running into André ever again.* Zoya looked bitterly in his direction.

André sat down at their once favorite table near the

window and was calmly sipping a coffee while flipping through a book. *So he doesn't care about me at all,* Zoya thought. *All right, then. He probably still doesn't know de Vigny is in Pittsburgh, and just thinks I am weird and made it all up.*

"Zoya!" Evan was trying to get her attention.

"Huh? Oh, sorry, I was thinking." She was so deep in her thoughts about André that she hardly knew where she was.

"Let's go, I gotta take my mom shopping," said Evan, looking sullen.

"Of course, let's get outta here." Zoya glanced one last time in the direction of André, who was still sitting at the table by the window, immersed in a book. As Zoya and Evan left the Beehive, she turned back and saw the curtain move, as if André was watching her.

# CHAPTER 23

July 7th, 1994

Zoya arrived at Upper Hill Psych, heading swiftly through the corridors to the children's center. It was Elizabeth's first day in the office after her vacation, which she had timed around the July Fourth holiday.

"We're going to my in-laws' house at the Outer Banks," Elizabeth had announced back in mid-June. "It's right on the beach." She complained that finding the perfect swimsuit was impossible, she didn't want to spend so much time with her mother-in-law, and apparently a week at the beach would cause her unspeakable misery.

Elizabeth had asked Zoya to come to work early that morning, because they would need to 'clear the backlog' and prepare for an audit, which was crucial to the survival of the center.

Since the start of summer break, Zoya had been spending her Thursdays at Upper Hill Psych. The last quarter of the eleventh grade had kept Zoya incredibly busy. She had the constant feeling that she was about to run out of time, as if she might forget something important, and that, having completed one task, she was sure to miss something else, of equal or greater importance to her future.

Working at the library in the evenings took up valuable time Zoya could have used for volunteering, or for developing some other talents and hobbies to help her get into a prestigious university. But she needed the money, and her parents were now paying off the mortgage. Her father's salary was low. Zoya liked her volunteer job at Upper Hill Psych, where she continued going on Thursdays, despite the unfortunate interaction with Ben, the programmer from CMU, whom she continued to run into from time to time.

Once the school year ended, Zoya felt incredible relief. She immediately switched to a summer schedule. Now she worked at the library three days a week, and dedicated her Thursdays to volunteering.

Zoya got used to the hospital and knew exactly what time she had to go to the cafeteria to cash in her food vouchers. The woman who worked at the cafeteria, who had seemed menacing and rude to Zoya at first, now knew her by name, called her a 'sweetheart', and always gave her free refills. Zoya was surprised at how her attitude toward the hospital had changed for the better, and she was glad of it.

Her fourth summer in America, and Zoya had finally gotten used to the humid and hot weather. She now considered herself a real American. It was with a feeling of tenderness mixed with self-disdain that Zoya looked back at 1991, her first year in Pittsburgh, when every day was a challenge, making new friends was a quest and she hated going to school. But now, Zoya had everything: excellent grades, a coveted job at the library, friends, and, of course, raves, that made her happy.

"Zoya, good morning! Thank you for coming in early!" Elizabeth smiled. Zoya noticed that there was sunburn on her boss' arms. "We have so much work, so much work!" Elizabeth sighed and headed for her office. "And we have reports to prepare – the grant renewal is coming up. Mrs. Kendle is coming in half an hour, she's the accountant, we have to have everything ready for her, I'm so worried!"

Elizabeth fussed, while Zoya focused on her work. She loved contributing to the center's success: sorting the drawings into folders, tagging, and organizing materials. *I am so lucky that I found this place. I get to do something interesting and useful and I'll have something to show on my college applications,* Zoya thought. She heard the door to the center open and then muffled voices. *That must be the accountant,* Zoya decided. She was about to put the remaining drawings away, when suddenly she heard a shriek:

"How terrible! Ah! It just can't be!"

Zoya peaked around the corner and saw Elizabeth, who was shaking her head at an elderly lady with glasses and a tiny tuft of hair on the back of her head, who was sitting across the desk. Zoya perked her ears up.

"But how is that possible? Disappeared just like that?" Elizabeth sounded perplexed.

"Yes, yes, I was supposed to do an audit the day before yesterday, and there's a grant, just like yours, so it was all according to plan, all according to plan. Tuesday morning, I went to their office, and it was all locked up. Well, I thought, of course... After all, it was the day after Independence Day, and everybody celebrates the Fourth of July, but such a great man. And his receptionist was nice, too. I even suggested they move the audit to mid-July; nobody wants it right after the holidays, that's understandable."

Mrs. Kendle threw a guilty look at Elizabeth. "But you know, since the fiscal year ends on June 30th, there's nothing I can do, so we have to make do with early July, especially for people like us. Those grants don't just audit themselves, and we gotta hold everyone accountable! No exceptions!" Mrs. Kendle continued.

"Of course, of course!" Elizabeth chimed in, darting her eyes.

"Unfortunately, not all the departments are as responsible as yours; but that doctor, he suggested I do the audit on July 5th, that was his idea!"

"Wow!"

"But you know, that's because he is French, he even made a joke, and I remember very well, that the Fourteenth of July was more important for him, and he was even going to Paris to celebrate Bastille Day." The tuft of hair on the back of Mrs. Kendle's head shook with laughter, and Zoya froze. *It can't be; are they really talking about de Vigny? There might be other Frenchmen working at the hospital.* Zoya stopped rustling her papers and devoted all her energies to eavesdropping on her boss's conversation.

"I'd like to go to France one day, too!" Elizabeth remarked.

"Well, I was very surprised that he asked for an early audit. But since the man asked… And so, on the fifth of July I came in and the door was locked. I waited for an hour, and then I went to look for him. And guess what, no one could find him. HR was running around all morning, and they even called his landlord."

"Wow!" Elizabeth gasped.

"Yes! And what do you think? He's really missing! I never thought I'd be involved in such a thing. He lived alone, he didn't have a girlfriend," Mrs. Kendle whispered confidentially, as if regretting the opportunity. *Is it de Vigny? Surely he wouldn't have a girlfriend in Pittsburgh, he's married to André's mother,* Zoya thought, digging her nails into her skin in order to stay calm.

"So now what will happen?"

"I don't know. His landlord was supposed to meet him to collect July rent on Friday evening. He lived in Shadyside, you know, those lovely new condos on Fifth Avenue. And he never showed up. Of course, my audit had to be postponed; now I don't know when I'll be able to finish it."

"So did they find him in the end?"

"No, nothing! He's gone. I think they notified the police and filed a missing person's report!"

"Wow, what a story!" Elizabeth nodded.

"Yes! And right here, in Pittsburgh! I don't know anything else. But he's just gone!"

"How terrible? You don't think it was foul play? But Pittsburgh is such a nice, quiet town."

"I just don't know. I doubt it, he was such a smart man, a luminary I heard, and the hoops that our hospital jumped through to get him to come to Pittsburgh. And what incredible research he did, how he took care of young women; groundbreaking work I heard! But of course, I am just an accountant, I don't know much about these things." Mrs. Kendle shook her head and the tuft of hair bounced in unison.

"Yes, terrible indeed."

"And now, of course that whole project he was doing, his partner, you know, Dr. Mirani," Mrs. Kendle lowered her voice and Zoya could barely hear the accountant's words: "No one thinks that Dr. Mirani can pull the research off on her own. It was all his work, his ideas."

"Dr. Mirani… that doesn't ring a bell," Elizabeth remarked. Zoya noticed how the supervisor tactfully avoided gossiping about another doctor. "Mrs. Kendle, don't get upset, it's probably just a misunderstanding."

"Yes, what a story! But of course, that's not why I am here!" Mrs. Kendle turned to the folders and smiled as she looked over the piles of papers Elizabeth had prepared for her.

"Of course, we've been expecting you!" Elizabeth called: "Zoya, Zoya, come here, please!" Zoya jumped up and rushed into the office, pretending that she was just now distracted from her work, and had not spent the last fifteen minutes eavesdropping on a fascinating conversation about the disappearance of her nemesis.

"This is my volunteer; by the way, it is so cost effective: we don't waste any donor funding on bureaucratic work at all," Elizabeth explained. "Zoya is a high school student, comes here once a week and organizes everything for me, so I have all the accounting in order. Zoya, please show Mrs. Kendle the files."

Elizabeth had a look of combat readiness on her face. Zoya did not want to let her boss down, especially after the woman had generously rewarded her with food vouchers and bus passes. Elizabeth had also promised to write Zoya a recommendation for college, when the time came.

"I've got everything right here." Zoya produced a pile of folders and papers and showed them to Mrs. Kendle, whose face took on the look of a hound on a fox trail.

As Zoya handed over the documents, she tried to not give away her excitement. *Is de Vigny actually gone? Is it really over? Did André do it? But he's been in France all summer, and André isn't capable of murder.* Zoya thought. *Or is this what Alum meant? That I needn't worry about de Vigny?*

Zoya remembered how André had left Pittsburgh for the whole summer and how their relationship had fallen apart after his departure, and clenched her fists in anger: *It was because of de Vigny and his mother that our relationship got all weird. If André hadn't left last summer, I wouldn't have gone to that first rave and made friends with Evan, we might still be together,* Zoya thought.

The idea shook her, and thoughts of André, which she had managed to suppress, came flooding into her mind. Zoya tried to imagine an idyllic scene, but instead she thought of her friends and the fun she had at raves. *If André hadn't left, I wouldn't have met Evan. I wouldn't have gotten to know Soup or Nikki, or have these friends in my life. Or have gone to raves.*

She imagined how boring and monotonous her life would have been without the raves, without Evan's steady presence. *Even finding this volunteer thing came about through Soup ending up at Upper Hill Psych at the time. And the $500 I got all thanks to Soup and her grandma.*

Imagining the alternative, she pictured herself happily paired with André, but with no friends, no volunteering, and no prospects of studying outside of Pittsburgh.

Zoya had already planned a trip to Philadelphia, where she would visit the University of Pennsylvania. She had called ahead to register for a tour for applicants, and even bought a bus ticket to get to the city in advance.

*So did I always have to choose between André and raves? Was our break-up the right thing for me? Would he have held me back?* Zoya's eyes widened at the thought. *So I'm better off without André? But he was so wonderful, and I felt so good with him... Although, maybe he wasn't so wonderful?* Zoya thought, remembering the episode with the green T-shirt and how he dismissed her sometimes. She'd donated the green T-shirt, unable to wear it without thinking of her ex-boyfriend.

At this thought, Zoya realized she had been holding the same folder for several minutes and had attracted the attention of Mrs. Kendle, who was giving her a curious stare.

Upon returning home that afternoon, Zoya rushed to watch The Simpsons. She turned on the TV, which was turned to Channel 11, a tell-tale sign that her mother had watched the morning news before leaving for work. Zoya lifted the remote to switch to Fox 53, but suddenly her hand froze in place. On the screen, she saw the familiar ugly face. A long nose hovered ominously over an upturned upper lip, the clever eyes stared unkindly.

It was none other than de Vigny, the very same photo that Zoya had seen in the Upper Hill Psych brochure advertising his research.

A second more and she would collapse on the couch. She

leaned against the wall. Black circles swam before her eyes, as she listened to the measured voice of the announcer:

*Jean-Marie de Vigny, the accomplished French psychiatrist who worked in Pittsburgh, disappeared on July 1ˢᵗ, 1994. He is a man in his fifties, six feet tall, weighing about two hundred pounds. He was last seen wearing a gray suit and a pink tie. If you have any information about this case, please call* **412-555-4963**.

*Now, for the weather.*

Zoya grabbed the remote again and switched on The Simpsons. The familiar theme song played, as the cartoon family, one by one, plopped on to their couch. Zoya held on to the wall, as she sat down and exhaled.

# EPILOGUE

Zoya zipped up her backpack, stuffing her notebooks and her economics textbook in it. Her exam was coming up, her first one at the University of Pennsylvania, and she decided that she would spend the weekend at the library studying. Zoya dressed as usual – in jeans and her favorite pink sweater – ate a sandwich and drank tea, which she always brewed ahead of time in her dorm room.

Early Saturday morning, the university campus was still asleep, and Zoya made her way from the Quad, where her dorm was, to the Fisher Fine Arts library. She no longer went to raves on weekends. The Philadelphia rave scene was not as welcoming as the Pittsburgh one, and Zoya couldn't find the right crowd. So getting up early on weekends was no longer a problem for her.

She'd spotted the Fisher Fine Arts library on her first visit to Penn, in August 1994, and had dreamt of studying in the reading room since the day she first saw it. The library was built of red brick in the Venetian neo-Gothic style; a half-palace and a half-fortress.

Inside the library, everything was full of magic and mysticism: dark corridors, massive vaults, lace railings – the whole building breathed antiquity and knowledge, and felt like just by virtue of being there one would get smarter. It often made her think of Alum and feel comforted by the idea of having guardian angels – she wasn't sure she would ever know if it was real or all in her mind.

Every weekend, Zoya would enter the magical reading room with the clear intention to dedicate herself to homework. But her focus only lasted for the first hour and a half. Then her thoughts drifted away, into a fantasy world. Zoya regularly admired the ceiling, the lamps, the beauty of the red brick and the tomes that filled the shelves of the library. The desire to stay in the beautiful reading room was stronger than anything else, and Zoya continued her futile attempts to study at the library for hours at a time.

Entering the familiar hall, Zoya surveyed the space. She was one of the first to enter and could choose almost any table. The selection was important and one had to choose wisely: it was best to sit not too close to the entrance, so as not to be distracted, but also not in the deepest part of the room, so that one could walk outside and stretch, if necessary.

Zoya chose a table in the middle of the room and sat near the wall. Racks of antique books hovered over her, a lamp shone comfortably overhead, and Gothic beauty reigned all around. She laid out her notebooks, and wanted to pinch herself: *I can't believe I am here! Five years ago, I didn't even know that I'd be living in America. Now, I'm studying at one of the best universities in the country!*

Zoya was filled with pride for everything that she'd been able to accomplish. For the difficulties she had overcome and the tough decisions she had taken. She had managed to convince her parents that moving to Philadelphia was the right thing to do, and here she was, at this prestigious university. In early September, the Kassatkins drove their daughter to Philadelphia in their Chevrolet Caprice Classic, which decided to cooperate during the six-hour drive. They were due to visit soon and she was looking forward to seeing them. All she had to do was to get good grades so that she could keep her scholarship, and then find a job after graduation.

Two hours later, Zoya had managed to get through three whole chapters of the textbook she was reading and even went over her notes from the beginning of the semester. She congratulated herself on a morning well spent, and decided that it was time for lunch. Her stomach rumbled, and she hurriedly started to pack.

As she was stuffing her last notebook into her backpack, she felt someone staring. It was a blonde guy, who was sitting straight across from her. She had noticed him earlier, but hadn't paid much attention to him – his face was down, glued to the book in his hands. As soon as Zoya looked up, the young man immediately averted his gaze and stared at his textbook. She tried to sneak a peek at what he was reading. On one of the books, which were strewn on the table at his side, she saw black letters on a white background: *Immanuel Kant*. Zoya shuddered.

*He must be super smart*, she decided. Taking advantage of the fact that he was immersed in reading a book, Zoya took another look at the young man. His features were handsome, though a little delicate. Big eyes and straight eyebrows, thin lips, a strong-willed chin. *I guess he is kind of cute*, Zoya thought, but tried not to stare, afraid that he would notice her interest. She had just managed to look away, when she caught the blonde man's point-blank stare.

As the blush crept up her cheeks, she tried to pretend not to notice, but it made her blush even more. Feeling terribly embarrassed, she decided she had to get out of the library right away so she could save herself from further humiliation. Zoya grabbed her bag and hurried to the exit. She walked past the counter, deftly maneuvered through the turnstile, swung open the front door, and went outside.

At the door, Zoya stopped before going down the steps

and exhaled. *Nice and sunny today*, she thought and fixed her hair. Since moving to Philadelphia, Zoya had been pleasantly surprised by the number of sunny days compared to the foggy and cloudy Pittsburgh.

"My name is Chris." She heard the male voice behind her.

Zoya jumped, catching her breath. Even before she turned around, she knew it had to be the blonde man from the library.

"And I'm Zoya," she croaked, turning around. Up close, the blonde man was even more handsome. His eyes were bright blue, deep and thoughtful.

"Zoya? What a beautiful name! It means 'life' in Greek!" The man looked at Zoya questioningly.

"Yes, that's right. How did you know?" The only other person to ever mention the meaning of her name was her mother.

"I took Ancient Greek in high school." Chris shrugged and gave Zoya a smile.

"Ancient Greek? Wow!"

"Yes, I've always been interested in philosophy, and I thought I could understand it better if I could read the ancient philosophers in the original," Chris said

Zoya's mouth dropped. She wanted to impress Chris, too. *But how?* She had just started the most basic economics course.

"But enough about me. What about you? And how did you get such a beautiful and rare name?"

"Umm, my name?" Zoya felt her cheeks turn red from embarrassment.

"Yeah. Why did they call you that?"

"I don't know; my mom chose it because she liked that it meant 'life' and she thought it sounded nice."

"Well, that's cool." Chris' smile seemed sincere. Zoya's breath slowed down to normal. "Listen, what are you doing tonight?" Chris asked after a pause.

Zoya widened her eyes. The events of the morning were unfolding like in a romantic comedy! A handsome stranger just asked her out, then they would happily date for several years, then he would propose by giving her a huge engagement ring, they would then get married; have a beautiful wedding, children, friends, a house with a dog. Zoya's fantasies had already transported her ten years into the future, and then she realized that she had never answered Chris' question. With tremendous effort, she forced herself back down to Earth.

"I don't know yet; my friends and I were going out, but we didn't agree exactly what we'll do." Zoya remembered that in response to an invitation from a guy, it was best to be vague and to hint at an active social life and to never, ever agree to meet the very same evening. At any rate, not right away.

"Oh, so I'm having a little get-together at my place; why don't you come by?"

"Oh cool!" Zoya couldn't help herself and reacted with joy and sincerity.

"Yes, I have a friend coming over from New York today; he wants to go to Wharton and is going to see the university. He works at an investment bank, so it's right up his alley."

"Wow," Zoya said. Wharton, as she had discovered since coming to Penn, was the most prestigious branch of the university and the best business school in America. A select few who would eventually make millions on Wall Street studied there.

"Yeah, we're very different, even though we've been friends for a long time." Chris shrugged.

"Did you go to high school together?" Zoya had gotten used to the fact that Americans were very attached to their school friends, and in spite of frequent moves, kept in touch with them.

"No, I met him when I was an exchange student in Paris,"

answered Chris. Zoya wanted to tell him that she also spoke French and had been to Paris, but she was too shy. "Well, I don't want to keep you. I hope to see you tonight. Here's the address — I live in Center City." Chris scribbled on a piece of paper and handed it to her.

Zoya had never met anyone who lived off campus before. Not only did Chris appear very smart, but he was also an insanely interesting person who lived in the coolest part of Philadelphia – Center City!

*Could such a great guy really be interested in me?* Zoya thought, peering at the piece of paper with Chris's address on it. Just then she realized that he hadn't asked for her number, and felt uneasy. Zoya sighed on the way to the Quad. *I should just skip this get-together, just forget it.* But she remembered Chris's intelligent, beautiful eyes, and really wanted to get to know him. In the hallway, walking into the dormitory, Zoya bumped into her roommate and immediately blurted out:

"Erika, come with me tonight, please, I met this grad student, he's having a party!"

Erika had a boyfriend who lived in Hawaii, and she was supposedly crazy about him, but that didn't stop her from going to all kinds of parties and actively hitting on guys.

"Sure, let's go! What time?" Erika asked, tossing back her red curls.

"I don't know," Zoya yelped, suddenly realizing that Chris did not mention the exact time of the party.

"Let's go at seven, it's the best thing to do. Not too early, not too late," Erika remarked, nodding wisely.

Zoya had gotten used to relying on her roommate's opinion, since she considered Erika to be more experienced in dealing with men.

The rest of the day, Zoya spent in nervous anticipation of the evening. She could not concentrate on anything at all, and had to stop herself from daydreaming about the beautiful Chris.

At six o'clock, Erika asked, "So, are you ready?" She was dressed in tiny shorts that completely exposed her long, tanned legs. Erika refused to dress for the weather, and had planned to go through the entire Philadelphia fall in short shorts. For Chris's party, Zoya decided to dress as usual: jeans and a low-cut tank top, which she immediately covered with a warm sweater. Zoya thought of putting on the amber bracelet Yegor Vlasov had given her, but decided against it. She hadn't worn it since moving to Philadelphia.

They could have walked to Center City, but Erika complained about the cold and suggested they take the university shuttle. Zoya had no choice, but to agree, though she would have much rather preferred to walk — she adored walking around campus and breathing the fresh air. The closer they were to Center City, the more nervous Zoya got. She felt a lump form in her throat. Erika chirped incessantly about her boyfriend, his surfing and how that made it difficult for him to live anywhere but Hawaii. Finally, they arrived at a gleaming high-rise.

"Wow! Is this where he lives?!" Erika looked at the imposing building and her mouth gaped open.

"Yeah, I think so." Zoya looked at the paper Chris had given her and checked the address. Her palms were sweaty, and if it weren't for Erika, Zoya would have turned around and run away long ago.

"So, let's go in? Do you know the apartment number?" Erika asked, businesslike.

"Yes, it says right here." Zoya looked at the paper for the tenth time.

Erika confidently approached the concierge sitting behind the counter – an elderly man with a long mustache.

"We're going to apartment 37 please," Erika said, coquettishly fixing her curls.

Zoya caught her reflection in the huge wall mirror behind them. Scanning her outfit, she felt the nerves start to settle.

She looked good, the colors suited her skin and her eyes shone brightly. Smiling at her mirror self, she took a steady breath and turned back to her friend.

"Sure, come on in; take the elevator to the third floor and go right down the hall." The concierge wrote something down in a little book. Erika confidently walked to the elevators and pushed the call button.

"Have you been here before?" Zoya asked, widening her eyes.

"No, of course not, but who cares? This is so that the concierge thinks we know where we are going." Erika shrugged.

They went up to the third floor and immediately saw a half-open door to one of the apartments down the hall. Loud voices and laughter reached their ears. Zoya and Erika exchanged glances and Zoya froze in place.

"What are you doing? Come on, this is the apartment!" Erika immediately pulled her along. Zoya moved forward, though her legs were tumbling underneath her with fear.

Erika looked at her with a frown. "We're about to go meet some guys. Come on, straighten up."

Zoya exhaled and did her best to calm down. She did not understand why she was so anxious. It was as if she had a premonition that something incredibly important was about to happen. They got to the door, and Erika went straight in, while Zoya remained standing on the threshold. In the middle of the crowded living room was a group of people discussing something animatedly. Zoya was just getting her bearings, when she saw Chris emerge. He smiled in recognition, walked over and gave her a hug:

"You made it! Zoya! Hi!"

"Hi!" replied Zoya. Being next to Chris felt good. "I brought a friend." She waved toward Erika, who smiled playfully and fluffed her red curls. Chris nodded at Erika but immediately turned his full attention back to Zoya, which flattered her.

"I'm so glad you could make it. Here, want a beer?" He handed Zoya a bottle of Corona, which she accepted with a polite smile.

"Thanks for the invitation," she said, taking a sip.

"Oh yeah, my friend, the one who's the reason for this whole thing, is coming over. He just got in from New York, the train was late. I hope he won't miss the party I am throwing for him!" Chris looked around the room, and there was a sense of pride in his eyes. Zoya noticed that Erika had already managed to surround herself with several men, and was laughing.

"There he is!" Chris exclaimed.

Zoya turned around and felt her knees start to shake, as she saw André walk into the apartment. He looked thinner than she remembered, and his face was haggard. He was wearing a leather jacket and black jeans. It also looked like he hadn't shaved in several days. But there was no doubt: it was him. André threw a black gym bag at the entrance, and rushed over to Chris.

"Hey, bro! Philly's such a dump! I can't believe I am here," he chortled.

Zoya retreated into the darkest corner of the room and tried to figure out what to do next. She had to slip out of the apartment as quickly as possible, before André would see her.

"I thought you'd never make it! Finally graced me with a visit." Chris gave André a pat on the back.

"I didn't think I'd make the train, had so much work! I did it all for you, bro."

"Nah, you just wanna see Wharton!"

"Oh yeah! As soon as I get that bonus, I am outta there. Gotta just wait till end of December. That's what it's all about." André happily rubbed his palms.

Zoya noticed an unhealthy glint in his eyes at the mention

of money and felt a sinking feeling in her stomach: *Is this the same André I suffered so much over? Was he like this before and I just didn't notice?*

"Alright, alright, keep waiting for your bonus, but in the meantime you can throw your stuff in there." Chris pointed in the direction of the bedroom, and Zoya noticed a huge bed that took up more than half the room. Her palms were suddenly clammy, as if the bed served as yet another reminder of what she had wanted with André. Zoya made her way towards the exit so she could run out of the apartment, when she heard a familiar voice.

"Zoé? No way!" Zoya turned her head to the side, pretending not to hear, but the voice insisted: "Small world, Zoé!"

Slowly, she turned around. Her heart was ready to jump out of her chest and she felt blood drain from her face. Standing there was André, who had turned into a phantom in her mind, whom she once considered to be her one and only true love and soul mate, for whom she had suffered and agonized, and who had accused her of being on drugs.

"Hi," Zoya whispered. She felt her lips turn white. The aftertaste of the Corona made her feel nauseous.

"What in the world are you doing here?" André asked.

"I live here," said Zoya.

"You live where?"

"In Philly."

"So you moved here from Pittsburgh?" André stared at her with amazement.

"Yes," Zoya nodded in response. She didn't have the strength for more. She darted her eyes, trying to find Erika, but it was as if her friend had vanished into thin air.

"Oh! So you two already met!" Chris came up to them and put his arm around André's shoulders. "André, this is Zoya, a student at Penn. She is studying economics, I spied on her this morning. Zoya, this is the friend I told you about; he's going to Wharton next year. Well, if he gets in!"

"Oh, we met before." André squinted at her.

"For real?" Chris smiled so broadly and sincerely that Zoya felt guilty about wanting to run away without saying goodbye.

"Oh yeah, Zoé here thinks that we knew each other in past lives," said André with a smirk.

Zoya stiffened: she had long ago put aside her theories about the Templars and past incarnations, though she took comfort in possibly having guardian angels who guided her. Too many times she'd gnawed at herself for sharing her theory with André and thus ruining their idyllic love! *That's it. It's all over now,* Zoya thought. *Now Chris won't want to see me again.* Dejectedly, she stared at the floor, trying not to attract attention.

"Past lives? Wow!" Chris responded, looking not the least bit uncomfortable. Instead, he had a look of fascination on his face.

"Don't you want to explain how we'd met in a past life, Zoé?" André smirked again.

"No, I don't think that's a good idea." The tips of her fingers had grown cold with fear.

"I've often thought about past lives," said Chris. "I think reincarnation makes a lot of sense. It's very interesting to me as a philosopher. What happens to the soul after death? And then, if you think about it, reincarnation explains different levels of consciousness. How else to explain why some of us are born with a completely mature understanding of the world, while others remain total idiots even in old age?" Chris winked at Zoya then looked at André with a smile.

"You never told me you believed in this nonsense!" André tried to sound ironic, but Zoya could tell that he was uncomfortable.

"Why nonsense? Even Plato thought it possible. And if

Plato believed in reincarnation, then why shouldn't we? Isn't that right, Zoya?" Chris said and smiled, baring his beautiful white teeth.

"Yes." Zoya sighed in relief.

"I came across a book the other day, it was written by a woman who does past lives regression therapy," said Chris.

"Oh I know about it! Is it the one by Dolores Cannon?" Zoya blurted out, as something clicked in her mind and she recalled Fatima Mbia and their conversation in a hotel in Paris. *But it had been a dream, hadn't it? None of it is real.* Zoya's mind raced, but then she heard Chris say:

"Yes! That's the one! I want to go to Arkansas to have her do a past life regression on me. I'd love to do it. Maybe we could go see her together, huh, Zoya?" Chris' eyes lit up.

"Chris, bro, are you out of your mind?" André's face twisted in anger. "You're kidding, right? Dolores what? And why did you get mixed up with Zoya anyway? She fried her brains out going to raves a long time ago. You don't want anything to do with this junkie.

"André! Why? Why do you want to ruin my life?!" A wave of indignation rose up in Zoya. Not thinking about the consequences, she clenched her fists and lunged at her former boyfriend.

—

"Zoya! Zoya!" She opened her eyes. Her face was streaked with tears, and her hair was tangled. She must have been twisting on the pillow all night. Next to her, she saw the concerned face of her beloved. "Was it that dream again?"

"Again, yes, I had the same nightmare. And again it was André, all gaunt and angry." Zoya forced a laugh, but it turned into a scowl. The dream was still too fresh in her mind.

"He was visiting from New York again, right?" Chris looked at her sympathetically.

"Yes, from New York. I was studying at Fisher Fine Arts, and you came up to me, like the time we met. He came to visit Wharton, and we ran into each other at your party; it was so strange, I didn't want to go. And the apartment was yours, it was this one."

"My apartment?"

"Yes! And the building matched, and the concierge, and he came here. Even the apartment number matched, number 37."

"Interesting; so we were all together in your dream, huh? I know you were having a nightmare, but you jumped up like you wanted to attack me."

"I thought it was him. In the nightmare, I almost scratched his eyes out." Zoya turned her eyes away in shame.

"I see." Chris gave her another kiss and wiped the tears from her face.

"But, there was one thing, in my dream you told me that Plato believed in past lives. Maybe it's true?" Zoya looked up at Chris hopefully and then buried her face in his chest.

"We should check it out." Chris kissed the top of her head. "My beautiful girl." Chris snuggled up to her and covered her face with kisses. "It's all your parallel branches and past incarnations, my enchantress. Let's go to Arkansas for Christmas, huh? To see Dolores Cannon?"

"Yes!!! Okay!" Zoya happily laid her head on her lover's shoulder and soon fell asleep.

The End

*Thank you for reading 'Zoya: Rupture'. If you enjoyed it, I would love your honest review on Amazon. Why am I asking for reviews? For an indie author like myself, each review means I can get more books to other readers who enjoy stories written in the magical realism style. This is why every single review means a huge amount to me.*

*Thank you for your support. And above all, happy reading.*

# ACKNOWLEDGMENTS

This book is about transformation, and I would like to thank my parents, Leonid Kazakov and Leonora Pugachevsky, for our own transformative experience of becoming new Americans. We were in it together and I am certain that it was only thanks to our strong bond and commitment to each other that we managed to survive.

I would also like to thank Natalia Piadushkina. I believe that there are no accidents in life, and I am grateful to this day for our seemingly chance meeting over twenty years ago, and for our friendship, that we have carried through the years.

I am grateful to my high school, Taylor Allderdice. Two teachers from Allderdice stand out: Dr. David Clark and Mrs. Kogut. I was incredibly lucky to have been in Dr. Clark's art class for two years. He saw me as a person and that made all the difference in the world. Mrs. Kogut, my sophomore English teacher, was an incredible force, and in one year managed to instill in us all the basics of grammar, vocabulary and good writing. I still have the checklist she used to help her students improve their writing.

There was one more incredible teacher in my life, Igor Olegovich Rodin. He taught Russian literature and grammar in my elementary school in Moscow, and introduced us, 10-year-old kids, to the Iliad, the Odyssey, Plautus, Chaucer and Robert Burns. If it weren't for him, I doubt I would have ever had the same appreciation of literature as I do today.

I would like to thank the city of Pittsburgh, which you can

see on the cover of this book. Pittsburgh welcomed me and became my first American home. I couldn't help but fall in love with it, and have carried this love through the years. To this day, I am always drawn to Pittsburgh and its charm, no matter where I am in the world.

# EXCLUSIVE FREE BOOK

*YOUR FREE BOOK IS WAITING…*
Download your exclusive free copy of 'One Day in the Life of Yegor Vlasov' and learn the bully's side of the story.

---

**Connect with the author**
Website: sashkina.com
Email: sasha@sashkina.com

# ABOUT THE AUTHOR

Alexandra Pugachevsky has always believed that magical elements exist in all aspects of our lives and reality is multidimensional. She writes in the magical realism genre.

Having immigrated to the United States from Moscow in her teens, Alexandra fell in love with the city of Pittsburgh, and has retained that love until now. She can't help but write about Pittsburgh. Another city she loves is Paris, which also features prominently in her work.

Alexandra Pugachevsky holds a BA in International Relations and French from the University of Pennsylvania and a Master's in Foreign Service from Georgetown University.

An international development professional by day, Alexandra has made Washington, DC Metropolitan area her home for the last 25 years.